Meant to MEET

HAZEL HELLIWELL

AuthorHouse™ UK Ltd.
1663 Liberty Drive
Bloomington, IN 47403 USA
www.authorhouse.co.uk
Phone: 0800.197.4150

© 2014 Hazel Helliwell. All rights reserved.

No part of this book may be reproduced, stored in a retrieval system, or transmitted by any means without the written permission of the author.

Published by AuthorHouse 06/24/2014

ISBN: 978-1-4969-8521-7 (sc)
ISBN: 978-1-4969-8522-4 (e)

Any people depicted in stock imagery provided by Thinkstock are models, and such images are being used for illustrative purposes only. Certain stock imagery © Thinkstock.

This book is printed on acid-free paper.

Because of the dynamic nature of the Internet, any web addresses or links contained in this book may have changed since publication and may no longer be valid. The views expressed in this work are solely those of the author and do not necessarily reflect the views of the publisher, and the publisher hereby disclaims any responsibility for them.

With best wishes to my friends, old and new.

All the characters in this book have no existence outside the imagination of the author, and have no relation whatsoever to anyone bearing the same name or names. They are not even distantly inspired by any individual known or unknown to the author, and all the incidents are pure invention.

Please place your order at W H Smith, Waterstones and Amazon to ensure you'll not be waiting. Proceeds going to Derbyshire Guide Dogs for the Blind and RNIB (Royal Institute for the Blind)

Kindle e-book and e-book platforms such as for Ipad's, Sony Kobo, Barnes&Noble Nook etc. distributed by Author house to Amazon and all the major book sellers.

My auto-biography Out of the Shadows was emotionally difficult to write and also a challenge, but I needed to glorify God in testimony for how he has helped me throughout my life.

Autobiography Out of the Shadows**

Other books using pen name Samantha Arran
  Trilogy: Love Never Fails*
  Unfailing love,
  A New Beginning*
  Mademoiselle Fleur*

Love is in the air*
Available from Amazon, Waterstones and all good book shops on order.

** Available from above as is this book, also produced as an e-book.

Chapter One

One very hot summer afternoon in June 1896 Katherine Hindley a seamstress at the age of seventeen went from the dressmakers shop on the outskirts of a mining village in North Derbyshire, to give Lady Derbyshire of The Hall a final fitting for her gown they had made for the Annual Ball. Getting off the little bus and walking up the long drive carefully carrying the gown covered with white cotton and enjoying the beauty of the tree lined drive where colourful birds and butterflies flew around and perfumes permeating the air, despite midges trying to attack her.

Although being fit and with strong arms through cutting out, machine sewing and carrying materials about, the gown hung very heavily on her arm. As she was transferring it to her other arm she heard a car engine and glancing behind her saw an open top car driven by a young man with very fair curly hair. She continued walking looking the opposite way as he slowed down at her side. 'Good afternoon. I'm Andrew

Derbyshire. I guess that is my mother's gown for the ball?'

'Yes sir.'

'It looks heavy. Would you like a lift?'

'No thank you, I'm quite comfortable.'

Jumping over the low door took the gown from her carefully laying it out on the back seat. Opening the door she hesitantly got in. 'Are you enjoying this beautiful weather, Miss..?'

'Katherine Hindley. Yes, I am.'

'Have you come on the bus?'

'Yes sir.' He liked her innate modesty.

'I will give you a lift back to the bus. What time?'

'Thank you but no. This would be most inappropriate.'

'Inappropriate? My mother should have provided you with transport up this long drive at least, especially as it's so hot. I'll have a word with her.'

'Please sir, don't. She'll think I'm a trouble maker.'

'I doubt you are. I'll take you back to the bus. I insist.'

Pulling up at the front entrance she quickly said, 'no, sir, I go to the back entrance.' Taking her round and lifting the gown out said, 'see you at five.'

'Thank you, but I'm not happy with this. I'll be fine. I won't have the gown.'

'Begin walking and I'll take you to the bus stop,' he insisted. 'You are a breath of fresh air.'

Lady Derbyshire was satisfied with the completed gown and her butler escorted Katherine to the kitchen for a cup of tea before going home. She gazed round the big kitchen with its huge range, furniture and the pottery and pans. The cook and staff chattered to her in a friendly manner as they worked. It was almost five o'clock so Katherine took her leave. Putting her straw hat on began to run down the drive hoping to avoid Andrew. Laughing he pulled up and she reluctantly got in.

'Would you like a country side run this evening, Miss Hindley?'

'Thank you but no sir.'

'I was looking forward to your company. It's so boring here with my mother and sisters on and on about this wretched ball.'

Katherine had to laugh and thought, "why not?"

Arranging to pick her up and he was waiting. Two black Labradors were sat on the back seat. Katherine greeted them.

'Have you been to Chatsworth House, Miss Hindley?'

'No sir, but I've read about it and seen photographs.'

'For goodness sake please stop calling me sir. I'm only 22 years old. My name is Andrew.' He drove on asking if she had siblings.

'No. I'm an only child.'

He pulled up and hurried to open her door, instructed the dogs to come out and led her into a field. 'Look, there's Chatsworth.'

Looking down and across she had a wonderful view of the house in all its splendour. The lake, fountain and the manicured lawns were clearly visible in the beautiful evening.

'It's so glorious. If I could paint, I'd capture all this,' she said in awe.

Waiting until she moved they began walking down the field keeping the dogs under control, so they didn't disturb the sheep and lambs.

At nine o'clock he took her back. The bus didn't run at this time of night. She asked him to drop her on the outskirt a distance away the small village. 'Are you free tomorrow evening?' he asked.

'I could be.'

'Same time, same place, another run.'

'Thank you.' She spoke to the dogs.

She went home excited but didn't tell her parents. The next day for the first time dragged for her. Her parents were surprised she was going out again, but trusted her.

This time Andrew showed her different views and again took her back for nine o'clock. Her parent's enquired and she had to tell them that she had met a young man and was meeting him to-morrow evening.

At the last stop Graham the bus driver watched her walk gracefully as usual but again eagerly going around the corner. She carried only her handbag. The bus was empty as always, the walkers and dogs got off at the previous stops to go on the walks where the dogs wouldn't upset the animals. The bus only came this far during the summer months. He drove past the crossroads signs and pulled into a lay bye for his usual quick cup of tea from his flask, sandwich and a leak behind the thick bushes, before picking up passengers along the way back to the village.

Seeing the open top car pass him and recognising the driver as Andrew, Lord and Lady Derbyshire's son. He wondered but knowing his wife Grace, a cleaner at The Hall, had mentioned several times that Katherine came to alter or give Lady Derbyshire a final fitting of her gowns and clothes, he thought Master Andrew as the villagers still called him despite his now being 22 years old, must be giving her a lift.

The next evening Katherine got out and hurried round the corner. Again he saw the car with Andrew and Katherine in shoot past him. She wasn't on the bus the next evening but Grace had told him it was the evening of the Annual Ball. Katherine was back on the following evening and again after scuttling round the corner, went past in the car.

Graham thought this was serious. He suspected Katherine's parents wouldn't know of these secret meetings. Having the greatest respect for them and for Katherine having seen her grow up as a sensible good hard working Christian girl he knew Lord and Lady Derbyshire would forbid Andrew marrying below his class if she got pregnant. Thinking long and hard about this situation knew he couldn't remain silent. "Did he tell Katherine's parents? No, it was Andrew's parents who had to know."

He told Grace and asked her to let Lady Derbyshire know but in full secrecy. He trusted his wife. She was very concerned and understood what the outcome could be if they continued meeting in these hot summer evenings.

'Leave it with me, Graham. I'll think of something. I can't make an appointment to see Lady Derbyshire without asking the housekeeper's permission, and I can't tell her in The Hall as there are always listening ears. But I often meet her when I'm coming down the drive for your bus as she walks the dogs after lunch.'

As they walked in the shade of the wood, Katherine and Andrew turned to each other in longing and kissed. He tenderly laid her down on the grass kissing her passionately with the dogs laid nearby. Katherine couldn't help herself and gave him her virginity. This was a first also for Andrew and they were filled with wonder.

Grace did meet Lady Derbyshire in the drive the next afternoon. The area was deserted, so asked her, 'excuse me your Ladyship, can I have a private word?'

Surprised she said, 'of course, you are?'

'Grace Arnett one of your cleaners ma'am.' She passed on the message from Graham.

Lady Derbyshire was shocked but knew Andrew had been missing these evenings after eating his dinner earlier. 'I'll tell my husband, thank you Mrs Arnett. Please don't gossip about this.'

'My husband's and my lips are sealed, ma'am. We're both concerned about Miss Hindley and her parents. They're a very respectable Christian living family and adore their only child.'

'Of course Mrs Arnett, forgive me. I was thinking of Andrew and his career.'

Grace thought, "Yes you would, selfish cow." She rebuked herself. Lady Derbyshire must have wanted more heirs.

'Do your hours here suit you, Mrs Arnett?'

'Yes ma'am. I'm able to attend to my children before school, and am home when they come home. They take a packed lunch as Mrs Bakewell allows this.'

'How many children have you?'

'I've three boys, Lady Derbyshire.'

'You are very fortunate.'

That evening Andrew was waiting for Katherine but hadn't his car. He looked agitated. Her heart sank. 'My parents have found out about our meeting and are very angry with me, Katherine. I told them you are a beautiful refined young lady, but they have taken my car away from me and are sending me abroad tomorrow until it's time to go back to University. I could kill myself.'

'Hush, don't speak so. I knew this would happen. You're their only son and heir. I'm just a village girl. I understand them Andrew. I'm not your class. You could never marry me.'

'Why not?'

'I haven't the social graces you need to be your hostess. You've a career with responsibilities and a position to maintain in this community. You'll be the Lord Derbyshire.'

'I'll give all this up for me, my darling Katherine. I could work.'

'No, no, I'm proud of your achievements and you'll be a wonderful compassionate politician. We'll need you. The bus is coming back soon. I'll go home and will always remember these precious evenings. I'll never regret giving you my virginity.'

'Please, please promise you will correspond with me.'

'No Andrew,' she firmly said. 'This is goodbye. You know it has to be. I wish you all happiness in your future life.' Her heart was breaking as she spoke but knew she had to be strong. She would always love him and now life without him would be agony.

Andrew with his breeding and training had to concur with her. 'I'll never forget you, my darling.

Whatever life brings I'll always have these memories of you. Promise me if you are ever in need to contact me.'

She didn't answer. They kissed but tore themselves apart as the little bus was chugging into sight. It had no other passengers as before at this last stop and after waving to Andrew, she sat on the back seat and cried. Passengers were waiting at the next stop. She dried her face and put a smile on.

Over the next few days her parents were worried seeing sadness in her face, but realized she was seventeen years and guessed she must have fallen out with her boy friend.

Katherine woke feeling bilious and was sick in her toilet bucket. She carried it down to empty in the outside privy midden. Her parents were as always up for her Dad to have a nourishing breakfast before his day down at the pit. Seeing her white face tinged with green and the bucket Rupert took it from her and emptied it down the midden covering with the provided powder chemical to dry the waste for regular collection.

Rupert returned and questioned her. Weeping, she admitted she had given her virginity to a young man but just the once.

'Did you use a protection?' her Mam asked. Katherine didn't understand what she meant. Janet knew they had been remiss not discussing such matters with her. At school girls had said 'he should have put something on the end of it' when discussing neighbours who were pregnant again and hadn't understood that, but didn't ask. 'You're very likely pregnant, darling.

Your Dad and I know you aren't common and cheap and you must love him.'

'He was a virgin too, Mam. I love him but it's over, my choice.'

They were shocked. 'We'll take care of you,' her Dad promised. 'If you're pregnant this baby will be welcomed and loved. Go back to bed and your Mam will bring tea and toast.'

'Thank you Dad but no, I'm well now and I must go to work.' They both admired her for this. Rupert went to work with a heavy heart.

Gossip was rife in the village as expected. Other village girls had been pregnant and hastily married unless the father was a married man, but Katherine had always appeared to be different.

At Sunday Church the minister knowing of this gossip began his sermon to the packed congregation with, 'my text for this evening is: Let him who is without sin cast the first stone.' The gossip ceased.

Lady Derbyshire told Mrs Harris, the owner of the dressmaker's shop, she needed Miss Hindley to make her some alterations. 'Miss Hindley isn't well, ma'am, and is only working in the shop for now. I'll come,' she promised.

As she pinned Lady Derbyshire's gown she queried, 'Is Miss Hindley's illness serious.'

'No ma'am, she's pregnant. She's a good Christian young lady. Her lover was a traveller and will never return here as he isn't free. She must have loved him to give him her virginity. We and her parents are supporting her.'

Knowing with all certainty that Andrew was the father admired Miss Hindley for not discrediting his career. Discussing this with her husband he agreed Andrew had changed about that time. 'We must ensure he doesn't spend his holidays here for the time being.'

She agreed, and then voiced her fears, 'what if the baby is a boy and resembles Andrew? The villagers are discerning and will soon spot this.'

'He can't marry her, Dorothy. If she, as you say, has told her parents her lover was a traveller and will never return here as he isn't free, leave it at that.' He admired Miss Hindley for her choice of words. Andrew yes was a traveller and he wasn't free. He had a moment of regret. Miss Hindley by her reputation and standing in the community would perhaps be a good wife to him. With being the local Member of Parliament he knew of her and her family. 'If it's a boy he should be Andrew's heir. What if Andrew doesn't marry nor has no sons? What a mess.'

'We need to ask our solicitor about this, dear,' she suggested.

'Perhaps we ought to wait until it's born. It may be a girl, prayerfully, or she may lose it but God forbid that. He must love her as he's always so responsible.' They both went quiet. 'Keep enquiring how she is, no one will suspect as she was your seamstress.'

'I will, dear.'

Mrs Harris gave Katherine light work and in the latter weeks Katherine embroidered flowers in the small squares of a new style hand knitted cardigan which was very popular. At home she and her Mam knitted baby clothes and made long gowns for the baby to sleep in. Janet had saved the pram, cot and bath and other items including clothes she had used for Katherine in the loft hoping she would have more children.

To Lord and Lady Derbyshire's relief Katherine bore a daughter. They both had a longing to see her as did Andrew. June had black straight hair but classical features as Andrew had.

June was almost two years old when Katherine received a letter from the local solicitor asking her to make an appointment. Naturally wondering what it was all about she did. After she had been given a cup of tea, Mr Sykes told her Mr Andrew Derbyshire had set up for her in complete secrecy, a lease to last her lifetime or if she moved out, on "Honeysuckle Cottage" on the outskirts of the village a few miles away.

He showed her a photograph of the cottage with thatched roof and told her it had two generous sized bedrooms, kitchen and sitting room, outside privy midden, and wash house. A lawn ran down to a small stream. She was weeping and her heart overflowed at this generous gift proving he still cared for her and her daughter. They never met at her request for not wanting to let any scandal fall on him, but she read and listened on the radio to everything there was about him in his successful career. She never kept a diary of these events but stored them in her mind. Unknown to her this cottage lease was from a Trust Fund Andrew had received from his Grandfather on reaching his 25th year.

Katherine and her parent's moved into "Honeysuckle Cottage" and loved it. It had quite a large garden with a shed. Rupert planned to build a small greenhouse as there was a vegetable growing area. They loved the lawn area also at the back of the cottage where June could have a swing and safely run about with their supervision until older.

With her earned savings Katherine's paid off the small mortgage on her parent's terraced house. From the sale of this she bought a little shop in the village which had stood empty for a long time. She asked her Dad to retire from his pit work. His lungs had suffered with working in the coal dust.

Having no mortgage or rent and growing their own vegetables and her mother baking, they would be enabled to live comfortably from her earnings. Rupert would get a pension in a few years. She and her Dad cleaned and decorated the shop. An odd job man painted the inside and outside as Katherine wouldn't allow her Dad to do this with fear of the paint irritating his lungs. She named it "June."

Buying her other needs second hand and with her treadle sewing machine she had had for years, began her own dressmaking business including curtain making. She worked mornings only whilst June was at the Church playgroup she took her to en route to her shop whilst Janet did the washing and cooked them a nourishing lunch. Rupert fetched her home.

Whilst June, Rupert and Janet slept after lunch Katherine ironed their clothes then played with June and her dolls on the lawn in the beautiful summer weather. Katherine was able to hand sew and embroider for her customer's needs before preparing tea whilst her dad took June for a walk on the country lanes or watched her paddle in the stream at the bottom of the garden.

June intelligent and very popular at school began sewing at an early age and went on to be a seamstress working with her mother, and was able to use her skills with embroidery. Katherine and her parents, Janet and Rupert, adored her and were so proud of her. Most people in their village admired her as she had an innate quiet dignity as her mother had.

World war one broke out and life in the village changed and women had to work. Men were killed also four young lady nurses. The miners at the little colliery were **exempt** on the grounds they were essential to the war effort at home.

The field where Kathryn, Janet, Rupert and June had always picked blackberries for their jam and preserves had been ploughed to grow potatoes in the war shortage.

Walking on until they came across a fruitful hedge where lots of people were busy gathering. Rupert asked the young man near them if he may borrow his stick he was using to lower his branches. Percy Markham, a 20 year old colliery worker, gladly obliged and they began talking about the colliery where Rupert had worked, Rupert introduced his wife, daughter and granddaughter. Percy and 17 year old June both fell in love at first sight.

Approving of him and his reputation after Rupert had enquired in the pub Kathryn invited him to Sunday lunch. Percy couldn't believe his good fortune; although he was a quiet very respectable Christian man thought he wasn't good enough for June. She was so beautiful and intelligent.

Rupert, when he and Percy were alone told him, 'June or my wife and I don't know who her father is.

My daughter must have loved him and he must have been respectable.'

'I'm very thankful she was born, Mr Hindley. I thank God every day that we met.' Rupert's admiration for him grew even more.

People in Percy's village recognised there was something special about June; probably inherited from her unknown father.

Katherine wondered if Percy filled the empty space June had being fatherless, and she loved him as a son.

Percy's mother had died shortly after giving birth to him and their neighbour Mrs Stephenson an elderly widow with no children, cooked and washed for him and his Dad. With the coal dust as a miner getting into his lungs and with not being strong his Dad died when Percy was a 15 years old miner, who then lived with Mrs Stephenson who loved him as a son.

Percy rented an allotment and supplied Mrs Stephenson and her neighbour Mrs Knowles with his produce. Any excess he sold or left for people to help themselves leaving a tin for the money. Two retired miners were near his allotment during the day but most people were honest. After meeting June he planted a row of flower seeds and a Gypsphilla which would grow into a bush. June knew Percy was her man and they planned to marry.

He asked Mr Dingle senior, his employer at the pit if he may have first chance of an empty colliery house. Mr Dingle had had the middens replaced with water flushing toilets.

Meant To Meet

When he was twenty three Percy came home from work and saw Mrs Stephenson sat in her armchair in front of the fire which had burned away. Dismay filled him. Gently shaking her shoulder knew she had died. Cuddling her he wept broken heartedly. He went to next door and Mrs Knowles also was shocked.

'Tell the doctor, Percy.' Percy quickly cleaned his hands, hair and face as best he could with the cold water in the outhouse and ran to the doctor who came and made the undertaker arrangements, and Mrs Stephenson's body was taken away. Percy was still dazed. Mrs Knowles had made his fire with pans of water heating for his bath. She gave him a mug of tea and after his bath fed him in her home telling him, 'Mrs Stephenson made funeral arrangements Percy. The undertaker will come to see us. Fetch box from under bed.' She found the insurance papers. Percy knew Mrs Stephenson had no family left.

'Now Percy, I know you're in shock but she's lived to a good age, you've kept her going. You and June want to marry so ask Mr Dingle if you can have this house.'

'Will this be disrespectful?'

'No, this would make her happy.'

The undertaker came and he had notified the insurance company.

June and family were also shocked but agreed Percy should take this opportunity for the house. Asking Mr Dingle senior before starting work the next morning, knowing what a respectable capable young man he was and with already living in it gave Percy permission to rent it.

At tea time the insurance man came and told Percy and Mrs Knowles the amount due. Chapel Minister

Lincoln came also and Percy gave him Mrs Stephenson's chosen hymns and bible reading for her service.

Mrs Knowles cooked his breakfast and tea, packed his snap tin and filled his billy can, kept the fire going and had the water ready for his bath whilst Percy continued living in the house. Mrs Knowles firmly told Percy when he offered to pay for all this, 'nay, lad, you've always been good to me never taking owt for all the vegetables and flowers you've grown me.' She knew he would continue doing this. June washed and ironed his clothes. There was a bit of money left from the funeral expenses which Percy gave to the Chapel Minister.

Janet had taught June to cook using simple ingredients and Mrs Stephenson had shown her how to use the coal range ovens which were the same in all the pit houses. June kept the mangle with the big wooden rollers which stood in the little outhouse and Mrs Stephenson had showed her how to adjust the handles on top for the space needed between the rollers when June was helping her, and the other washing needs. Percy and June kept the scrubbed wooden kitchen table with two drawers, three wooden chairs and a kitchen cupboard, two high backed easy chairs in the front room June later would clean and make covers matching the curtains. Mr Benson who owned the second hand shop took away what they didn't need. Mrs Knowles did accept this small amount.

Percy, June, her Mam and Grandparents cleaned throughout and Percy and June palmared the walls and painted the woodwork. They were so proud of their own future home. Percy took flowers from his allotment to Mrs Stephenson's grave every week and planted a rose bush he had grafted from another. He greatly missed her.

Katherine and June made curtains, bedding, table cloths and aprons from remnants of material from the market. June made pillow cases and filled them with off cuts of washable foam pieces the foam man had on his Saturday market stall she could wash. She, Katherine and Janet had been knitted squares to sew together to make blankets.

June and Katherine's customers gave money as wedding presents as did Katherine, Rupert and Janet. June spent the money wisely on everyday crockery, preserving jars, a new zinc bath and a galvanised meat safe with a wired front keeping insects and mice out as it stood on the concrete floor in the cool pantry. She and Percy bought a new bed and the utensils June needed for cooking and baking from the money Percy had saved through work and selling his allotment produce.

Katherine made her beautiful gown and veil and she looked radiant knowing she was still a virgin. Katherine wept that Andrew couldn't see her or be with them. She had never lost her love for him. June wept that her unknown father wasn't "giving her away" to Percy. She had asked Katherine again who he was, but she just shook her head. Her Granddad carried out this honour.

They didn't go away on honeymoon. Whilst June washed the clothes, cleaned and cooked a nourishing dinner Percy worked on his allotment and brought their and Mrs Knowles needs. In the afternoons they either went up to the allotment with sandwiches and cake with Percy mashing their tea on the primus stove, or they caught the little bus into Chatsworth area taking sandwiches and a bottle of water. Mrs Knowles never interfered with them, just greeting them when outside. Percy proudly went shopping with June into the market town on Saturday afternoons when she bought her needs and then meat and provisions for Percy's nourishing breakfast. They went to Katherine's for Sunday roast lunch after being at the allotment as several faithful customers including children with their farthing, came to buy flowers for visiting or graves. Percy wouldn't sell anything else on Sundays.

With June being intelligent and thrifty Percy gave her his wage packet. After setting aside what she would need, gave him a little spending money and invested the remainder with the allotment takings in the Co-operative Society Bank. She and Percy had a cosy home they took pride in and loved it. When the dark evenings drew in they sat at the table pegging a rug with pieces of cloth from coats and jackets no-one wanted at the jumble sales so June bought some, washed and cut them up. In her spare day time hours she made cushion covers and embroidered them for her Mam's shop.

June became pregnant in November 1920 and Percy and the family were delighted. After a month of morning sickness she had a comfortable pregnancy with being strong and fit. It was a long labour but a healthy boy was born featuring Percy and June, they were weeping with joy and named him Matthew. After four more healthy good looking sons featuring their parents also and named Mark, Luke, John, and James, each one deeply loved. Violet was born on Monday 6th May 1932 and June, Percy and the family were thrilled. Very feminine with her small ears, rosebud mouth; long lashes already fanning her little chubby cheeks and the classic shape features and fair curls following Andrew Derbyshire's lineage. Marvelling at her but decided not to have more children. June had fed all her children until sharp teeth enforced her to wean them. Adoring each other Percy never recovered from June falling in love with him as he was opposite to her genteel manner.

Not being used to a girl baby her brothers loved Violet but got on with their lives. She was a happy baby and lay in her pram or on the pegged rug in front of the fire waving her arms and legs, chortling. As her hair began to grow she had white curls and June's classical features, Andrew's lineage lived on. Percy knew June wouldn't have been unfaithful to him but their sons all had straight black hair as he, June and her Mam had. People as they do, gossiped about this despite having respect for her and the way she cared for her family.

June was a refined woman, she kept their miner's little terraced home immaculate and despaired of her sons who after she had carefully ironed their shirts took no care of them or the jerseys and pullovers she knitted them, but she adored them as Percy did. Her shining black hair she cut herself was always neat in a pinned roll coming up behind her ears very becomingly. She also cut Percy's and her son's hair so theirs was always shining and neat too. She and Percy had thanked God for the gift of a daughter and with her expertise in knitting, sewing and embroidery June began to make Violet her little dresses and knitted cardigans, socks and outdoor clothes.

Violet started talking at ten months and walked at eleven months. As she matured she loved to crayon and look at books with animals and birds in. She also loved being read to. Percy made her a doll's cot and painted it and June sewed a pillow and counterpane with a bow on each. Violet loved her little doll and dressed her in June's hand made clothes after she had bathed her in a bowl of water. Her brothers spoke to her but let her get on with these activities.

Being very protective of her did take her in her pram for walks in the fields and woods and on the disused railway lines, also down by the side of the river where all the young village children went to play in the school holidays. The girls made "houses" with circles of stones taking their doll, pieces of pegged rugs, sandwiches and bottles of water with them. The boys swam in the river, climbed the trees and ran up the sleep slope leading to the railway lines waiting for the trains passing.

When Violet was almost two years old the wages clerk at the Colliery was waiting for Percy coming up on the lift and smiling at him, gave his an envelope and left him. As he was covered in coal dust Percy ran home for June to open it. She had the zinc bath in front of the fire ready as always to fill it from the boiling water in the pans on the fire. After going to the outside toilet he washed his hands and face from the cold tap in the outhouse.

June poured him his mug of tea then opened the envelope and read out: 'Percy, my brother and I are giving you to-morrow off with pay as we need to see you in my office 10 a.m. Wendell and Glynn Dingle.' Percy and June naturally wondered what it was about but he assured her saying Robin the wages clerk had been smiling kindly at him. June prayed it was promotion, he deserved it.

Meant To Meet

June put the tall clothes horse with sheets on for Percy's privacy and he poured the water into his bath and sat in it, cleaning himself. June took his clothes outside and shook them free of the coal dust then went back in to wash his back. Their boys had come home from school and after washing their hands and face, changed their clothes and with an orange each went out to play with their pals, taking Violet fastened in her pram to watch them.

As he stood up June gave him a bowl warm water to rinse his hair and body as she had from being married to him. She had a towel and his clean clothes ready on the fire guard. Although it was summer, she needed the fire to cook on and also to try and keep the house from more damp with being built on ashes and having no cellar. Putting warmed oven shelves in beds also continued.

Before she served them their nourishing cooked meal and suet pudding with currants in, affectionately known as 'spotted dick' and sweet white sauce, Violet was in her high chair next to June for her to feed her with the same food, Percy told them about the letter. Matthew suggested, 'it sounds as though you're going to be promoted, Dad.'

'We'll soon know,' Percy laughed. 'It can't be anything to worry about as the wages clerk was smiling at me.' He repeated as he had told June, 'and no one else had one.' He washed the pots, pans and cutlery and the boys dried as usual. June cleared them away. They all then went to their allotment. Percy pushing Violet in her pram for June to choose the supplies she needed for the next day before she returned quickly to bath Violet in her small bath and put her in her cot.

Percy brought the zinc bath in using the water that was ready. After they all brushed their teeth with salt June crushed from a big block she bought, Luke, John and James bathed together using red carbolic soap and as they stood up June rinsed their hair and body, and then dried them before they put their pyjamas on. With clean water in the bath Matthew and Mark followed the same procedure but with Percy giving them the rinsing water. Percy covered the warmed oven shelves and put them in their beds.

Sat in front of the fire in their pyjamas June made them their mug of cocoa before they had a prayer time, kissed their parents and went to bed. Percy brought the oven shelves back down and poured the water into the bath for June. She always washed her hair separately at the sink and washed and changed her dress and apron after lunch. Before getting in bed June took Percy's suit and best shirt down and hung them from the ceiling clothes dryer.

The next morning she was still up before five feeling strange not having to pack Percy his lunch or fill his billy can. They all breakfasted together and when the boys had set off for school and she had attended to Violet, June cut Percy's hair and then washed and rinsed it as he stood over the sink. He had given his best shoes another polish although they didn't need it. When dressed in his Sunday Chapel suit and white shirt and striped tie, clean shaven, he looked very handsome and fit and she told him so. He kissed her and Violet and then set off. They had prayed together as a family at breakfast about this meeting, but as he set off June thanked God for him and prayed again it would be good news.

Going up the stairs to the offices, he knocked on Mr Dingle seniors' door. He called, 'come in' and then shaking his hand smiling at him said, 'Good morning Percy.' His son known as Mr Glynn shook his hand and they all sat down.

'We'd like you to accept the job as our foreman, Percy. I'm nearing retirement and we need you to support my son.' He told him how much more money he would receive but expected him to work Saturday mornings with extra pay. Percy's heart leapt thinking he would be able to provide more for June and their family.

After discussing what it would entail and Percy said, 'thank you both, I accept with pleasure and will do my very best.'

'We know that Percy. Good man,' Mr Dingle replied.

Mr Glynn then asked, 'Would you like a glass of beer, Percy?' Drinking their beer Mr Dingle enquired about his family and then shook hands again. 'You'll now be eager to go home and tell your wife?' He knew how much in love they were and how well June looked after him.

'Yes please sir. I'll make my time up,'

'No you've earned a bit of time off, Percy,' he laughed. They had always admired how he had applied himself, being faithful and never causing trouble as other men did.

Passing people as he ran home full of excitement at this honour and the extra money June would use to better the family, he was laughing so they knew there wasn't anything wrong but were curious. June hearing him running and flew to the door. He swung her round and round and told her the good news. She was cuddling and telling him proud she was of him and was also very relieved that he would no longer get as much coal dust on his lungs. She made a pot of tea and they both sat drinking as he told her what it entailed. Her morning housework routine had gone to pot not being able to concentrate when he had left.

Percy went to meet his sons coming home for lunch. They were cuddling and congratulating him. They told their pals as they all walked together. Human nature being what it is some of the boys was jealous. Back for the afternoon lessons they proudly told their teachers of this promotion and they also were very pleased. Each one of them had the highest respect for this family. The Chapel Minister came to see Percy to congratulate him.

To celebrate when the boys came out of school caught the little local bus and had a run into the beautiful countryside near Chatsworth House, returning home to a nourishing casserole and pudding June had safely left cooking. Percy for once had a bottle of beer with his meal. After eating Percy told the boys, 'it's thanks to your Mam I've been promoted. How she's always looked after me and fed me as she does you. I'd be nothing without your Mam.' He and June exchanged a loving smile, she was close to tears. He wasn't one for making flowery speeches.

Jealous boys at school tried to bully Matthew and Mark, but they were strong and fit with June's cooking and being rugby players. Percy and June saw the black eyes and bruises but they never told tales. The teachers at school knew who the trouble makers were with Mr Markham being promoted without being told. Their admiration for these boys went up. The bullying stopped.

Meant To Meet

With their Dad now working Saturday mornings Matthew, Mark, Luke and John went proudly up to the allotment to sell his products. There was a used blue bag in the shed for if they got stung or bitten. As their Dad had taught them, bunched the flowers with wool June gave them. Percy wrote the price of the vegetables with a piece of chalk on a piece of slate. Everyone brought their bag or basket for these. Some of their school pals did the same for their Dads, but most of the men wasn't as committed and only used their allotment to get out of the house until pub time.

Matthew, Mark, Luke and John were boisterous rugby, football and all sports players but James was very quiet and loved to draw or write on the wallpaper off cuts June was given by the market trader, but they were good pals together. James now his Dad was working did his jobs at home, cleaning the windows leaning out with his arm though the hinges, scrubbing the steps and swilling the paths.

Sunday mornings rain or shine Percy took Violet in her pram to his allotment only selling flowers to his neighbours to take to graves or hospital. The boys went to Chapel for Sunday school. Not allowed to play out on Sundays, returning home changed out of their "best clothes" and eagerly waited for their Grand Mam and Great Grandparents coming. They all enjoyed their always special Sunday roast dinner with Yorkshire pudding soaked in gravy first, then a plateful of meat, roast and boiled potatoes with lots of vegetables from their allotment and a glass of Dandelion and Burdock. This was followed by fruit pie with ice cream they each fetched in a cup from the van which came round every Sunday summer afternoon. Katherine and her parents paid for the meat, Percy and Katherine had protested by they insisted. Not having enough chairs Percy had made a wooden form and Mark, Luke, John, James sat close together on this. Matthew being the eldest had a chair and Violet had her high chair.

Percy washed up the boys dried. Katherine and her parents then went home to give the family time to prepare for Chapel after Katherine gave each grandson a farthing. June wouldn't allow her to give more as she gave them a thro pence (three pennies) for the work they had done for her and their Dad, to save to buy or make Christmas and birthday presents or spend. Percy filled June's copper with six buckets of water ready for her washing the next day, then went to bed. Violet slept in her pram whilst June read the weeks' newspapers her Mam brought her and her sons did their homework or looked through their comics they had bought from their spending money.

After a salad tea with gammon June had simmered all night in the oven after soaking, saving the remainder for Percy's next day's packing up with a little mustard she made from powder, they all went to the 6 pm Chapel service. After a walk when the weather was fine, they returned home to bread and dripping from the roast and then a beaker of cocoa. June bathed and put Violet to bed and read to her, whilst Percy and the boys with them not needing a bath, listened to "This is your story teller- the man in Black." It was scary and John and James hid under the table but they wouldn't go to bed without listening and then they wouldn't go upstairs on their own!

Chapter Two

The colliery terraced houses were condemned with being built on ashes and no cellars and had always been damp. The miners were able to buy coal at a reduced price and they needed a fire night and day even during the hot weather to keep the homes from more damp.

New pit houses were to be built nearby and the Messrs Dingle gave the thirty workers the opportunity to buy or rent. With the money June had thriftily saved they could afford to buy and Percy before he committed himself, asked for him and his wife to have their choice.

With his position and their respect for him and how June had cared for their colliery home, in privacy they showed him the plans and he chose a four bedroom house to be built at the end of a row and on a corner where there would be a front garden and land running down the side of the house and a back garden. It would have a low wall. It was at the side of a quiet road. Neighbours would walk past but Percy and June didn't object to this as they were part of the community.

Percy and June had the opportunity to have an extra bathroom and toilet built downstairs at the side of the house where the plumbing ran down from the upstairs bathroom and separate toilet and would be accessible from the hall. With the plumbing set up it was a very reasonable quote. Katherine who had diligently saved gave them a sum of money. June's Grandparents did the same for them to buy new beds and wardrobes. As Rupert said, 'this money would come to you when we die, so enjoy it now.' They were all excited as were the others at this new beginning. Whilst being built they walked round the area watching the developments.

The family sat at the table and June with her notebook planned who would sleep where. Percy and June had the largest bedroom where Violet would continue having her cot. James and John would share with new twin beds, as would Mark and Luke. Matthew had the smallest bedroom on his own as the eldest and would soon be starting work and paying his bed and board. June, Katherine and Janet were busy making sheets, pillow cases and curtains from end of rolls and remnants from the market and the materials shop, and knitting the squares for the washable blankets.

In the school holiday Percy had the miner's weeks' holiday with pay and excitedly they went to the Co-operative Store to choose their new beds, wardrobes and a three piece suite for the "front room" which had a small mosaic fireplace in. June ordered lino to fit every room and the stairs and then paid for everything with the money her Grandfather had given them and made up from her Co-operative Savings investment, after she had asked for a discount with buying everything from them. Seeing how she had diligently saved in her book, they agreed. Percy and the boys admired her for this and how respectful she had been and they with her.

June had left a nourishing casserole cooking in the range "slow" oven for their return as her Mam had booked them afternoon tea in the market town café as a celebration. Two tables had been joined up and a high chair for June had been provided. After tucking into the freshly made sandwiches the waitress smiling brought more and refilled their glasses of fresh orange juice. A selection of cakes and pastries were brought and Percy and June were served a pot of tea and then a refill.

It was a lovely first time they had eaten in a café. June in her thrift had at first thought this was an extravagance, but when she saw her beloved children and Percy enjoying themselves so much, she had a thankful heart for her Mam.

'These plates are lovely, Mam.' Matthew said. 'Ours don't match.'

'That doesn't matter,' June quickly said. 'It's what's on the plates that matters. When ours are cracked I don't used them.'

The family helped June to do her work and washing each morning for the remainder of the week. After their bowl of soup from the vegetables Percy grew, June packed sandwiches and scones to take to their allotment, and Percy filled bottles with water for the children to drink. Boiling water on his primus stove he made June and him self a pot of tea. They loved being there. June sat knitting with Violet sat in her push chair happily waving her arms and legs and talking. The boy's helped their Dad do jobs and proudly sold the spare produce when people asked. They were a very happy, contended family.

The walls of the newly built houses had to dry out for six months before decorating. For their other needs June and Percy gradually bought second hand furniture being careful it hadn't woodworm. She arranged for their beds to be collected after they had moved out, and was promised a good price when this work had been carried out.

June was thrilled to find a large drop leaf table for the kitchen covered with washable Formica which would clean easily and be cool to roll her pastry out on.

In the kitchen with its red brick floor the large range with four ovens fed by the coal had been installed. It needed 'black leading' but June took pride in continuing doing this job on Friday mornings. There was a separate gas oven with rings, a gas boiler for boiling clothes, wooden draining board, and a deep white sink with hot and water taps. The pantry with shelves and a big stone slab and concrete floor was under the stairs, in the hall opposite where the front door was a row of clothes pegs sat on a wooden rail.

Percy was keeping his allotment but also planned to grow at home as well. His sons, as June said, had "hollow legs." He planned for June to have a lawn at the back of the house where Violet could play safely and flowers would be grown around the sides and where June's washing lines would be.

Women grumbled at the husbands for spending all their money on beer and not saving to buy as Mr and Mrs Markham had. In all this new beginning violence was still part of the community. Some of the wives had to be careful as with their violent husband's temper when drunk, they were hit. Sons were beaten with the belt or cane bearing their father's frustrations. One boy had always been so badly beaten by his father, when he was strong enough he turned on him and murdered him.

Percy often had difficulty controlling the men at work but he remained strong and they soon realised he was no pushover and would sack them if they went too far. If their complaint was valid he took it to his employer's, if not he dismissed it. Despite all this families and neighbours cared for the vulnerable and elderly.

To celebrate before moving into the new homes the women organised a street party. Each family brought sandwiches, cakes, tarts, and Messrs Dingle provided a bottle beer for each man and soft drinks and bottled water for the children and women. With permission Percy invited them to join them and they brought their wives and children. After they had eaten Mr Dingle senior stood and wished them all good luck in their new homes. The grown ups all stood and clapped him and his brother. As they mixed with everyone, Percy proudly introduced June and his family.

Everyone enjoyed themselves. All the children ran about excited and were given an orange and an apple to take home.

When the condemned houses had been demolished, the pit employees were allowed to take bricks or slates or whatever they needed, and when cleared the area was dug over and grass was sown to make an outdoor community centre. When grown, Messrs Dingle had a children's play area with swings, roundabout, and a sand pit put in with seats spread all round in the play area, the grass area and round the paths laid for cycling on or pram pushers. It was a haven for everyone being in the fresh clean air and named "Green Pastures." Retired couples sat round enjoying company and young mothers sat knitting or sewing whilst their children played in the sand pit having fellowship. A ladies' and a gent's toilet and a water drinking facility was available.

A second world war was forecast casting a dark shadow over the village and the air raid shelters were built. Everyone was aware this would be a different war with the aeroplanes and technology the Germans had. Percy and June both knew their beloved Matthew would have to join up, but they prayed and remained strong enjoying each day as it came.

Matthew had almost completed his second year as an apprentice as a lathe operator for Witts Limited, the local reputable engineering works. Percy was pleased he had chosen this career and not gone down the pit as this was an uncertain time. Collieries were closed and closing and a miner's strike was discussed in the Great Depression of the 1930's. Despite this new washing machines were made, electricity was laid, new automobiles and cinemas built.

June continued to go into the market town on the little bus on Saturday afternoons taking Violet and James, whilst Percy supported his sons in turn at the local sports where they were taking part or watched their local team. She bought the dried pulses and lentils she used in her soups and casseroles, the roast for next day's lunch and lumps of suet for the dumplings and puddings during the week.

Percy always called at the market which remained open until late, even in the winter months and cheaply bought stewing meat, kidneys, liver, sausages, bacon, pieces of meats and gammon to cook for sandwiches, bones for her soups, chickens. The butcher knowing he

Meant To Meet

would be coming, always put the best on one side and whatever else he thought Mrs Markham would use knowing how she looked after her family. She always gave him her appreciation which he didn't often get, quite the reserve over his prices. He often thought if he gave some women their meat, they'd still find something to grumble about.

June waited to eat with Percy after putting his shopping in her meat safe under her stone slab in the pantry. Being fresh everything kept well in this coolness.

She often said her sons had hollow legs! To fill them and Percy up she made them a sweet pudding every day except Sunday and Monday varying the ingredients, boiled wrapped in a pristine white cloth she re-used and tied tightly with string, serving with her custard. They all laughed when she announced, "spotted Dick to-day" as the currant pudding was called but no one no one knew why. She made sweet white sauce to accompany this. Monday's she minced the meat left from Sunday and made a nourishing meal with this and vegetables from the allotment as always. For quickness in her busiest day she made a rhubarb fruit crumble or from fresh fruit or her preserves, and custard.

The fish man came on Friday afternoons so it was fish, chips and mushy peas she had pre-soaked, with bread and butter. Saturday mornings a local man sold skinned and boned rabbits he had caught and June always bought two plump ones. She always checked for small bones and then made a nourishing casserole cooking in her "slow" range oven whilst she was shopping.

When almost five years sat on June's knee as she was reading to her Violet said a word, she stopped reading and Violet read the next few words. It was a new book.

After tea when everyone was still sat round the table June gave Violet the book and she read a sentence. Her Dad and brothers were amazed at this and they all cuddled her.

Mark began working for the nearby reputable building firm, Colyton Limited, training to be a joiner and from early September they sent him to the local Technical College. June had his packing up and flask ready and made sure he had had a nourishing breakfast as Percy and Matthew had.

Percy and June hadn't slept knowing Violet was starting her first day at school. June walked with her and Luke, John and James and waited until she had walked into the girl's section where a teacher was waiting. The boys were segregated from the girls.

Bringing Violet home for lunch she chatted at what she had done and that she had stood and read out loud. Her brothers proudly took her back to school whilst June got her Monday work done. She was, of course, fetching Violet home as the older classes finished later.

Mrs Whittington the school secretary saw Violet was sobbing and rushed into the cloakroom. 'What ever is wrong, Violet?'

'Millie said my Mam is wicked and she's a bastard. What's a bastard, please?' Millie and the other girls were looking scared.

'Come with me, Violet, I'll take you to Mrs Bakewell.' Knocking on the Head's door, she called 'come.'

Violet was still sobbing. Mrs Whittington quickly told her. 'Fetch her brother Luke please.' Mrs Whittington hurried off.

'Would you like a glass of milk or an apple, Violet?' she kindly asked.

'No thank you. I want my Mam.'

After a knock on the door Mrs Bakewell again saying, 'come.'

Luke came bursting in. Seeing Violet crying, he picked her up and cuddled her. Mrs Bakewell told him Millie has upset her. Then asked Violet, 'do you want to go home or stay in your class with Miss Peterson? She's looking forward to hearing you read again.'

Violet looked at Luke. 'Please stay Violet. You're five years old and have begun school. Millie is a silly jealous girl because you can read.'

'I promise you Violet, no-one will be unkind to you again.' Looking at Luke she told him, 'I'm sending for Millie's mother to come and see me tomorrow morning. I'll not tolerate this bullying.'

'Thank you Mrs Bakewell. Violet's a brave girl,' Luke told her.

'What's a bastard?' Violet again asked. Luke looked horrified.

Mrs Bakewell looked at him shaking her head, 'it's a very naughty swear word Violet, forget it and think of beautiful words, will you please?' Violet nodded. 'Would you a glass of milk now?'

'Yes please, Mrs Bakewell.'

'Luke, please ask your teacher if she can spare you for half an hour. I want you to take a note to your mother. I need to see her half an hour before taking Violet home.' He thanked her and left after kissing

Violet who had quietened but still looked upset. As she drank her milk Mrs Bakewell asked, 'you like to read, Violet?'

'Yes, Mrs Bakewell.'

'There are some books in the school library you may like to borrow. Mrs Whittington will help you for the first time. Can you write your name?'

'Yes, Mrs Bakewell.' She passed her a pencil and paper. Violet wrote down her name and address. Mrs Bakewell recognised the potential in Violet and would need careful nurturing. She took Violet back to her class.

Mrs Whittington brought June to Mrs Bakewell and left them. 'Please sit down Mrs Markham.' Luke had told her what had happened so she repeated this Mrs Bakewell to save time.

'This is very unfortunate, especially on Violet's first day at school. In assembly tomorrow morning I'll remind the school that I'll not have any jealousy and bullying, I need to be more firm and have sent a note to Millie's mother to come and see me. Please rest assured Violet will encounter no more trouble or the girls will be expelled. Millie and her sisters have had repeated warnings but their targets have been older girls who can retaliate. I could have expelled them but know they come from a difficult home life, but that is no excuse. I can only apologise again Mrs Markham. We look forward to teaching Violet here and have already recognised that she's a very clever girl. She will, in a few weeks, to be moved up into the year older class. We'll make sure she's happy there.'

'Thank you Mrs Bakewell. Matthew and Mark always enjoyed coming to this school as do my other sons now.'

'And we delight in them, Mrs Markham. They're all a credit to you and your husband.' Mrs Bakewell was again admiring June's composure and manner, and how neat she looked knowing Mondays were a big wash day, her shining black hair parted down the middle and pinned into a roll emphasised her classical features very becomingly. She was slim and fit from her hard work and when it was the school sports day the races she entered she won. Mrs Bakewell thought, "Goodness shines from her."

Standing up they shook hands, then taking her to the library where with Mrs Whittington's help, Violet had chosen a book and was already reading from it. Violet looked happy again and June cuddled her before walking home hand in hand listening to Violet tell her what she had done that afternoon. June was very proud of her. Walking home Luke had told his brothers what had occurred and asked them to not say anything at home in front of Violet. They were especially loving to her and telling her they were proud of her reading out loud asking her to read for them.

In the next morning's assembly Mrs Bakewell very firmly told the school she wouldn't tolerate any bullying, especially with the new children beginning school.

Mrs Whittington brought Mrs Barlow to Mrs Bakewell. She invited her to sit down. Mrs Whittington left. Looking sternly at Mrs Barlow she told her what had transpired the previous day and that she wouldn't tolerate any bullying.

'I suppose Millie won't have a chance here now.'

'What do you mean by this,' Mrs Bakewell asked sharply. She shrugged her shoulders. 'Every child here is treated the same. If Violet or any student shows potential we encourage this. That's our job and what we're paid for. I'm telling you straight Mrs Barlow, Millie has been destructive, insolent and surly from starting school in January. I'm recommending that she sees a school psychiatrist.'

'Please Mrs Bakewell don't. She's a difficult child but has a lot to put up at home. My husband is a bully. This would destroy me. Please help us to give Millie confidence.'

Mrs Bakewell sat thinking then said, 'other children encounter difficulties at home but they aren't destructive. Do you read to Millie and encourage her to read to you.'

'No ma'am. I can't read.'

'It appears to me Millie's unhappiness begins at home. Do you set her a good example?'

'No Mrs Bakewell, I don't and my husband is also jealous of anyone who's getting on well.'

'Do you think you could both change before it's too late?'

'We'll have to, ma'am. My husband's been depressed. He argues with everyone. He's the opposite of the man I married. With his temper he was sacked from the pit last year. He'd been warned several times I was told and now can't get another job.'

'So he's unemployed?'

'Yes ma'am. He does odd jobs for next to nothing.'

'That's generous of him Mrs Barlow. I've a vacancy soon for the school caretaker BUT it requires good references.'

'He's never stolen, Mrs Bakewell.' She began to brighten up. "Will you please help him?'

'I'd like to help you all but I haven't the final say. Ask him to come to see me.' Looking in her diary said, 'say tomorrow 4.30?'

'He'll be here Mrs Bakewell. Thank you.'

'I can't guarantee it, but there is hope.'

'I'll talk to Millie, ma'am. You won't have any more trouble. If Geoff gets this job this would be a new start for the family.'

'I appreciate this, Mrs Barlow. Very good, let's see how Millie behaves in the next month. If she doesn't change, it will be serious and I'll have to ask you to take her away from this school.'

'Should I apologise to Mrs Markham?'

'By all means but Millie should apologise and mean it.' They said goodbye. When she'd left, Mrs Bakewell sighed heavily.

Mrs Barlow went home and thoroughly cleaned the kitchen then washed herself and put on a clean ironed dress and brushed her hair.

Millie and her sisters came home for lunch and she told Millie she had to behave or Mrs Bakewell wouldn't let her go to school.

Geoff then came and was surprised seeing the clean tidy kitchen and his wife looking neat and clean, the table set with a small cloth. 'Wash up Geoff. I've some news for you.'

As she cooked him chips and two fried eggs, she told him about the possible job and Mrs Bakewell wanting to see him to-morrow afternoon. He cheered up at this. 'I'll have my hair cut. Will you press my suit and wash my white shirt. I'll polish my shoes. I'll put new heels on them. I've got a piece of rubber.'

'Mrs Bakewell said she can't promise you'll get the job, but there's hope.' She told him about Millie's bad behaviour.

'When she comes home I'll give her some strap.'

'NO, NO, you won't. That's not the way. You are teaching her to bully. We've to be quiet and well mannered like Mr and Mrs Markham.' She told him she and Millie were going to apologise to Mrs Markham and Violet.

'Ok, Cassie. Tell you what, when you come back I'll take the girls for a walk. Pack us some bread and jam and a bottle of water.'

'I will. I'm going to scrub the bedroom floors now.'

'I'll clean the windows,' he offered. The middle windows opened wide enough on their hinges to get an arm through to clean. He also scrubbed the concrete window sills. He then swilled and brushed the paths. They were both happy for the first time in years. The house began to sparkle.

Women were passing; one cheekily teased him, 'has she got you at it?'

'She has that,' he laughed. They couldn't believe it. They thought he would swear at her as he had before.

After much discussion he was taken on as school caretaker on a three month trial. The family was turned around at this, each determined to support each other and set a good example. There wasn't any further spitefulness and all the new girls went happily to school, learned and mixed at "play time." The boys who deliberately misbehaved had a stroke of the cane across the palm of their hand.

Meant To Meet

Rumours of war were anxiously heard. Percy, June and Katherine knew life would never be the same again as Matthew and then Mark would have to go and possibly not come back. They made the best of each day and Violet flourished at school and had to be moved up a class. When she was 7 years old she began to grow taller and was very graceful.

As feared war broke out in 1939 and in the rationing produce in the allotments was stolen during the nights. There was no excuse as several were available through deaths and old age. Two retired miners took it in turns to stay in their sheds with their dogs during the "Indian summer" hot weather. Two men were caught and the police dealt with them. There was no further stealing. Percy and the other miners at the pit were **exempt**, on the grounds that they were essential to the war effort at home.

Before leaving school in 1940 Luke had applied for a job at the Colliery and Mr Glynn willingly employed him. The miners were pleased. Percy and June accepted his decision as this was what he had wanted from being a small boy. Percy was thankful life at the pit wasn't as hard as when he began at Luke's age, now they had technology and machines to help. They breakfasted and walked to the Colliery together with the other workers.

In 1940 Matthew had to enlist and he opted for the Air Force. Percy, June and the whole family missed him very much as did several young ladies. He came home on leave in his uniform and gave June money. She put it in the Cooperative Savings Bank for his saving for a car. He was friendly with the village girls but that was all.

James passed his 11plus examination easily. Before setting off the first morning attending the Grammar School, June stood smiling at him and he smiled back. Sheer love flowed through her. He was a different personality to his brothers and this is how God had made him, but still masculine. She thought, "It would be a funny world if we were all the same."

The nightmare telegram came in 1941. Matthew had been killed in a raid. Percy couldn't go to work and he, June and the boys and Violet sat holding hands sobbing. Minister Lincoln came but they couldn't accept any comfort from him or his prayers. He understood and quietly left them. The children didn't go to school.

Mrs Bakewell as arranged, came to see them as she had and was visiting all the bereaved. June had a tea tray ready. She was very impressed how June cared for their home. They all wept together. Mr Witt senior came and expressed their sorrow not only for their son and brother, but also their own loss of a brilliant engineer. He tentatively told Percy he had brought Matthew's tool box. Percy went to the car with him and accepted it with thanks. Mr Witt shook his hand warmly and left. Percy quietly took the tool box up into Matthew's bedroom, weeping again.

Lord Derbyshire arranged also to meet with the bereaved. He was still the Member of Parliament for the area. He knew June from her being born was his son Andrew's daughter. He was used to meeting June out and about with her children. When he told Percy and June how much Messrs Witt regretted his death as he had a good engineering future in front of him, both Percy and June lost their composure and broke down. He was nearly crying himself as June stood comforting her husband and the children were cuddling them both.

A pang went through him. Had he and his wife denied Andrew happiness? Katherine had never revealed he was the father of June. Seeing June and Percy and recognising their bond of love he had a sadness. He and his wife despite getting on well together never had had this closeness. Andrew who had married when he was 30 to produce male heirs as was his duty, but he and his wife also weren't close. She went her own way living a life around horses but bore two sons for him, heir and a spare. Andrew always had an air of loneliness about him but threw himself into his work. Lord Derbyshire thought it prudent to leave them to their grief but would keep in touch as he would with the other bereaved families.

Percy and June knew life had to go on as the other bereaved families did. Order was restored and Percy went back to work, the boys and Violet back to school but they were all subdued, a light had gone out of their lives. Percy and June heard their sons and Violet crying at night in bed.

Automatically rubbing a little Vaseline into her hands her Mam always bought her for her birthday with a tablet of slightly scented toilet soap, as the bowl filled sprinkled a little soda in to wash the breakfast pots and pans. Staring into the water she saw Matthew eagerly running to her waving the shopping bag he had left with her shopping list and money at Mrs Denholm's to collect on his way home for the first time. She saw him running home eager to see if his siblings had been born, turning the heavy handle whilst she put the clothes through the big wooden rollers. She saw him eagerly waiting to watch the grinder man sharpening knives, scissors, axes, and garden tools, twice a year. Matthew sat with all of them round the kitchen table as they pegged rugs, painstakingly cutting up strips of material she bought and washed from the jumble sales. Memories, memories, she shouted at God, "Whatever did he do? Whatever have I done for you to take my precious first born?" She knew she was losing her mind. Realizing she was crouching on the floor she knew she had to get control back.

Like a sleepwalker she walked up to his bedroom and opened the door no-one had touched since he was killed. Going in and seeing the made up bed ready for his coming home on leave, sobbing she gathered up his bedding smelling the fragrance of the red carbolic soap they washed with, sobbing, sobbing until she was spent.

Going to his cupboard she took out the cardboard box the official from the War Office had brought of Matthew's personal belongings and laying it on the tumbled bedding she took off the lid. On the top was an envelope addressed to her. With trembling hands she opened it. It was a birthday card with a picture of her favourite flowers, violets. Inside she read, "I love you Mam, you've been everything to me a loving Mam could be. Please take care of yourself, my loving Dad, my precious brothers and Violet. God bless you all. See you soon. Love and kisses from Matthew." She knew he had prepared this for one of his brother to give her.

Standing there she told him how much she loved him, how much she had loved him before he was born;

how she would always love him and how much she appreciated what a wonderful son he'd been. Feeling calmer she put the card back in the box and returned it to the cupboard.

Wrapping up his pyjamas she put them in his cupboard. She knew instead of passing these down with his other clothes he had outgrown to Mark in her thrifty way as her boys grew she passed the clothes down making or buying new for Matthew. His brothers couldn't have cared less. All they wanted was a good plate full of food!

Folding his bedding she opened his window, then went down and put more coal on the fire to heat the ovens, washed the pots and pans and tidied the sink. Taking off her crumbled apron and dress she combed her hair, washed her hands, arms and face and put on a clean dress and apron. She put her cooled bread away and got out the ingredients for the family's favourite coconut jam tarts and mixed the pastry. She stirred the pan of simmering soup on the hob she had made just after 5 o'clock for the children's lunch, and when everything was baked she went upstairs working though her routine of bed making and cleaning before her children came home for lunch.

Stock taking her home made preservatives in the cool pantry with dismay she heard a knock on the door. She didn't want to see anyone just now but couldn't hide and with no doors having locks, people opened them and she couldn't hide. It was the Chapel Minister.

'I won't delay you in your busy morning. How are you?' He could see the emotions etched on her face and her eyes and swollen lids red with weeping.

'Please sit down, would you like a cup of tea?' He never had refused and he was eyeing the cooling tarts. 'Would you like one, Minister?'

'Yes please.' They settled down. 'How are you Mrs Markham?'

'I've had a bad morning,' crying again.

He waited. She blew her nose. 'I've been shouting at God for taking our beloved Matthew.

'Yes, I can understand why. But God doesn't send wars. You know the bible, Mrs Markham. How in Genesis God made a perfect world for each one of us, but sin came in.' He was putting this into his memory to use in his sermon on Sunday.

'Yes he did. I repent of my words.'

Praying together June couldn't stop her self from crying again. He stood behind her saying 'tears of healing.' After waiting for a few minutes said, 'I've to go now for my next call.' He was looking at the tarts again.

'Would you take two, Minister?'

'I would please.' She wrapped them and he carefully put them in his bag thanking her and bidding her goodbye.

Finishing checking her stock she put the tarts away in a tin then laid the table for her children coming home just in time as she heard them calling as they came into the yard, 'Mam. Mam, we're home.' She as always cuddled them. They had brought her bag of groceries she needed for the next day.

June decided to do her washing when the children had set off for school. 'Darling, will you come home with me after school instead of our walk to-day?' she asked Violet.

'Yes Mam.'

Meant To Meet

'Thank you.' Off they went and June quickly got her machine out and filled it. She loved this little small washing machine with attached rollers and manual paddle and it had a tap. She always saved the water for her scrubbing. June had seen it advertised in her weekly magazine and Percy said, 'Go to Mr Williams and ask if they can get you one and deliver.'

She took her magazine. Mr Williams promised, 'I could get you one and deliver at a price cheaper than this. You can pay weekly.'

She had thanked him and said, 'I'll pay. I don't have credit. If I can't pay, I don't buy.' Still thrifty she kept to her budget saving as much money as she could. Reading the instructions she noted the emphasis stating when lifting the rollers up for use, they must be secured or they could drop down on fingers or hands and cause damage. Mr Williams had put a free box of Oxydol washing powder in the tub.

June continued using her tub for soaking the sports clothes and Percy's pit clothes before dolly pegging or used her washboard for stubborn stains after rubbing carbolic or hard white soap from pieces off the market before putting them through the machine. Then she used her mangle with the wooden rollers she wouldn't be without after she had adjusted the handles on top for the space she needed between the rollers. She put their pyjamas, shirts and trousers through she always made and sewed rubber buttons on and the bedding and other items she didn't need to iron, repeatedly putting them through until they were almost dry. Washing was now much easier having instant hot water with the gas water heater over the sink instead of having to boil all the water, and using the Oxydol powder. She often thought of the women who had had to carry every drop of water to their home.

She didn't wash on Friday mornings unless she had her son's sports clothes they needed again for Saturday, with making enough bread dough to cover Saturday, and fruit cakes, coconut loaves and seed loaves known as "mouse cake" to cover the weekend. Black leading her range whilst the dough rose, then whilst the cakes baked she scrubbed the kitchen red tiles, outside steps and toilet, as she did also Monday and Wednesdays with her water after she had boiled the white clothes. Percy when he wasn't working Saturday mornings scrubbed the outside window sills up stairs and down and cleaned the windows inside and out. Her boys swilled and brushed the yard and path.

Her big washes with the bedding were Mondays after she had changed the beds on Saturday only putting top sheet to bottom in the winter, and she also washed Tuesday, Wednesday and Thursdays including Percy's pit clothes and the boys' sports clothes. When it was raining Percy helped her fill up the ceiling clothes dryer he wound down for her and wound up when she had loaded it before he went to bed.

Rushing to get tidied up before fetching Violet home hadn't had time to get all the dried washing in. In no way was she still having it out when the boys and Percy came home. No one did. Violet enjoyed helping her fetch it in and the lines. June checked the chicken casserole in the slow oven

Enjoying the tarts after their substantial casserole with dumplings, June had kept four back for Mark's and her beloved husband's next day packing up. They laughed when she told them the Minister had taken two with him. 'He'll be coming more often,' Percy teased her. He knew from her eyes she had been crying again, but waited until they were in bed to talk to her in privacy.

June had always from marrying Percy been up washed and dressed before 5 o'clock, apart from when she suffered morning sickness in the first month of being pregnant with the males. She hadn't suffered morning sickness with Violet which had led her to believe this one was a girl. She cleaned out the fire and putting more coal on, packed Percy's lunch and filled his flask and had a beaker of tea from the pot. She gave him a nourishing breakfast as always and sent him out to work with a loving cuddle and kiss telling him she loved him. He kissed her back telling her he loved her and was proud of her. Next she packed Mark's lunch box and filled him a flask of tea. He came and enjoyed his usual nourishing breakfast before he caught the bus.

Violet and June had a bowl of porridge but neither she nor Violet had the fried breakfast the males had. They had either an egg boiled, poached or scrambled with bread and butter.

After tea June asked Mark, 'as the elder son now and working, will you have Matthew's bedroom?'

'Can I think about this Mam?'

'Of course Mark.'

After a talk with his brothers they all agreed their Mam and Dad should have their own bedroom and they stay in the twin bedded rooms and let Violet have Matthew's room so she could spread her "girlie" toys about.

Suggesting this to their Mam and Dad who agreed if this was what they wanted and thanked them for their thoughtfulness. Violet was excited about having her own room.

'I'll decorate it and make new curtains,' June promised her. 'We'll choose the wallpaper and material on Saturday afternoon.'

Percy looked at his boys in thankfulness. This would now help June in her grief, planning something different.

'I'll help peg a rug,' James offered.

'I'll ask the College as my next project for my exams if I can make you a desk, Violet,' Mark promised. She excitedly cuddled him.

He proudly had given June a rolling pin he had made for her. He also made her a bowl and at home he varnished it and June kept fruit in it. She had thrilled both times and loved using them. He was enjoying learning to be a joiner and was aware he had been chosen from a lot of applicants. At 18 years as expected, Mark had to enlist. He chose the Navy.

Chapter Three

The second nightmare telegram came when Mark had served almost two years. His ship had been torpedoed and every life was lost. June went into shock, Katherine came and stayed, she was heartbroken for their family's loss. For three days June didn't eat, she didn't let her children leave the home keeping them close to her, constantly checking their breathing during the nights. The Chapel Minister and Mrs Bakewell came and tried talking to her, but to no avail. Percy in his heartbreak for their two sons being killed was now fearful for June as was Katherine. She was like a zombie. Mr Colyton senior came and gave them his condolences. He could see they were heartbroken over losing two sons. He quietly left. Percy walked with him to his car and Mr Colyton hesitantly gave him Mark's tools expressing his own sorrow at losing Mark. Percy quietly sobbing put the box upstairs.

The doctor came and took Percy and Katherine outside and told them, 'you'll both have to be strong with her and make her see sense. She can't go on like this.' Percy and Katherine already knew this.

Percy went back in and taking her in his arms, he was stern with her for the first time. 'You've to let go June, you're heartbroken we know this, but so are we. You're destroying our children's confidence; do you want to make them nervous wrecks? Mark knew the dangers when he enlisted.' He didn't know what to say.

She spoke through cracked lips, 'the silly fools. Why didn't they join the Army?'

'Soldiers are being killed daily, June. It's the evil of the war. You must see sense.'

His words broke through her mind; she looked at him for the first time in the three days and saw his suffering, his eyes blood shot and lids swollen with crying, his drawn face. She saw her children's frightened white faces. Giving a loud cry she gathered them all to her, sobbing, 'I'm sorry, I'm sorry. Please forgive me, please forgive me.' They and Katherine all cried together.

Unknown to them Katherine was heartbroken also for Andrew who had lost his eldest son and heir. Only she, Andrew, his parents, and Grace and Albert Arnett the bus driver and his wife, knew the blood connection this young man had with June and Mark. She made a pot of tea and forced June to drink it; then stiffly standing June began to prepare them a meal. The children and Percy relaxed; Percy was silently thanking God for his helping them. They stayed at home the remainder of the day then Percy and Luke went back to work and the children to school the next day. Katherine went home knowing she had so June in her duties would regain her mind.

Meant To Meet

Katherine knew she would have to support her family at the Memorial Service the village held for the killed also in the 1914-1918 war. Jeremy Derbyshire's, Mark's and the other men and women from the village would be added to Matthew's on the monument under the names of the men and the four young nurses killed in the First World War. She had to prepare for meeting Andrew, now Lord Derbyshire on his father's death and his family, and hoped in her heart that Andrew would take strength from her in his bereavement of his heir. She knew he would recognise her and June as his daughter, Violet as his granddaughter. Matthew and Mark had been his Grandsons. Her thoughts were chasing round and round until she made herself control them. The important fact was they were both honouring the fallen.

Chapel Minister Lincoln introduced Percy, June and their family to Andrew. Dowager Lady Derbyshire and Andrew's wife were mingling. Katherine saw emotion go through his face on meeting June and he looked closely at Violet recognising his Granddaughter. 'I'm so sorry you've lost two sons, Mr and Mrs Markham. I'm informed what fine young men they both were. I regret I was unable to come to Matthew's Memorial service, I couldn't leave an urgent meeting in the House.'

June said to him, 'thank you sir for your letter. We appreciated it. We're all deeply sorry you've lost your elder son.' He was looking at her, his daughter and she didn't know, recognising the hint of culture that was in her voice.

He asked Percy, 'you're the foreman at the Colliery, Mr Markham?'

'Yes sir.' He introduced Luke, 'Luke works in the colliery.'

'Good man,' Andrew replied. Percy then introduced John and James.

'Congratulations James on passing your 11 plus examination. What's your ambition?'

'I'd like to teach, Lord Derbyshire.'

'Excellent. Do you know the subjects yet?'

'My favourites are mathematics, English, history or languages.'

'Good man.'

Looking at John he asked, 'have you chosen your career, John?'

'Yes sir. I leave school at Christmas and have been accepted as an apprentice gardener at The Hall. I've always wanted to be a gardener, Lord Derbyshire.'

'Excellent, excellent, John. I look forward to your progress.' He already knew John was going to be their apprentice but wanted to include him. He was thinking how well mannered his Grandsons were and how he would love them to know this relationship. He smiled and nodded at them both.

Smiling at June and Percy, he said, 'you both have set your family a good example.' They thanked him.

He said 'hello' to Violet.

She stood holding June's hand, 'I'm Violet. I'm ten.' Katherine knew he was delighted with her. Squatting down he said, 'You're a very beautiful young lady.' She was smiling at him. He had to restrain gathering her up into his arms, his little Granddaughter.

Standing up he then spoke to Katherine, 'How are you?'

'I'm so sorry you've lost your son, sir.' They were both remembering when he had asked her not to call him sir, all those years ago. His hair was now grey, his face was lined and his bright eyes were dull.

He stood looking at her. Briefly they gazed into each other's eyes conveying the message, "I love you." Abruptly turning away before his urge to gather her to his heart overcame him, went to speak to the other families. Katherine felt a glow in her heart, he still loved her and he now knew that she still loved him. She prayed he would take comfort from this. Rupert and Janet re-joined the family and they left.

June began to mix again with the community supporting the other mothers who had lost their sons. A shadow hung over the little village but they got on with their lives as best they could. They were all together in the air raid shelters as Sheffield was badly blitzed, the women and girls knitting throughout these nights for the armed forces. Girls in the village were grieving at losing the young men.

Several more men and women in the village were killed or injured but thankfully the war ended in 1945.

When he was 21 years, Luke got engaged to a young lady from the next village. June and Percy were unsure about her but made her welcome as Luke loved her. One evening he came home earlier. He was never out late with going to bed early for the early morning working day. He looked upset. June made him a mug of cocoa as he sat quiet at the table. Eventually he told them she had ditched him deciding he wasn't exciting enough. His family and friends supported him but he was unhappy for a while.

A quiet young lady came to Chapel on the Sunday evening and left immediately the service ended. The Chapel Minister told June in confidence, knowing she would sensitively welcome her that Mrs Berwick's husband had been killed in the war and she was still heartbroken. For a new beginning she had applied for the post as teacher of the nine year old boys in the local school becoming vacant as the male teacher was retiring. She was given the post and bought a new two bedroom house from the eight built on the outskirts of the village with wonderful views of the countryside. Mrs Berwick came regularly to Chapel but didn't mingle.

Asking Luke a question and he helped her and they chatted for a few minutes. Their friendship continued and Luke was happier again and doing well at work. Luke didn't go to her home but after several months he asked June if she could come for tea before Chapel? June willingly agreed and they all had a lovely time after Mrs Berwick had lost her shyness. Three years later when she came to tea Luke said, 'Angela and I are going to marry next summer. We're getting engaged.' She was blushing as they all congratulated them.

Luke when she had agreed to marry him told her he didn't feel comfortable moving into the home she had bought from the money her husband had left her. Being intelligent she understood and they made enquiries about a three bedroom bungalow being built also on the outskirts of the village but at the opposite end. The six bungalows each had a large garden. They bought it between them with Angela's savings from her teaching job. She sold the house and invested the money with what remained of her husband's legacy for their children. Regretfully for all of them, Angela didn't become pregnant but she and Luke was happily married and she continued working at the village school and they both enjoyed their garden. Luke had made a lawn and the remainder of the land he grew vegetables as his dad did, but he also planted fruit trees and bushes.

Rupert died after a bad dose of influenza. With the coal dust he had inhaled his lungs had weakened as he got older.

Janet asked Percy 'would you like Rupert's greenhouse?' He was thrilled. It was easy to dismantle with Rupert having made it. Archie Benson the owner of the second hand shop and Percy fetched it and Rupert's garden equipment and taking it to the allotment Percy told him, 'I'm going to put a guttering round the greenhouse to catch the rain water. Mr Hindley didn't need to do this with the stream at the bottom of the garden.'

'Tell you what Percy; I can get you a couple of big wooden barrels with taps. You'll just need to make a hole for the down pipe.'

He was thrilled again. 'How much are they Archie?'

'Nowt to you, don't tell anybody else though. I made a good deal with your beds,' he laughed. 'Give us a bunch of your flowers if you will, Percy, for wife. It's her birthday.' Percy laughed.

The men were all interested as this was the first greenhouse and they were pleased for him. Nearly all of them as Percy made their own garden frame with old windows. Percy was able to grow his seeds in the little greenhouse instead of on the window bottoms at home and fitted a length of hose pipe to each tap, so didn't have to carry the watering can about.

Shortly afterwards Janet was diagnosed with breast cancer and because she had kept quiet with caring for her husband this had quickly spread, but mercifully she didn't suffer too long before she died peacefully.

June begged her Mam to come and live with them. They all wanted her to do this. Thanking them but said she was happy for the time being with her good neighbours. June noticed her face looked drawn but knew she was bereaving her parents.

After a month still looking pale and tired, June urged her to see the doctor and she promised that she would. They walked with her to the bus stop. The next evening a policeman startling them came. Katherine had died sat in her chair in the garden. Her neighbour as always had taken the early evening local newspaper round, Katherine bought a morning paper and they swopped, Katherine saving them to take to June on the Sunday, found her thinking she was asleep. The doctor signed the death certificate as "heart failure." June and the family couldn't stop weeping. In just a few months they had suffered three bereavements.

June found papers at the top of Katherine's tin box stating her wishes for the Church service and funeral and to be buried near her parents. June wasn't surprised knowing how her Mam liked to be organised and had paid an insurance policy covering this. The spare with Katherine's Co-operative savings June invested for her children.

There wasn't a male stranger at the funeral service but on Katherine's coffin with the other flowers, a most beautiful bouquet sat. Afterwards looking at the flowers at the side of the grave June hoped there was a name, but was disappointed. The funeral director came enquiring if she wanted to take any. June asked him, 'do you know who sent this?'

'Yes, Mrs Markham, it came from The Hall. Your Mam did a lot of sewing for the Dowager Lady Derbyshire.' As expected Andrew had had to come back to The Hall when his father died to carry on with the tradition of running it and the estate. He, like his father had been, was the local Member of Parliament.

Gazing and overwhelmed by the beauty of the flowers June saw Lord Andrew Derbyshire's face in it. She thought it was her imagination. Of course, why had she not realized this before? **He** was her father. The classic features she and Violet had, Violet's fair curly hair, Violet and James' intelligence. June thought, "My Mam is sending me the message." She immediately dismissed this, it wasn't Christian. Yes, love lived on, but only love. She remembered he hadn't married until he was 30 years and he always looked unhappy in the newspaper photographs when he was a London lawyer. He loved my Mam. She now, like her Mam, would take this secret to her grave. Percy thought she had stood grieving long enough over the coffin and gently urged her away.

Quickly emptying Honeysuckle Cottage, June had her Grandparents wardrobe and dressing table and Violet had Katherine's. The boys had the radio. Archie took the beds and other items away June and Percy didn't need. June wouldn't take payment as he had helped Percy with his greenhouse and was now helping them free of charge. June had Katherine's personal things including her sewing machine, reels of cottons and materials also everything from the kitchen and washing clothes equipment.

Percy and the boys emptying the shed found two old wooden washing tubs under a cover. Percy was happy with these as he would be able to root another white Gypsophila bush and a rose pink for his many requests. June took her wedding dress and veil her Mam had carefully covered and taken care of for if she had a daughter.

Katherine had told her years ago that it was leased for her lifetime and June knew in her heart that it was Lord Andrew who had paid this. June wept for him knowing he must have loved her Mam, but not free in his position, to do so. If it hadn't been for him, she wouldn't have been born. Her Mam perhaps would have had a different life. She had to stop these thoughts, thankful that she had been born.

In the sixth form, James concentrated on French and German for the higher school certificate. He did sufficiently well in the exams to secure a place in the modern language department at the University of Durham.

After three years of study, James gained a degree in modern languages. Since he wanted to become a teacher, he was transferred to the Education Department at Durham, where he learned how best to present his material to students. He gained a Diploma in Education, enabling him to apply for school teaching posts and was offered three opportunities to teach through retirement or illness. Carefully laterally thinking as he always did, in his loyalty to the opportunities he had been given and also his loyalty to the village, he chose his local Grammar School to teach his specialised languages. He was gladly accepted knowing the students would require these languages in the changing cosmopolitan world and he was very popular with the staff and students.

Percy, June and John were so pleased he was staying at home with them, but in no way would they have held him back knowing how hard he had worked. Needless to say, they were very proud of him and June always made sure he looked immaculate in his pressed suit and the white shirts she washed separately and rinsed with the "blue bag."

James loved his work nurturing young minds and made them aware of the privilege of learning for their future. Hearing on the "grape vine" he had come from a working class family and worked hard to teach, the students greatly respected him.

June as always happily cared for James, John and her beloved Percy. John had bought a car and took his Dad, Luke and James to the Saturday afternoon matches.

Whilst they did this Angela, Luke's wife, took June in her car to the market town shopping then went to the café for tea before buying their meat to last until Thursday. Mr Richards gave June a discreet discount with Percy not now coming. June loved Angela as her own daughter, and Angela loved her. She called her Mam and Percy, Dad. Angela and Luke went for Sunday lunch with her family who were so pleased and thankful she was happy again with him and his family, before returning for Chapel.

Violet gained all her qualifications and was given a place at Cambridge University paid for by grants as James had for Durham, to gain the qualifications needed to be a teacher of English and Mathematics. She met Robin Forrest three years older who was studying to be a lawyer and they fell in love. Violet and Robin married when she was 23 years old. Robin's parents being wealthy bought them a small home in London. She continued teaching until she was pregnant. Both sets of parents were thrilled and she sailed through the pregnancy but complications arose during labour, and it was a long difficult time when the doctors in the private hospital saying she would need a Caesarean.

Being strong and fit Violet persevered and a beautiful baby boy was born naturally. Everyone rejoiced. With the noise of his crying he had good lungs! The doctors regretfully told Robin and Violet there would be no more children. They wept as did the family when told, but were so thankful Violet had survived and Clive was a healthy happy baby they all adored him. Rita, Robin's mother with living near visited daily.

Percy had a day holiday and he and June travelled on the train to London where Robin met them and took them to the hospital. They were thrilled with the baby and June gave Violet the baby clothes she had made. Violet being strong and fit quickly recovered and was able to go home where she had a nanny for Clive and a housekeeper. When Clive was eleven months and his sharp teeth were coming through Violet reluctantly had to wean him. He had Andrew Derbyshire's features and fair curly hair.

She cooked as her Mam (now calling her Mother) had taught her and Clive thrived. When he was one year old he went into the child nursery in the school where she taught mornings only taking him home with her. She and Robin were very much in love and he prospered in his career. They visited June and Percy who adored Clive and he adored them, in the school holidays.

John when he was 29 years old married Honoria. She had told him she didn't want children as she who was being trained to take over the role as housekeeper at The Hall. Loving her so much he agreed but was disappointed as were June and Percy, but they loved each other and were happy and that was all June and Percy had ever wanted for their children. Honoria cooked John a nourishing breakfast and she travelled with him to The Hall. She made sure he had a hearty lunch with them in The Hall kitchen.

Sunday morning's John came to help his Dad in his allotment along with James and the three of them had a "man" time whilst June cooked her usual delicious Sunday roast, still using her beloved range. John always brought her beautiful flowers and fresh fruit from The Hall he was allowed to buy with a discount. Honoria slept in these mornings as she was up early the other mornings now being The Hall housekeeper, and came on the bus to join her husband and his family for lunch. They all loved her and she had a wonderful sense of humour. She shared humourous happenings that had occurred at The Hall among the staff and they laughed and laughed. She washed the dinner pots and pans and John and Luke dried. Then she and John went home,

Percy went to bed, Luke marked his student's homework and June watched a television film and knitted.

The following Sunday after June had cooked she put her new jumper on she had knitted in 3 ply wool. Honiara told her, 'you look lovely in your jumper Mam. What's the pattern?'

June explained, 'it's what is known as "feather and fan." She had used this pattern time and time again for herself, her Mam and Violet. Honiara repeatedly looked admiringly so June asked her, 'would you like me to knit you one?'

'Yes please, Mam. Perhaps I should have two to wear against each other.' They all laughed at this.

'I will,' June promised. 'I saw some multi coloured wool I think you will like.'

'Wonderful. Thanks Mam, I'll give you the money.'

June now had an automatic washing machine but still used her wooden rollers mangle to get all the wet out and an electric iron and refrigerator. Life had begun to be so different but she thought time after time she would gladly have gone back to the days when she had no "aids" to have Matthew and Mark back.

Chapter Four

Clive Forrest was clever and went to Cambridge University where his parents Robin and Violet had gained their degrees. They as Robin's parents had funded Clive with being affluent. Clive's ambition from being a young boy was to own a hotel. No one in the families knew where this came from but he worked hard and learned Business Studies, Finance and other qualifications he would need. From a Trust Fund his paternal Grandparents had set up for him when he was 21 years and which he had kept this gaining interest, at the age of 25 years he bought and renovated one in London naming it Gresley Wood in memory of his North Derbyshire ancestor's.

Through this hotel Clive met Jill a secretary when he was 25 years and they fell in love and married. Jill helped him run Gresley Wood and they had a son Sebastian again born with Andrew Derbyshire's features and white curls. Also going to Cambridge University he also gained the qualifications needed to help his dad run the hotel and now the one they had also renovated named Cobden Wood. His paternal Grandfather died first then when his Grandmother died the home and money was left to Robin, Violet and Clive.

Percy retired at 65 years, Mr Glynn Dingle appreciating how he had made his work easier after his father had died, asked him to stay on as Percy was fit and strong. June put her foot down. 'You've worked hard long enough, darling. I want you to be with me enjoying our years together.' Mr Glynn understood and he had Luke as a proficient foreman when Percy was made production manager.

Percy helped June do her washing which had lessened with only James being at home and Percy not getting his clothes as dirty. With James having a good meal at school she cooked a nourishing meal for Percy and herself for 12 noon. The afternoons they spent up at the allotment where June happily sat knitting or sewing and then home her supplies for the next day, or in the home garden or when raining went for walks on the country lanes outside the village or having a trip out on the little bus. June did sick visiting for the Chapel on Wednesday afternoons. They had a filling pudding at tea time with James after a light tea.

June picked up the viscious flu virus that was going around and died in the hospital isolation ward. Percy and the family were devastated. John and Honiara moved in to look after him and James. Jill and Clive came and they all wept broken heartedly. Violet knowing Honiara was capable and loving her as a sister as did Honiara her, took comfort from this and returned to London until the funeral. It was a very traumatic day. Percy, Luke, John, James, Clive and Archie Benson carried the coffin.

Violet arranged a buffet lunch the village pub provided just for the family at home, to take pressure from their heartbroken Dad. He lost his will to live without his beloved June and John found him dead in bed. The family were thankful at least their parents had enjoyed nine years of their Dad's retirement.

After a good discussion John, Honoria and James voted to live in the home as it had two bathrooms, separate toilets, and the big garden. There was only a minimum amount to pay for rates.

Mr Glynn Dingle came to see them. He'd been twice a week to see Percy and each time he'd been shocked at his deteriorating. John told him, 'my wife, I and James are going to live in this home, sir.'

'Good. I'm happy for you all.' Emotionally he said, 'Percy was a wonderful man and you both and Violet are a credit to him and your Mam as your dead brothers were.'

Finishing his glass of beer he quietly left them as the three of them were crying broken heartedly. He sat in his car crying. He had never cried so much in his life until Percy had died.

The family arranged to meet at home. Honiara cooked her nourishing casserole; John brought different fruits from the Hall to have for pudding with cheese and biscuits. Meeting up they all wept together. After lunch

John passed the cafetière round the table and everyone helped themselves.

John told them, 'Honoria, James and I suggest that we live in this home and we mentioned this to Mr Glynn Dingle.' The others were pleased at this and thankful James would be taken care of.

'Now we need to get the value and share this between you four.' Clive said, 'thank you John. With Jill and I having my parents' money, please keep this. Each one of you has always worked hard.'

"As Sebastian is our parents only Grandchild, I think he should have your share invested,' James said.

His brothers and wives agreed with this wholeheartedly. Clive and Jill thanked them.

'Now there's Dad's allotment,' John next said. 'I'm gardening all day as you know so don't want to take it on.'

'I have so much preparatory work and homework, also paperwork, I really haven't time,'

James told them.

'I'd love it please,' Luke broke in. 'Angela, as James, has so much work to do at home in the evenings she'll stop feeling guilty if I'm at the allotment with the men.'

'Thank you Luke, I'm very thankful of this. We'll continue the links with our growing up and all the happy times Dad, Mam and we had.' James broke down again as they all did.

'From being foreman when Dad was made production manager, I haven't had the same fellowship with the men not working alongside them. Now I've proved myself to Mr Glynn, I'm going to be promoted to production manager,' Luke announced. They all cuddled him and Angela. The men then had a glass of beer and the females a glass of white wine.

Discussing the buffet lunch, Honiara told them, 'the Chapel Hall isn't booked.'

'Please book it. May I get the pub caterers as for our Mam?' Violet asked.

'Yes, please Violet; more food as the men are coming and bottles of beer.' Honiara answered. 'I've a list of who to invite.'

'I'll attend to this,' Angela offered. This was accepted with gratitude. James quickly put two pans of water over the fire to boil for a cup of tea.

'Now there's another matter to discuss,' John told them. 'Mr Glynn came and told us Dad and Mam had invested the pension scheme money when he retired for us.' They all, including Clive, began to cry again at their unselfishness as always. Not one of them had known about this. Luke was in the pension scheme but his Dad had never discussed it.

Clive thanked them for all they were doing and told them, 'we are a family and we must continue being close to each other. Jill and I are in London unfortunately but with modern technology now there is no problem.' They all agreed on that. John then mentioned the money from their Dad's funeral insurance. He agreed to their request to pay for the funeral and any over, as their Mam's, to give to the Chapel.

James and Luke prepared the pots of tea and whilst they drank and relaxed, Honiara lovingly asked them, 'when John and I have sold our home may I update this? A vital help I need is a gas Aga range to help me with cooking as I work full time. John and I have a nourishing lunch at The Hall and James does also at school, but in the winter we'll need a more substantial tea. I'll be able to set the ovens. And there's the cooking at the weekends. I'd have to get rid of this range.'

'I agree Honoria,' Luke immediately answered. 'Angela wouldn't be able to manage without her modern aids. We'll never forget our happy childhood and the memories.'

Honoria looked round the table with tears in her eyes, 'Mam and Dad would be happy seeing us together.'

Violet, Jill and Clive left to go back to London, first going at Mam's grave with flowers.

Walking up to the allotment to find Mr Searle, the allotment owner who was usually in the shed shop which sold seeds and the gardener's other requirements. After greetings Luke asked him, 'can I continue renting Dad's allotment please Mr Searle?'

'With pleasure, lad, your Dad would be pleased.'

Angela then invited him to the buffet lunch after the funeral, and he gratefully responded. 'Your Dad, as you all know, was one of the finest men that ever lived,' he emotionally said. This set the family off again. He stood looking at Luke, John and James remembering when they and their dead brothers were growing up and how respectful and well mannered they had always been. How they had all eagerly worked helping Percy. He thought with tears welling up in him, "whatever will they do without their Mam and Dad?" Thanking him again they went and invited the men who were there

Meant To Meet

and asked them to invite the others to the buffet lunch and a glass of beer.

As expected it was another traumatic day and when they saw Percy's helmet sat on the coffin, everyone including hardened men wept at this. Luke, John, James, Clive, Archie and one of the bearers carried his coffin. Percy was buried at the side of June and the family had a headstone put up in the middle of them.

After a few days James suggested they make a Will leaving their home to whoever was left after death. When they were all deceased he again suggested they leave their home to Sebastian. Clive and Jill accepted this loving thought.

James paid his board. John and Honoria still paying the mortgage on their home put it up for sale.

Honoria's youthful mother came on Monday and Tuesdays to do their washing and ironing. She as June had, took great care of James' shirts and starched his collar and cuffs with a thin starch she mixed from granules. Staying together worked out very well and having spare money Honoria employed Mrs Hope, a very reliable village woman to black lead the range and clean the house as she worked full time and often had to work Saturday mornings when at The Hall they were entertaining. The three of them were determined to keep the home immaculate in respect of June.

James continued on Saturday mornings cleaning the windows, scrubbing the sills and steps and swilling the paths, enjoying this physical work after teaching, preparing work and all the marking of homework. He travelled to different parts of France on coach trips in the school holidays when he was able to converse in their language. He was now getting affluent also in Japanese knowing in the changing world this would be useful.

Saturday afternoons the three of them went for a countryside run calling at a pub for a glass of beer and a gin and tonic for Honoria, before going into the market town for her shopping needs. Calling at their village shop they bought freshly cooked fish, chips and peas enjoying these for their tea with bread and butter. After clearing everything away the three of them went into the front room to watch television. James made their beaker of cocoa before he left them to have his bath and bed.

In the long summer holiday James flew to Japan for a month to become more proficient with their language. He knew when he had passed the final exams he would be able to teach this language needed in the changing world trade they now had with Japan. Honoria and John stayed with her parents whilst the home was updated with central heating and a big Aga type gas cooking range, carpeted throughout apart from the bathrooms and kitchen and decorated. John and James both had a garage built either side of the path and John brought climbing plants from The Hall to cover the sides.

When Sebastian, Jill and Clive's son was almost 23 years he met Tanya also a secretary. It was love at first sight and they married. They had a son Grant, born also with the white curls and classical features.

Sebastian loved to ski and had gone often to the Alps with two friends from Cambridge University. They

Meant To Meet

contacted Sebastian asking if he wanted to join them as an "old students get together." Tanya in her unselfish love for him knew he wanted to go and insisted he did. Setting off from the top of the mountain as numerous times previously, an unexpected severe freak storm met them and he was thrown damaging his lungs. He was lucky not to have been killed as his friends, also expert skiers, were. The rescuers eventually found him but with being frozen and the shock of it all, Sebastian suffered pneumonia and other complications including being unable to father more children. The surgeons recommended he went to live in Switzerland. Grant was 13 months at the time and his parents had wanted a large family but Tanya was just so thankful her precious husband hadn't been killed and they had Grant.

Tanya devoted her life to her beloved husband and son and with technology helped Sebastian run the hotels from Switzerland with Clive and Jill in London.

Grant was a wonderful son from being very small doing everything he could to help his mother and father, and they adored him as he did them. He was a quiet studious boy and man as James had been and went to a Switzerland University gaining a Masters Degree with Honours in Business Management.

Jill died when Grant was 27 years old and Clive died two years later. Sebastian, Tanya and Grant were the only members of the family left.

Grant, age 27 years saw 24 year old Faye Harvey when he was staying in her parent's hotel she helped run in Portugal after she had completed University and Finishing School. Grant had been recommended to see this hotel and get ideas for renovating Gresley Wood and Cobden Wood, the hotels his Dad and he now owned. He fell in love with her. She was beautiful with auburn hair and gorgeous sparkling green eyes.

Faye fell in love with Grant and after a few days he plucked up courage to ask her if she would like to go to a popular show running nearby which she gladly accepted. Didi, Faye's mother wasn't pleased.

Sharing time in Portugal, Grant didn't invite her to London as he felt this wasn't etiquette to be on her own with him away from her parents. After three months they knew they were going to marry. Sebastian and Tanya were thrilled for him and longed to meet her. Grant regularly had sent photographs and videos.

Didi was furious with her. 'How can you even think of marrying that common man? His ancestors were pit workers with no class.'

'How do you know this?' Faye shouted. Grant had spoken to her of his family. She never dreamed she would hate her mummy but in this moment she did. 'They were all respectable hard working people and children. They weren't born "privileged" so how dare you pull them down? They left a legacy of strength and hope setting a good example. I'm proud I'm marrying into Grant's family. I wish I had known them. What adversity have you known, mother? Leave Grant and me alone if all you can do is try to destroy our happiness. I adore him and I'm very proud of him.'

'His grandmother five generations back was illegitimate. She didn't even know who her father was.'

'I didn't know this, but it makes no difference. Grant wasn't even born then. That's it isn't it?' she challenged, 'you regret him being born. How do you know all this rubbish? Whoever you are talking with isn't a nice person. I don't want my mind polluting with this slander.' Faye was longing for Grant. 'I'm still a virgin. That says something about how honourable Grant is. Were you?' she challenged. Didi couldn't answer because she hadn't been. She was amazed at this new Faye as she hadn't seen any of this previously.

Shrugging her shoulders Didi said, 'so you are going to defy me and marry him?'

'Yes, I am.'

Right, that's it then. Don't say I didn't warn you.' She stormed off furious that she hadn't got her own way.

Faye wept broken heartedly. Her papa knocked and came in. 'Please don't leave, darling. Your mummy will get over it.'

Faye snorted and kept silent with her thoughts.

Russell sighed. He knew if he defied Didi with her being financially independent as his business partner, she would leave him. He adored her but didn't like the fact that she was a snob. Sick in stomach he sat in the armchair in front of the window, Faye remained sat on her bed. 'Let's have a drink, darling. Would you like a glass of wine?

'Thank you no, papa, I'd love a coffee.' He rang the housekeeper.

As they were drinking he saw Didi drive off in a cloud of dust. He sighed. He liked and admired Grant who obviously worshipped Faye.

'Now precious, may we have a serious talk?'

'Yes papa.' She adored him. 'Let's go for a walk?'

'Yes darling. I've something to tell you now you are going to be married.' They set off. 'Thankfully my parents were organised and they worshipped you, you know this?'

'Yes, papa, and I adored them.' Didi had never been maternal and Russell's parents knew this. Faye had spent her vacations with them in London choosing Cambridge University to get her degrees in hotel running and languages to be near them. Determined Didi wouldn't get their wealth from their jewellery and gold businesses they had built up from being married, they left everything to Faye. She had no idea of this, hadn't even thought of it.

To relax and being keen sailors they went out on their yacht with four friends in a competition. In a choppy sea another yacht accidentally crashed into them and their yacht had overturned in the strong current. Their bodies were quickly recovered but they were all dead. Faye and Russell were devastated. Faye was at a Paris Finishing school.

'They made you their sole heiress, darling, with me as your Power of Attorney, Trustee and Executor. I had their money invested for you when you were either 25 years or getting married, which you are now. There are devious men around, darling, and you've been sheltered. But you'll be secure with Grant.'

Faye understood his reasoning and hope flared in her heart. She had no idea what the amount was but she would share whatever with Grant.

'What's happening to Holly House papa?' It had been empty for almost four years since their death, unknown to Faye waiting for her either marrying or living there in her career as she loved it so.

'It's yours, if you want it.'

'Yes, I do, papa. I loved my times there.'

'Birdie is still taking care of it. Your Grandparents left it to you hoping you would live there. We need to go to their solicitors in London.'

Faye rang Grant. He was thrilled they were coming and would meet them at the airport. Russell listened with pain in his heart to their words of love before ringing off.

'Now, my precious, you know how my parents loved the sea and taking advantage with having a trustworthy manager in their shop, went on cruises when you were at school and university, and spent money on yachts?'

'Yes, papa, I'm so thankful they did didn't wait until they retired. They must have worked hard building their business up.'

'Yes, they did, darling.' They both walked in silence with their memories.

Russell invited Didi to go to London with them, but she was angry again now Russell had told Faye of this inheritance instead of continuing being dependent on them.

That evening when Grant rang, Faye told him of Holly House and being her Grandparents sole heiress. His heart sank knowing Didi would throw this in their faces that he was marrying Faye for her money. Good sense prevailed realising they had planned to marry before Faye knew of this inheritance.

After Russell made the appointment with the London solicitors, he booked their flight after Didi again refused to go with them. Grant was waiting for them at the airport and took them to the solicitors.

When completing the business of transferring Holly House to Faye, the solicitor told them the financial amount Faye had been left from the sale of the shop, contents and the amount of money Russell had invested. Grandparents Harvey had spent as they earned but Grant again was uncomfortable at the amount. Faye firmly told him they would be able to buy or build a hotel for their and hopefully their children's future. The solicitor approved of this plan. 'Much better investing your money in bricks than in stocks and shares,' he smilingly advised Faye.

Faye then surprised them all by asking if a Will should be drawn up.

'This is very wise thinking, Miss Harvey. Thankfully, your Grandparents were diligent making their Will so you would benefit. There may have been problems otherwise.' He was thinking of Faye's mother. 'God please forbid you both or either of you being killed or die. Who would you leave everything to Miss Harvey?'

'Mr Grant Forrest.'

'And you, Mr Forrest?'

'Miss Faye Harvey, my future wife.' The solicitor smiled.

'If you both?'

'Mr Forrest's parents, our children or my papa in the event of not having any,' Faye answered. Each one of them was thinking, 'it's better to make the most of each day.'

'Good, good, I'll get this prepared.' They made a further appointment to sign and would again after they were married. After everything was sealed and signed Faye felt exhausted with the emotions of all this and Didi being so cruel to her.

As arranged they went to Holly House with Faye directing Grant. Going through the security gates Faye breathed a sigh of relief, she had come home and this was where she and Grant would live and prayerfully have their family. Grant was looking round in amazement. Miss Bird, Birdie as she was affectionately called and staff rushed outside to greet them. Birdie cuddled Faye who proudly introduced Grant and she greeted him with warmth. She liked him. After freshening up, they met up and had a glass of wine. Russell was sad Didi wasn't with them. He had invited her but she had abruptly refused. Grant was sad she had been so cruel to Faye and voiced his thoughts.

'She'll come round. Please don't let her spoil your happiness.' They felt much better after a delicious nourishing lunch. Grant and Faye took Russell back to the airport.

Birdie took Faye under her wing whilst she and Grant when he came daily, finalised the quiet wedding and had the Master Suite refurbished. Tanya came to the wedding and was re-assured with Faye and loving her immediately, but Sebastian wasn't able to travel. After a few days honeymoon at Holly House Grant took Faye to spend a short time with Sebastian and Tanya. Sebastian also loved her and was happy that his son had a wife who loved him and would continue to do so as Tanya had him. They were all surprised at Faye's expert knowledge of running hotels.

Didi didn't "come round." She enforced Russell to leave Portugal and live in Bermuda where they bought a luxury boutique hotel.

Chapter Five

Faye and Grant settled very happily in Holly House and with her inheritance from her Grandparents they bought two run down hotels and began to renovate naming them Bow Wood and Clough Wood she helped him run taking pressure from his father. Just over a year married to everyone's delight, Faye became pregnant.

Loving to knit but restricted for colours with not knowing the sex of her baby, at eight months pregnant had the urge to knit a Fair Isle cardigan from the pattern in her magazine. Grant in his adoration indulged her as always and took her to the store where she bought the wools.

Returning home a powerful motorbike shot out of a side street and crashed into Faye. People rang for the ambulance, Grant was in shock. The young man and Faye were dead. A member of the ambulance crew heard the baby's heartbeat and led with a siren police car rushed Faye's body to the nearest maternity hospital where they immediately performed a Caesarean and in two minutes had lifted the baby girl out and put her into the special care unit.

Grant and the parents of the young man Ian were heartbroken. It was the first time Ian had been out on the big machine and he had obviously lost control. Grant had to be sedated and his parents came from Switzerland.

This tragedy was widely broadcast with Grant being a well known hotelier and the sheer miracle of the baby still being alive in her dead mother and surviving was made much of.

Grant's solicitor had contacted Faye's parents in Bermuda but they made no acknowledgement and didn't come to the funeral, or even send a card or flowers. Didi blamed Grant for Faye's death and then was furious again when learning Grant had inherited everything her parent's in law had left Faye, including Holly House.

Sebastian and Tanya were very disgusted with Didi and Russell but hid their feelings. Grant was disappointed not for himself, but thought they would have had some respect for their daughter and now granddaughter. Numerous cards and flowers were received at Holly House from sympathetic people including his hotel guests. When they suffered bereavement, Grant always sent a card.

Abbey with being a strong baby and having good lungs thrived and was able to go home where she was deeply loved and precious to Grant, his parents and Birdie. Private specialized nurses cared for her. Seeing Abbey drinking from the bottle, regret filled Grant again. Faye's breasts had been preparing to feed her baby and she had been looking forward to this bonding.

Sebastian even with special breathing apparatus and determination to support his son couldn't cope without the Swiss air so he and Tanya reluctantly went back to Switzerland.

For a long time Grant mentally tortured himself thinking that if he hadn't stopped for an elderly lady and her dog to cross the road, it wasn't even at a crossing, he wouldn't have been in line with the side street. With his father's accident and now Faye's death he had begun to think his family was fated. If it wasn't for the miracle of Abbey being born and the love and responsibility he had for his parents, he knew he would have committed suicide. Thankfully with his faith in God he was eventually able to overcome these dark thoughts knowing it had been, as his father's, a human accident. He over protected Abbey until he knew this was wrong and not fair on her and her nannies, but never drove again and grieved daily for his beloved Faye and Abbey without her mummy.

Grant felt very close to Faye in Holly House. He knew that she would be happy for Abbey to grow up in this secure home with Biddy and staff. Using the study with technology put in as an office as he couldn't sleep, worked in the early hours of the morning until he was exhausted and went to bed.

Going to the head office each morning leaned heavily on his PA and managers during this period. Each one of them and his staff were grateful for his trust, but knowing he was available if they needed him. After lunch at home he rested for an hour before spending time with Abbey. Weather permitting he took her in her pram in the grounds or wood exercising the dogs at the same time. She was very bright and full of curiosity looking around her. Whenever possible he was with her at bedtime to cuddle her before she was put in her cot. She had a happy disposition as she grew up surrounded by love and she adored her dada and Birdie.

From beginning to walk Abbey led her nannies a right dance! Always running off and her day nannies had a problem keeping up with her. Discussing this with Gerry the gardener, Grant had a section of the land in front of the house walled off with a gate and grass grown so Abbey and the dogs she loved and they loved her, ran about to her heart's content with the watching nanny being able to relax. Grant bought a swing, small slide and a sand pit was arranged and he loved to spend time there with her.

Not charging guests extortionate prices for Gresley, Cobden, Bow and Clough, they were booked up in advance all year round for the London entertainment, Wimbledon, Royal Ascot and Royal events they favoured. January was a slack time so Grant closed the hotels down for a "spring clean." The staff not needed was given half pay until the week before re-opening when they came back to help prepare. The offices remained open.

Grant was enabled to buy two larger hotels when Abbey was five years old and renovated these and naming them Ireton Wood and Linacre Wood. Again with being made comfortable the guests also became faithful even coming twice annually. He always made himself available for short periods and his guests appreciated this.

Ladies he met socially tried to tempt him but he always replied with good manners, "thank you, but no."

After being a weekly boarder at a private school in Berkshire, where she wasn't lonely and her needs including art, equestrian and languages were met Abbey at 11 years went to a private boarding school which included learning the skills needed to run the hotels and continuing her languages, art and music.

Questioning her dada about her mummy's family he told her. Abbey accepted it as she adored her dada and knew he lived for her, and she had her beloved paternal Grandparents and Birdie.

With her elegantly boned and structured face a heritage from her ancestor Andrew, she grew into a very beautiful young lady working hard at her education.

For her degrees to help her dada run the hotels and learn more languages she was accepted at a Switzerland University so was near her Grandparents. This reassured her dada who was very busy running the six hotels, but came to stay with them often. She went home in the long summer vacation and visited the hotels with him.

Before beginning her third year at the university, Grant discussed with Abbey and his parents how Bow Wood and Clough Wood were now surrounded with new high rise buildings so had become very enclosed and his plan to build a Boutique style 120 room hotel in central London with the proceeds from Bow and Clough where land was available for this and for Abbey to run this after completing her education and Finishing School. They approved of this new venture and Abbey was grateful for her dada's trust in her.

Grant's PA contacted every one of their faithful annual guests with his proposal to build a new hotel. Each reply said they would be happy in his new hotel agreeing Bow and Clough were now enclosed and traffic was getting a problem.

He was offered an excellent price for the area from the builders of the high rise apartments and offices and, after making enquiries from his trustworthy source, secured a higher price they had drawn up with deposit, so with Abbey's input began planning with the architects.

With this new venture Grant was satisfied he had done his very best for Abbey with the inheritance her mummy was left by her paternal Grandparents. He always went weekly to Faye's private grave taking fresh flowers. He had had a seat put so he could spend time with her and planted a weeping willow tree. Abbey also went with him when she was at home.

The hotel was completed and Abbey suggested they call it Whitwell Wood. She decided to do just one year at the Finishing School with wanting to start work.

Now working from the head office with her PA Lara, was a great help to her dada whilst she learned first hand about running the hotels. She received several invitations from young men and older, to lunch or dinner but said, 'thank you but I'm spending time with my dada, having been away being educated.'

After coming home with her dada for lunch then a stroll with the dogs, went back visiting the hotels in turn. The staff and guests were always pleased to see her.

'May we call at mummy's grave on our way back to work, dada?' Abbey asked.

'Let's do that, darling.'

Calling at the florist Abbey bought beautiful flowers as always. Grant always close to tears still over Faye's death, wept and Abbey joined him. 'If only your mummy was here, darling,' he said for what must have been over millions of times. She told her mummy how proud she was of her dada.

Wiping their faces Abbey told him, 'I looked our ancestor's up on line, dada, and I'm very proud to be part of the family.' Grant didn't mention he also had previously. 'If June hadn't been born you and I wouldn't either, would we dada?'

'No darling, we wouldn't. We come from a very hard working respectable family.' They went on to the head office

On their own Abbey said to Grant's PA, 'my dada looks tired, Lorraine.'

'He doesn't like this extremely hot weather, Miss Abbey. Our climate is a pain at times. One minute cold, then too hot,' she laughed. 'And your dada being brought up in Switzerland doesn't help.'

'No,' Abbey agreed. 'He needs to stay cool at home.'

'I could come to your home office in the mornings,' Lorraine offered. 'Now we have you here, Mr Forrest could take it easier.'

Abbey thought, "She loves him." Knowing her dada was still in love with her mummy, knew he would remain so. But he must at times be lonely.

'Right Lorraine, I'll take him in hand, Abbey laughed. 'Please come in the mornings and bring the managers if they have anything urgent. I'll ask Lara to also come and we'll all work together.'

'I'll attend to this Miss Abbey,' she promised.

Arriving home Birdie told her, 'your dada is resting. Pot of tea, darling?'

'Yes, please, on the patio,' Abbey replied cuddling her. She was typing in her laptop when Grant came out. Cuddling him, she said, 'this hot weather gets you down, dada?'

'Yes darling, it does.'

Abbey told him in a firm voice. 'I've arranged for Lorraine and any of the managers to come here for a few mornings. I'll work with you and Lara is coming. Then I suggest you have a time off until the weather is cooler, the staff will contact you when necessary. I want you to play golf some mornings before it turns too hot.'

Grant laughed, 'well that's me told. Ok, thank you darling, will do.'

'Next week, may I work mornings and then have the afternoons free when possible. I'd love to ride or walk in the wood with the dogs.'

'Do this, darling, set it up. You should have a holiday, do some painting.'

'Thank you, I will.' Abbey told him what she had been doing in the head office.

'Well done, darling.'

Later when Abbey rang her Grandparents as always, she told her Grandmama, 'dada is tired in the extreme hot weather we are having. I've told him to have a few days' holiday and have a game of golf early morning, meeting up with his pals.'

'Well done, darling, be firm with him,' her Grandmama laughed.

Abbey discussed a few business matters with her.

'I suspect Lorraine loves dada, Grandmama.'

'Yes, she does, she keeps it well hidden and your dada hasn't recognised this. She's not the only one. Young ladies wanted to marry him before he met your mummy and others have since.'

Hazel Helliwell

Abbey then spoke to her Granddada who as always was breathing with difficulty and coughing. She didn't put a strain on him so chatted to him. She adored her Grandparents as they did her.

Chapter Six

Having known 33 year old hotelier Andy Byrne through their Golf Club membership, Grant had always been impressed with Andy's manner and integrity. How he had built up his successful hotel business from hard work and no financial help apart from a Trust Fund from his Grandparents and parents. He hadn't seen him for over two years with Andy supervising his requested luxurious hotel being built in Kent and completing one in Dubai. He knew Andy had briefly been in London but their paths hadn't crossed.

Following his hotel progress with interest Grant was delighted to see Andy at the Golf Club as was Andy on meeting Grant.

'Good morning, sir. How are you?' Andy enquired. After exchanging pleasantries, he invited Grant to have a whiskey with him. 'Congratulations Mr Forrest on completing Whitwell Wood.'

'Thank you Andy. Bow and Clough were getting past it. I could have renovated but with all the new high rise buildings around them they became very enclosed. Traffic was a problem also. Our faithful guests have settled in Whitwell Wood satisfactorily, I didn't want to lose contact with them.

'Bristow's, you'll know Andy, bought the land to build yet more high rise apartments needed by business people, so I've been well recompensed.' He smiled at Andy.

'I'm so pleased to have met up with you, sir. I'm sorry I missed you on my recent flying visits.'

'Thank you Andy for enquiring about me. Are you on a flying visit this time?'

'No, I'm here for a while catching up on English Oak my new London hotel. Like, you sir, I have supportive staff, but it's time now to be around for a while. Modern technology is wonderful now for communicating.'

'Well, I'm not into this Andy,' he laughed, 'my daughter Abbey is She's being a wonderful help to me and my parents with her university qualifications.'

After discussing Andy's new hotels in Dubai and Kent, Grant invited him to lunch at Holly House. Andy, having the greatest respect and liking for Grant accepted the invitation with delight. He knew Grant had a 24 year old daughter although never having met her, had always known Grant lived for her.

Grant prepared Abbey that he had invited a hotel colleague and golf friend to lunch the next day.

Abbey had to go to the head office with Lara to find a record but quickly returned home in time to greet their guest.

Hearing voices from the sitting room was surprised to hear a younger man's as her dada had always before invited older colleagues and used the hotel's restaurants combining business with pleasure.

Going in she saw the guest stood slightly taller than her 6 ft dada, in a bespoke summer weight silver grey suit and grey highly polished shoes stood looking up at the oil painting she had done of her dada for her Masters Degree in art.

'Well done darling, to get back so quickly,' Grant congratulated her.

'Andy, this is my daughter Abbey,' he proudly introduced her.

'I'm very pleased to meet you Miss Forrest. Your dada has constantly spoken of you,' he smiled.

'I'm pleased to meet you Mr Byrne.' Shaking hands both felt their skin tingle at this first physical contact. Abbey experienced an awareness of sensual recognition as never in her life had she known before. She knew with a strange feeling that her life wouldn't be the same after meeting him.

With her artistic eyes she saw thick chestnut brown hair with an expert cut, brown eyes with a gold flecks in not the most sculptured handsome face she had seen, but he was very good looking and looked kind and sincere. Broad shoulders, lean body in his suit, pristine white shirt with silk burgundy tie with tiny blue diamond squares. He exuded health and fitness. It was the first time her dada had invited so young a man.

Andy also liked what he saw. He had seen photographs of her but they hadn't done her justice. In her heels four inches shorter than he, her pale blonde hair shone in a very becoming simple style cut to chin length and waved down the sides of her face ending in a row of curls. Her eyes were the most beautiful he had ever seen, sparkling green he felt he could drown in, beautifully shaped classic features with an English complexion radiating good health. Andrew Derbyshire's genes continued in her. Her shoulders were superb and her bare arms well toned with a slim but very shapely body that looked fit.

After introductions looking back up at Grant's portrait Andy told her, 'this is so wonderful, so lifelike. Congratulations Miss Forrest. You've captured your dada from your heart.'

'Thank you, Mr Byrne,' silently amazed at his discernment.

He began to look forward to getting to know her, but recognised that she was an inexperienced virgin.

Birdie came in smiling but hesitated not to intrude. Abbey greeted her and Grant introduced her to Andy. She had surmised this lunch was being used as an introduction between him and Abbey.

'Lunch is ready Miss Abbey.' Andy had assured Grant that he enjoyed any food.

'Would you like to remove your jacket, Andy?'

Looking at Abbey for permission when she nodded said, 'thank you sir.'

Birdie smilingly took it. Andy thanked her and they went into the dining room where the table looked gorgeous with the table settings and sparkling crystal glasses. A beautiful flower arrangement was set in the centre.

Andy held Abbey's chair, smiling up at him she thanked him catching a whiff of his cologne, liking it. She was surprised and pleased to see he wasn't wearing cuff links in his well fitted shirt which must have been tailor made for the fit round his broad shoulders and lean torso. He also didn't wear a ring but that could mean anything. She puzzled why her dada hadn't given her any details about him.

Pete the chef and Birdie brought the first course, fresh melon, pink and yellow grapefruit and strawberries with a mustard and vinegar and fresh mint dressing accompanied by the best quality white wine Andy recognised. He noticed that Pete poured Abbey only a small amount without asking, he was impressed with this.

After Birdie and Pete had served they left. Andy was enjoying talking about running hotels with Grant and Abbey. Grant encouraged Abbey to share her views. Andy discerned that she was shy but well trained as a hostess. Pete and Birdie then brought in the steaks grilled to their preference and Viola who couldn't take her gaze away from Andy brought the salads. Pete poured Andy and Grant a red wine, Abbey helped herself to a glass of water.

They tucked in but Grant ate sparingly. Abbey was concerned over his recent lack of appetite but he blamed the very hot weather.

Grant was relaxed seeing Andy and Abbey discussing the hotel business, Andy was really enjoying talking with Abbey recognising her high intelligence. She had begun to relax as Andy made her feel at ease and had begun to like him.

Andy said, 'this steak is so tasty and the salad is so fresh and delicious.'

'Would you like another steak, Mr Byrne?'

'Well,' he laughed, 'yes please.'

Abbey was glad Andy had eaten well as she had a good appetite, She texted Pete asking for this, also for another bowl of salad which she had more of but Grant refused. Andy's hands pleased her; his nails were cut short and not manicured.

After the second course as Viola again gazing at Andy and Birdie came to clear the pots away. Andy asked, 'may I compliment the chef on the delicious fresh food, Miss Bird?'

'Thank you, sir. I'll pass this on. Miss Abbey grew the salad ingredients.'

Abbey was blushing.

'I'd like to see your garden, please Miss Forrest,' Andy asked her.

'It's only tiny as yet. I have a small greenhouse.' She had inherited Percy and John from generations back love of gardening.

Waiting for the dessert in a little space, Grant told her, 'Andy has hotels Abbey.'

'Where are they, Mr Byrne?'

'One in Dubai, Dorset, Jersey and London and one almost completed in Kent which as requested is a luxury boutique spa as Dubai.

'My parents retired to Jersey, they're both active in sports. My dad, Quentin, was a solicitor carrying on my Grandfather's business. Dad is still involved in the administration. My mother, Melanie, was an attorney.

'I have an older brother, Marlon, who is a solicitor in the business; his wife, Sabrina, is a wedding planner. They have three boys who are at a boarding school which specialise in sports they love.

'My younger brother Stuart is also a solicitor in the business, his wife, Louise, owns a riding school and race horses in Gloucestershire. They haven't as yet, any children.

'I had a very happy secure childhood. I enjoyed boarding school, learning, playing sports, my teenage years, university.' Abbey felt a pang of loneliness go through her.

Birdie and Pete brought the rhubarb crumble and ice cream dessert in. Andy and Grant asked for water. When they had been served Birdie and Pete left, Abbey continued their conversation, 'didn't your parents want you to be in the family business, Mr Byrne?'

'Yes. When I was 12 years old we went on holiday to a four star hotel and my parents were grumbling and complaining as other guests were. I thought people looking forward to their holiday shouldn't be disappointed and have their expectations dashed. So, I began thinking that I'd buy a hotel and ensure holidaymakers, business people, whoever, would be comfortable. My parents were disappointed but never forced my brothers and me into anything.

'When I was 17 before university I worked in a hotel starting at the bottom and working my way up. At 18 with the Trust Fund my grandparents had set up for me, I bought a derelict hotel and had it re-built.

'From a young age I'd always been interested in how buildings were produced and thought I'd be a construction builder. In my holidays from university learning the business skills to run a hotel as you have, Miss Forrest, I laboured for the builders, digging and whatever, learning about wood which I love. I saved the money I earned waiting on tables and ever learning what made a hotel run satisfactorily. Whenever I had free time from studying at Cambridge I offered my services again waiting on tables or behind the bar!'

Abbey was so enjoying listening to his cultured deep voice with a youthful ring to it and him being so articulate. This was the first time she had eaten with her dada and a young man guest, usually they were older business colleagues of Grant's and lunched in one of their hotels, but Andy had quickly made her feel relaxed.

He continued, 'with my parent's Trust Fund when I was 21 years I bought another run down hotel and repeated the process. By the time I'd finished university the hotel I'd renovated had earned me enough to begin another.'

'Well done Andy,' Grant applauded.

'Yes, well done Mr Byrne,' Abbey echoed. Her admiration for him was ever growing.

He encouraged her to talk about her University Masters Degrees with Honours in Business Studies Management, and Business Administration. As she told him he was enjoying her beautiful cultured voice and recognising how very intelligent she was.

'Congratulations, Miss Forrest, you must have worked very hard to gain such qualifications.' Looking at Grant he said, 'with my taking these degrees sir, I know what an achievement through sheer hard work and commitment it is.'

'Yes, thank you Andy. My parents and I are very proud of her.'

Passing her dada a glass of water, Andy saw the outline of her braless breast through the pleated silk bodice and desire shot through him. Small, full and soft, he knew this would keep him awake, but he puzzled that he hadn't seen a nipple.

Abbey caught him looking at her breasts and she blushed as for the first time in her life they awakened and swelled. Praying her nipple protectors didn't shoot off she knew he had awoken her sexuality. Grateful for this making her aware of her body, she thought, "I'll have to wear my sports bra if he comes again."

When she had been 18 she saw a lady doctor as she thought her nipples had grown too big compared with pictures and paintings she had seen. The doctor assured her that she had very healthy breasts and the size of the nipples was very common. 'Your babies will love these,' she had gently assured Abbey. Knowing she was a shy virgin she didn't mention that men also would.

Grant looked very relaxed but had only eaten a little from each course. 'Shall we have coffee outside, darling?' he asked Abbey.

'Is this ok with you, Mr Byrne?'

'Yes please. It's glorious out there.'

'Are you riding this afternoon, darling?' Grant then asked her.

'No dada, I need to go back to the office to complete the VAT returns.' Andy and Grant groaned. Abbey laughed and said, 'I'll ride after dinner.'

'Abbey plays the piano for me before dinner,' he told Andy.

'Do you ride, Mr Byrne?' Abbey asked.

'As often as I can.'

'Are we free on Sunday, Abbey?'

'Up to now we are dada.'

'Would you like to come for a ride on Sunday afternoon, Andy? Have lunch first? We've a stallion our groomsman rides.'

'Thank you very much Mr Forrest, I'd love to come.'

'Dress code?' he asked Abbey.

'I wear jeans,' she laughed.

'Hard hat necessary?'

'If you prefer but I wear my cowboy hat for going through the wood. Please excuse me. I'll see you both outside.' She ran up to her room and changed into a cotton brown and white small checked scooped neck sleeveless dress, teamed up with a red belt and matching wedge heeled shoes. She hurried back down. Her chauffeured car and bodyguard were waiting.

Grant and Andy stood as she approached them. She warmly kissed Grant on his cheek and said to Andy, 'see you Sunday.'

'Yes, indeed.' He watched her gracefully walk towards the car, her gorgeous shining blonde hair bouncing; her very shapely fit body and her long legs in her wedge shoes were very attractive. He felt another pull of the desire he had experienced from meeting her, and knew a sense of loss as she was leaving, which was a first for him. Abbey was filled with joy thinking about Andy. She hoped he liked her.

Todd the bodyguard handed her into the car as Andy closely watched her gracefully swing her legs together as taught at the Finishing School. With his knowledge of women he knew that she was an inexperienced virgin and she was like a breath of fresh air. In all his busy days of having not enough hours Sunday seemed a long way off. He was also looking forward to seeing her in her cowboy hat and jeans.

Grant took Andy to the downstairs bathroom facilities. Andy glanced up the stairs at the beautiful wheat coloured carpet and matching wallpaper decoration over wooden panels and then stopped. 'These carved doors, this stairway and panels are wonderful Grant. I love wood. Must be solid wood oak?'

'Yes, I remember this well. Everything is covered with UV Golden cured lacquer. Continues through the house, very pricey at the time, but made to last.'

'Indeed it is, sir, wonderful.'

Enjoying coffee on the patio under the sun awning, Grant asked him, 'do you like Abbey, Andy?'

'I do, very much indeed, Mr Forrest. She is very beautiful and graceful. I've never enjoyed a lunch as much as this one. Conversing with Abbey and her intelligence has been a delight. She's a wonderful hostess.'

'I'd be happy knowing she was safe with an honourable like minded man.'

'I can understand your concern, but Abbey is highly intelligent and full of sound sense. I'm positive you need have no concerns.'

'Knowing she'll be an heiress from me and my parents, there are very devious men about.' Andy identified with this concern. 'If only her mother had lived or she had siblings.'

'Young ladies don't always take advice, sir.' They went quiet. Andy knew more was coming; this invitation to lunch at Holly House and meet Abbey was a deliberate ploy of Grants.

'I have to tell you Andy, I've only a few months left. My heart is now failing fast. Abbey doesn't know, hence my concern. My parent's who live in Switzerland with my father's ill health don't now travel, also aren't aware of my condition as yet. They are all we have of our small family.' He didn't at his point, tell Andy about Faye's parents.

'I assure you, Mr Forrest.'

'Please Andy, call me Grant.'

'Thank you Grant. I assure you I'll discreetly keep Abbey safe. I need to build up her trust in me. We do have so much in common. She would make me a wonderful wife, hostess and prayerfully mother of my children. I'm at an age where I need to settle down.

'I don't feel honourable Grant. I've had women, not too many and only short-term, they had that understanding. But my wife would be the only one for me and treated with the greatest respect.'

'I know this Andy and I also know the integrity of you and your family. I wouldn't have invited you to meet Abbey if not. Don't concern yourself about the past, Andy. I had women before I met Faye. In the hotel business there are many temptations. I have been celibate since marrying Faye out of respect for her.

'You're coming on Sunday, that's good. It's a start of your friendship with Abbey and you both getting to know each other. I feel as though a big burden has been lifted from my shoulders. Let's have a glass of red- a small for me.

'Abbey insists I stay put at home just now. It may be too hot for me to play golf but I can spend time in the club and the chess club, catch up on some detective books and DVD's I've missed. I can happily watch

Inspector Morse over and over. John Thaw was a fine actor.'

'I watch him when I can,' Andy laughed. 'Does Abbey watch with you, Grant?'

'No,' he laughed, 'she's more the action girl. Riding or running with the dogs in the wood. She belongs to a tennis club and goes hiking with a group from our church, works out in her small gym, swims. I could do with a quarter of her energy.'

They were both feeling much happier. Andy with knowing how Grant adored his daughter felt very humbled that he was giving him this responsibility. He had been requested to supply the super luxury hotels but they were not his scene and left him feeling strangely dissatisfied with his life. He played more squash now than tennis but hopefully she would respond to his companionship and support, but knew he had to tread carefully for her not to suspect. Although she adored her dada she would back off if she knew he was planning who she would marry. He had discerned that she was no "pushover." He approved of that.

He and Grant had a short stroll then Birdie came to remind Grant that it was time for his rest. She was fully in the picture of his condition 'Mr Byrne is lunching with us on Sunday, Birdie.'

'Good, Do you like a roast, sir?' She had liked Andy's respectful manners.

'I do very much, please Miss Bird.'

Thanking them both again, they walked with him to his ordered waiting car with a bodyguard, and stood waving goodbye.

Setting off Andy thought, "Should I send Abbey a bouquet?" then decided not as it was Grant who had invited him. As he sat back he cast his mind back to the women he had known and enjoyed and they had known from the start they were just short term. Returning to his Penthouse suite he was aware how soulless it was. Groaning he knew he had to ring Sonya to end their fling. "Take her out to dinner as the others? No, Abbey would find out." Sighing he rang her.

'Sonya, how are you?' He listened whilst she prattled on; he could imagine her sat examining her nails whilst she complained about several inconsequential matters.

'Sonya,' he broke into her chatter, 'you know I never make any promises in my flings?'

'Yes.' She was filled with dread, but knew this would come.

'I'm ending ours, Sonya. I appreciate how much pleasure you've given me, darling, but it's now time to call it a day.' She was silent, which was unusual for her. 'Go to Harrods jewellers and buy yourself something, darling.'

'How much can I spend?'

'They'll tell you, Sonya.'

'Ok darling. I'll be discreet. If or when you need me, contact me.' He didn't reply to that, but then she didn't expect him to. After exchanging brief pleasantries they said bye.

Andy put his mobile thoughtfully down. He had accepted Sonya who had approached him and only two other women's invitation, but had invited several for a one night. He had always used protection and even so, had had regular check ups. He was thankful that he was and always had been clean. Doubts began to set in, perhaps Abbey wouldn't like him, and he was nine years older. When she knew he had had women,

Meant To Meet

he knew people would tell her with him being widely publicised in the magazines and press. Feeling unsettled he changed into his casuals and went down to the gym for a work out and swim his usual twelve lengths.

Returning, he sent down for food and opened his laptop dealing with the e-mails. There was just one problem with the new hotel in Kent he had to sort out. This was quickly resolved.

Whilst eating, he looked at the days Stocks and Shares on the television then put in a DVD of a detective film.

Arriving on Sunday the car from the firm Andy used for his hotel guests' needs with security left as he was let through the security gates. Grant and Abbey were sat on the patio with the day time guard dogs and Grant's Jack Russell, Smillie so named as he had a smiling mouth. Abbey came to meet him and introduced the dogs. She was relieved when the dogs accepted him. She looked gorgeous in her jeans discreetly showing her beautiful figure. She was thinking how dishy he looked in his obviously designer jeans and short sleeved polo shirt. She was amazed to see his firm arm muscles but had thought at the lunch he was well toned and must work out.

After the usual delicious roast lunch Grant went to rest. Brian took Andy up to a spare en-suite room to freshen up and left him. There was no furniture in the bedroom. Abbey took Andy to the stables for him to meet Oscar the groomsman and Jet the stallion Oscar exercised through the wood letting the dogs run about and her mare Babs. Oscar had both saddled. Setting off Abbey recognized Andy's expertise with horses.

Strolling through the wood discussing their favourite music, she began to relax with him and he was enjoying being with her very much. It had been a strain as this was the first time she had ridden on her own with a man other than her dada or Oscar or staff. With his sense of humour and natural innate manners she had quickly become at ease with him.

Like her Andy loved classical also both liked the singer Adele and other popular singers. 'I listen through my earphones whilst travelling Abbey.'

'Yes, you must spend hours travelling.'

'I'm able to ease off now Dubai is completed and Kent almost. I can have corporate meetings through video.'

'Yes, there is wonderful technology these days. Takes some keeping up with,' she laughed.

'To relax, I enjoy quizzes and crosswords.'

'So do I Andy, at the minute I'm working my way through a French crossword book to keep my brain working,' she laughed.

'I must get one,' Andy laughed. They discussed the languages they were both fluent in and then moving into the open fields galloped for a while.

Strolling back Abbey asked Andy where he rode in London. 'I go to my sister in law's stables in Gloucestershire. I've a cottage in the Cotswolds, Abbey. Also, I ride in Dubai.

'I prefer British weather. When it's pouring with rain and afterwards breathing in the fragrances in the air. I love the scent of wood smoke in the autumn.'

Abbey was being filled with joy identifying how she also loved these times and fragrances. Stopping at the stream running through the wood the horses and dogs had a drink. Abbey had brought bottles of spring water for her and Andy and they sat on the ground under the canopy of trees whilst the horses and dogs wandered about. She took off her Shady Brady cowboy hat and ran her fingers through her hair. Andy took his cowboy hat off also.

'Have you had any holiday time yet Abbey?'

'I'm having the afternoons off this week. After lunching with dada I'll ride in the wood or walk, do some gardening and I'm completing a painting in oils of Smillie for a surprise birthday present for dada. It doesn't sound very exciting, does it?'

'It sounds ideal, Abbey. Be thankful that you enjoy these healthy pleasures and not everlastingly craving being entertained and wasting your life away on fleeting past times. What would you prefer to do with these afternoons?'

'Ride in the wood or walk with the dogs, do some gardening and complete my painting of Smillie for dada's birthday present,' she laughed.

'Good girl.'

He was looking at her in admiration. Impulsively she asked, 'are you busy working, Andy? Oh dear, sorry, that's a stupid question.' She was blushing.

'I've a morning meeting and business lunch tomorrow and Tuesday. Then I'm heading off to my Cotswold Cottage to enjoy this glorious summer weather. Whenever I've a spare morning or a day, I fly from wherever I am to go there. I'll be doing what you are, apart from painting in oils,' he laughed. Then seriously he told her, 'but I would love to spend time here with you Abbey.'

She was filled with joy. 'Please come to-morrow afternoon. You've the spare en-suite for your use. Stay for dinner?' She then thought, "He won't want to do this."

Smiling warmly at her he said, 'thank you, Abbey, I accept with gratitude.' He was thankful that he had this spare time. He also was filled with happiness at the opportunity of spending more time with her. As she recognised this her uncertainty began to leave her.

Returning to the stables they both took their saddles off and rubbed their horses down before putting them into their stalls to enjoy their hay.

Andy had to shave as the dark pinpricks of persistent masculine stubble had been clearly visible. After freshening up, he joined Grant and Abbey on the patio for a delicious high tea. Grant was delighted when Abbey told him, 'dada, Andy is coming to-morrow afternoon and staying for dinner.'

'That's good, thank you Andy, I look forward to this.' He was also re-assured as they naturally called each other with their Christian names.

Abbey played the piano afterwards and included a classical piece of Brahms Andy had mentioned. His heart leapt. At 8 pm she walked with him to his waiting car and smiling at him said, 'bye, see you to-morrow.'

'Yes indeed. I'm looking forward to it.' She was also. They had arranged for him to see her small garden and he had offered to do some digging for her. Percy and John's love of gardening had been passed down to her.

Being with Andy she realised although she had been happy on her own which she was used to, he had made her aware that she had been a loner and lonely. Returning to Grant she kissed him. 'Goodnight dada, enjoy your detective.'

Knowing that she wouldn't sleep being excited thinking about Andy, she went to her art room and whilst the light was still good, worked on Smillie's portrait.

Although she was busy the morning dragged in her eagerness to be with Andy. After lunching with her dada and he had gone to his room to rest, she changed into a cream cotton vest top to absorb the heat. Being close fitting thought her breasts were too revealing so began again putting on one of her specially designed sports bras and completed with a loose silk blouse teamed up with lightweight beige cropped trousers, raffia sun hat with an upturned brim.

Andy arrived in designer business clothes and sunglasses looking every inch the successful hotel tycoon. He was carrying a holdall. Abbey thought he looked wonderful and was so proud of him for getting his success through his sheer hard work, loving him. She stopped short, "loving him?" Yes she did, she loved him.

Taking his sunglasses off he said, 'it's so good to be here Abbey, is your dada resting?'

'Yes Andy he is. He asks to be excused. You are very welcome.'

He was breathing in the fresh air. 'May I go and change now, Abbey.'

'You don't have to ask, Andy.' She wasn't surprised that he had with his immaculate good manners asked. 'Would you like a glass of wine?'

'Thank you, no, Abbey. I've had wine with the meal. I'd love a glass of water, please.' He shot off followed by the day dogs. They knew they were not allowed in the house so waited under the patio table for him.

He hadn't slept thinking of her. This was the first time thoughts of a woman had kept him awake. In the meetings he had also, for the first time, struggled to keep his concentration focused, and the morning had dragged.

Arriving at Holly House and seeing Abbey waiting for him he was filled with happiness and encouragement. He knew he loved her but also knew he had to be careful not showing his emotions until hopefully she knew him more. Grant had told him she hadn't had a boyfriend and was a virgin. He had discerned this on first meeting her and was very proud of her.

Quickly returning dressed in a dark brown fitted vest, Bermuda khaki shorts, sports shoes and a khaki sun hat, Abbey thought he looked gorgeous. His arms, legs and thighs were firm, muscular and had their glass of water and Abbey suggested, 'shall we take these bottles with us?'

'Good idea. Gardening is thirsty work,' he laughed. He was so relaxed and happy.

Abbey introduced him to Gerry the gardener. Looking inside a large area of lawn walled off at the side of her small garden and greenhouse, asked, 'what is this piece of land used for?'

'It was my safe place when I was a toddler and young child. I was such a live wire the nanny couldn't cope with me always running off,' Abbey answered.

He laughed. 'Yes, I can just imagine you.'

'I had play area facilities.' Gerry left them.

Brian had bought a stainless steel spade and fork for him at Abbey's request. He tested the weight of the spade and asked Abbey, 'where do you want me to dig?'

'From here to the blackberry bush, please.' She put her gardening gloves on. 'Do you want a pair, Andy?'

'Thank you, no, but if I may have a nail brush.'

She texted Birdie requesting one be put in his en-suite, then changed her hat for her patchwork trilby style sun hat.

'Love your hats, Abbey. This one is unusual.'

'Yes, it's so comfortable to work in. It's from Cotswold Outdoor shop. I bought it on line.' She picked up the hat she had taken off, 'this is also very comfortable made with raffia. But this patchwork stays put better.'

'You look very fetching in either.' She laughed and he joined in.

The rocket seeds Abbey grew in trays then cut were ready to eat and lettuce seeds had shot up in the greenhouse, so as Andy dug she transplanted them with her dibber. 'It's really too hot to put these out, but they grow with plenty of the rain water round their roots,' she chatted. Beginning to feel very uncomfortable in the extremely hot sunshine took her silk blouse off.

'That's better Abbey,' Andy told her looking at her very mischievously leaning on his spade. Abbey inwardly groaned as he looked so sexy. 'Do you wear shorts, Abbey?' he asked.

'Yes, I have shorts.'

'Good. I look forward to seeing you in a pair to-morrow.'

She had to laugh, 'you are so cheeky Andy Byrne.'

'Yes, I am,' he admitted.

As she worked she felt his eyes on her and was glad he was interested in her. She didn't look round but was thankful she had a good figure. Although having a hearty appetite with swimming, working out in her small gym, riding and gardening she hadn't any surplus fat but was well covered. Andy had to tear his eyes away enjoying Abbey's pliant body as she moved economically, her very shapely derriere and long legs showed in her trousers. He was proud of her and longed for the time when he could hold her in his arms.

Abbey felt him looking at her for a long time, bending down she glanced across at him. He was leaning on his spade. 'Ok Andy?'

'Thank you yes. You are the most beautiful young lady I've ever known.'

Blushing Abbey laughingly said, 'oh yes. Is this what you say to your other ladies?'

He went red. 'I've never said anything like this before, but I say it to you most sincerely.'

'Thank you.' To change the subject she said, 'it's good soil.'

'Yes, virgin.'

She couldn't help bursting into laughter and he joined in, he had a wonderful laugh. She continued watching him for a few minutes as he dug so methodically. Recognising he had had lots of practice her admiration for him shot up further, she then went back to her work.

Whilst he continued digging she took a couple of photographs. Andy had photographed her several times as she planted the lettuces out. They worked in compatible silence; the birds were singing their hearts out.

Viola came with a tray of a jug of freshly squeezed oranges, ice and glasses. She put it down on the small table. She used every opportunity to see Andy. "Thank you Viola, this is most welcome,' Abbey praised her. Andy also thanked her.

Andy refilled the dog's bowls with the remainder of the bottled spring water. They sat in the comfortable padded garden chairs under the sun parasol. Stretching out he said, 'this is the life, Abbey, time out from work.'

'Definitely is,' she agreed.

'Do you have to water night and morning in this weather?'

'Brian willingly does this for me, there isn't a lot.'

'Good.' He lay back and fell asleep.

Abbey laughed to herself. She felt her eyes closing, she hadn't slept thinking of him and being excited that he was coming. She woke to a wet nose rubbing her ankle, it was Barney one of the dogs. Andy still slept.

Quietly getting out her notebook quickly sketched him relaxed and asleep. She then again quietly got out of her chair and watered around the lettuces she had planted out. Her little greenhouse, despite the windows and door being open and shading was now too hot to go into.

Andy woke up and apologised, 'sorry Abbey, that was very rude of me to fall asleep.'

'Please never apologise Andy, I also slept,' she laughed.

'I hope I didn't snore.'

'Well, just loud enough to keep the insects away,' she teased. 'No, you didn't.'

Both feeling happy being at one together and refreshed, they washed their hands at the garden tap then went to freshen up before joining Grant on the patio for tea and sandwiches

Andy, thinking Grant would be interested with knowing them shared who he met with for his business lunch. 'They asked now I've almost completed the Kent hotel and as I've the hotel in Dorset, that I build another one in Poole.' Abbey and Grant knew this area.

'It's a wonderful holiday venue, Andy, and most suitable for children,' Grant said.

'Yes, it is,' he agreed, 'they requested a hotel catering for families.'

Contentedly lingering on the patio covered with the awning they conversed together about hotels and Andy told them some humourous stories of hotel life. Grant was very happy seeing Abbey and Andy so much in tune with each other. After a short stroll in the grounds with Grant they returned back to freshen up for dinner.

During dinner Abbey told Andy, 'Thursday morning I'm going to the local junior school. The head Mrs Hickman, wrote weeks ago asking me to help judge their submission for an art competition. I accepted and am very much looking forward to this. I've to be there for 8.30.'

'Congratulations Abbey. You'll enjoy using your art creative skills and you'll be impartial with not knowing any of them.'

'This is why they've invited me, I guess.'

Abbey again walked with Andy to his waiting car at 9 pm. 'Thank you Abbey for to-day, I've really enjoyed myself being with you and your dada. Goodnight, sleep well, see you to-morrow.'

Meant To Meet

'See you to-morrow, you sleep well also Andy.' She smiled at him and waved as his car set off.

Going back to her dada who was still sitting on the patio reading a newspaper with Smillie at his feet, she kissed and said, 'Goodnight dada.'

Guessing she wanted to think about Andy, replied, 'goodnight, darling. You've enjoyed your afternoon?'

'I have dada, very much so.' Then set off to do some more work on Smillie's portrait. As she painted and thinking of Andy, remembered she had bought three cotton jersey tops in Switzerland with the money her Grandparents had given her for her birthday two years preciously. She knew Andy wouldn't want her to dress unbecomingly and be uncomfortable, but he had been around.

Opening the drawer she lifted the sleeveless tops wrapped in tissue paper out and laid them on her bed. She had forgotten how lovely these were and knew Andy would like them.

They had been expensive but Abbey was glad she had bought them. A pale green, lemon, and lavender, each with an exclusive lace insert along the neckline between the thin straps, gathers around the sides and underneath her breasts. She hung them up in her wardrobe and ran her bath.

Soaking she began to be aware of her inexperience on how to keep Andy attracted to her and was filled with regret she hadn't her mummy or sisters, brothers or sisters in law, only her paternal Grandparents in Switzerland. At university in Switzerland working for the degrees to help her dada run the hotels there had been only one female from Japan amongst the other male students. Spending all her spare time with her

Grandparents, riding at the centre and painting her dada's and Grandparent's portraits, realised how much a loner she had been and began to sob. She needed her mummy or a family female to advise her. Thinking of the young wives in the church fellowship, decided not, she would talk with Andy. Sitting up at this thought, she began to feel emotionally stronger.

Yes, they had begun conversing and teasing each other. He would understand when she told him of not having any female relatives to advise her.

Getting into bed she fell asleep as soon as her head hit her pillow. Waking up just after 4 am feeling revitalised and excited that Andy was coming again to-day jumped out of bed and went into the Switzerland stores web site bringing up sleeveless tops in soft cotton was thrilled to see a few styles she loved. A peach covered with small butterflies and fruits of the forest pattern in vibrant colours. Zooming in she was very impressed with the pattern and fitting around the breasts, so ordered one in peach and one in mustard.

She then saw a dark brown with wonderful embroidery of vibrant coloured flowers on the slightly gathered yoke threaded on two narrow straps going over the shoulder and crossing to join the back. It had well shaped gathers under the breasts. Looking at a few more designs went back to the dark brown and added it to the list for the first time in her life dressing to please someone.

Next she brought up Bermuda shorts and cropped trousers. Looking at the colours she decided to keep to her favourite natural shorts which matched all the tops so ordered two pairs plus a pair of mint green well cut cropped trousers. Delighted, she sent the order. Having buying her clothes with the money she requested for her Grandparent's and her dada's birthday and Christmas presents, it was still the first time in her life when she had been extravagant with herself.

Putting her robe on over her cotton pyjamas quietly crept down to do more work on Smillie so it was almost completed. Examining it with critical eyes she was satisfied that she had captured Smillie's expression from her photographs and sketches.

Tim and his trainee assistant came before going to work to thin out and cut her hair in a downstairs room. This didn't take much time as she had it washed and conditioned ready.

Before breakfast Abbey asked Birdie, 'please ensure the rooms Mr Byrne is using are made as comfortable as possible and with the best quality towels et cetera. Please ask Brian to put an armchair in the bedroom, he won't be lingering upstairs but it will not look as sparse. If I look out a few watercolours, will you have them hung and put a vase of flowers on a table?'

'We'll all carry out these requests, Miss Abbey. Cheryl and Viola are hanging fresh curtains up as we speak.'

'Thank you, Birdie.'

Birdie was so happy for her knowing she wanted Mr Byrne to feel comfortable. Although she hadn't married after a broken engagement, she had been so happy serving Faye and Grant then Grant and Abbey, especially as Abbey was motherless. Now she was content feeling sure Abbey's future was with Mr Byrne they all admired very much.

Grant, in the hot weather continued spending the mornings in the Holly House office with his PA

Lorraine and the key managers coming. Abbey went into the head office when needed but as she was on "holiday" joined them with her PA Lara and between them cleared a lot of urgent business. The staff knew Grant was training Abbey to take over and left at noon.

She went to change for lunch putting on a thin silk blouse over her new cream top and beige lightweight trousers. She had suggested to Andy they exercised the horses on a clearing in the wood where she knew from experience, they wouldn't be bitten so much with the midges, and he welcomed this.

Sat on the patio with her dada waiting for Andy, he asked, 'you like Andy, darling?'

'I do dada. I'm so glad you invited him. Does he think I'm naïve?'

'No Abbey, he won't think that at all. He has known women, but I did before I met your mummy. All men do, darling, unless they are gay,' he laughed. 'Andy isn't a womaniser and his wife will have his full commitment. His reputation of honesty goes before him. He is highly respected amongst his peers of all ages. Just be your beautiful self, precious, don't think you have to be like the stupid girls.'

'How do you know stupid girls,' she teased him.

'Andy admires you as you are Abbey. Anytime you have doubts, tell me.'

'I will darling dada. Thank you.'

He couldn't answer her questions what her mummy was like as she grew up, and she had always needed these answers.

Her heart leapt when the guard dogs set off towards the gates. Smillie always stayed with Grant. She knew Andy had arrived and went to meet him.

Meant To Meet

Patting the dogs he looked gorgeous again in his tailored business clothes. Straightening he took off his designer sunglasses and smiling warmly at her said, 'hello Abbey, you look very beautiful. Have you had a good morning?'

'Yes thank you Andy, we've had a good constructive meeting. And you?'

'I've sorted quite a few things out. How is your dada?'

'He's wilting in this hot weather Andy. He has gone for his rest so asks again for you to excuse him.'

Waiting on the patio whilst Andy changed, Abbey was so happy looking forward to spending the afternoon with Andy.

Riding accompanied by the dogs which now followed Andy confirming to Abbey his integrity. Stopping again at the down flowing river he said, 'I'd love to spend the remainder of this week with you, Abbey, is this ok.'

'It is Andy, but what about your going to your Cottage?'

'I would rather spend time with you Abbey. Apart from painting in oils and gardening, I would be doing what you are but alone.' He would love to take her but it would be inappropriate with just meeting her and being a virgin. People knowing he had women would tar Abbey with the same brush.

'Come for lunch?' she excitedly asked.

'Thank you, love to.'

They were both filled with happiness. Andy was thinking "should he ask her to go to a London show with him?" but decided it was too early yet. Also, knowing

Grant's prognosis he knew he was also enjoying their times together.

'Use the swimming pool if you want Andy.'

'Will you be swimming with me?'

Blushing, she laughed 'well, no. I'll complete Smillie's portrait. I'll show you. They are coming to frame it next week whilst dada is having his afternoon rest. Feel free to use my small gym also, Andy. I'll show you where it is.'

'Thank you Abbey, will you exercise with me?'

'Ok.' They went quiet in compatible silence.

'I'm not a playboy, Abbey. Don't believe everything you read. This is the first time I've spent such quality time with a young lady. Yes, I admit I've had short term mistresses, but not many. I've taken them to dinner and then bed. Any normal red blooded man likes sex, Abbey.'

Abbey gasped at his openness but appreciated it. She was filled with jealousy of the women who had known his body and attention, but knew with all certainty that he would never do this again if he was committed to her. She would keep him happy and safe.

'Did you meet them in bars, Andy?'

'Well, connected to sports venues. Squash in particular.'

'You played squash with them?'

'No, but met in the bar.'

'You took them back to your penthouse suite?'

He was looking embarrassed, 'no, hotels.'

'If you had met me in different circumstances, would you have asked me to go on a date with you?'

'I'd have met you Abbey, through the hotel business. I'd have met you before but with being in Dubai and

Kent, I haven't been in London only very briefly for over two years. I certainly would have asked you out. We were meant to meet.'

'Where would you have taken me?'

'I'd have taken, with your permission, to dinner.'

'And then?'

'And then recognising you are an inexperienced virgin, I'd have brought you home. The next morning you would have received a bouquet from me, with a request to dine again. The ladies I've known I treated with respect, but you Abbey would have had my greatest respect, but I'd have wooed you.'

'Thank you.'

'Would you have liked me to woo you, Abbey?'

She looked at him with tears in her eyes, 'yes.'

'Haven't you recognised this is what I am doing?'

'No.'

'No darling, of course not, but I have and am doing so very sensitively.'

Having said that he asked how her portrait of Smillie was progressing. 'I'll have it completed and framed before Thursday week, dada's birthday.'

'What have you planned, Abbey?'

'I'm restricted with this spell of exceptional hot weather making him so tired and needing to rest in the afternoons. Also he isn't eating well as you know. He loves to play golf as you also know but I think not at the moment.' She was looking anxious.

Andy was thinking of several things but Grant wasn't strong enough so asked, 'do you think if I suggest I organise lunch at the Golf Club and invite a few of his closest golf friends?'

'Oh Andy, you are a darling.' She impulsively took hold of his hand and electricity again shot up both their arms. 'That would be perfect I'm sure. Please ask him, I'll pay. Men only?' she laughed.

'On this occasion I think so. Please allow me to cover this.' He held on to her hand and they sat at one with each other. Andy was so thankful that she was beginning to want to touch him.

Whilst they knew Grant was still resting, Abbey quickly showed Andy the portrait of Smillie. He was overwhelmed at the likeness and from a photograph! 'This is wonderful Abbey. Your dada will absolutely love this. You could be a world famous artist.' He was thinking Grant wouldn't be here very long to enjoy it, but it would be another memory for Abbey. His heart filled with compassion for them both.

'I enjoy painting Andy, but not full time and I need to support dada with the hotels. I enjoy this work also.'

'Good. You've all the qualifications.'

Knowing it was getting near the time to meet with Grant on the patio they hurried their separate ways to freshen up. Andy had to shave.

Over tea and Pete's home made granary bread sandwiches, Abbey shared with Grant what Andy was suggesting and he thanked him giving him the go-ahead. Andy rang the few players Grant wanted to ask, and they knowing Grant wasn't too well, responded willingly and cleared the time.

'There, Grant, they all wish to be remembered to you and are looking forward to seeing you.' He booked the lunch. Abbey was so thankful for this brilliant care, she though, "if I love him any more, I'll burst!"

'Abbey isn't included in this so we must think of something,' Andy laughed.

'I'm more than happy that dada is having lunch with you and his golf friends.'

'Abbey really means this, Andy. She has a generous heart always wanting other people to be happy.' The more Andy knew Abbey, the more he loved and admired her un-selfishness.

'I'll organise a special dinner for the three of us. Pete will be happy to make the cake.'

At 9 pm walking to the gates where Andy's car was waiting, he asked, 'What can I buy your dada as a personal present for his birthday Abbey, a bottle of whiskey?'

'Thank you Andy, he did mention that he likes your sun hat.'

'Ok. What size head?' She rang Birdie who laughingly told her. Andy rang the shop early next morning and they had one in. Telling them he would pick it up later this morning, he texted Abbey, "Will your dada be offended if I gave it to him to-day to wear in this exceptionally hot weather?"

She texted, "Thank you Andy. Yes please do that. He'll love it."

Andy arrived just before 1 pm. As he was patting the dogs and looking gorgeous in a designer cream polo shirt and natural lightweight trousers, Abbey stood smiling at him in welcome and loving him.

Andy picked this up and told her, 'thank you, this is the most wonderful welcome I've had in my life.'

Both filled with happiness joined Grant, Andy gave him his hat. Abbey had asked her dada's permission. Grant put it on and told him, 'this is the most comfortable hat I've ever had, Andy. Thank you very much. I really appreciate you giving it me now. We may, with our British climate, not get a lot more of this hot weather,' he laughed. He took it off and read the label, 'UV protection, repels rain, a secret pocket. This must have cost you.' Andy hadn't thought about the label but the price wasn't on it.

'It's a great pleasure Grant. Believe me it's nothing to what you are doing for me, welcoming me here, enjoying your and Abbey's company, and the food and wines.' They all laughed happily together.

'Good man,' Grant grunted.

Abbey asked, 'may I see the secret pocket?' Grant showed her.

'What is this for, credit card and money?'

'Yes,' Grant answered.

'What a brilliant idea.'

Abbey then told Andy, 'when I rang my Grandparents last night and told them how you are organising the birthday lunch, Granddada asks if they may pay for this, Andy. They had been wondering what to buy and dada has accepted this.'

'If that helps them, fair enough, and your parents will be part of your day.' Abbey looked at him in gratitude.

It was so extremely hot after lunch Andy and Abbey sat in her little garden under the sun parasol. She told him how she had cried missing not having a mother or siblings to talk to and being a loner.

'Louise and Sabrina my sisters in law are friendly and compassionate. You could talk to them but Abbey darling, you have me. Tell me your fears and doubts. You are losing your shyness with me aren't you?'

'Yes Andy. You are very easy to talk to. Being a virgin I'm afraid I'm not exciting enough for you.'

'Please don't change, darling, you are perfect as you are. Full of sex appeal and your clothes sense is spot on. I'm very proud of everything about you. You are very beautiful, gorgeous.

'I long to make love to you but I'll never pounce on you and wham bang, so you have nothing to fear.' She had to laugh at this. 'See, you have a wonderful sense of humour and are full of fun and very loving.

'I only use the spare en-suite bathroom but you've had it made so welcoming for me with the watercolours and chair. This is part of making love, darling, being thoughtful, our conversing about the hotels is a very valid thing, you being interested in my work and day.

'Our affinity in appreciating the same pleasures of riding and walking in all weathers, the rain on our face, smelling the perfumes of the woods in all seasons and the smoke from the garden fires. I could go on but do you understand what I mean, Abbey?'

'Yes, I do darling. Thank you very much. I feel much more confident now.'

'Good. Anytime please talk to me, ring me, text me.'

'I will, be sure of that.'

'There is more to relationships than having sex, I'm concerned that I'm not worthy of you, Abbey.'

'You are Andy. I admire everything about you. How hard you have worked for your success, but the money hasn't spoiled you. How you love to dig and enjoy the simple things of life. You are full of integrity and trust and have a great sense of responsibility and a warm heart.' She paused, 'I must also mention your sex appeal.'

He held her hand looking at her very lovingly, 'thank you, Abbey.'

They discussed the latest happenings in the hotels. 'It's so wonderful that I can have intelligent conversations with you Abbey.'

He then lay back in his chair and fell asleep! Abbey laughed and did the same.

Chapter Seven

Before preparing for bed Abbey, for her morning at the school helping to pick a winner in the art competition got out the three silk dresses she had bought in Switzerland with her Grandparent's birthday money. Deciding on her peach with small clusters of vibrantly colourful rosebuds and open roses scattered about with colourful butterflies and brown and wheat leaves interspersed. Narrow built up shoulder leaving her arms bare and a beautifully fitted bodice to the tight waist with gathers down to just above her knees, giving movement as she moved.

She teamed up with light carrot wedge heels and matching small shoulder bag, which echoed the small cinnamon, dark salmon, tangerine and fawn patio roses she loved on the material. She had two of these miniature rose bushes growing in her little garden after enquiring and buying at the garden centre.

Her dada had shared her early breakfast but feeling nervous, she had only managed a glass of fresh orange juice, a slice of toast and marmalade and coffee. Still feeling nervous she arrived at the school for 8.30 am as requested.

A lady was waiting for her and introduced herself as Miss Crosby the school secretary and welcomed her. Walking to the head's office she said, 'I love your dress Miss Forrest, haute couture?'

'No,' Abbey laughed, 'from a store in Switzerland.'

Reaching the office Miss Crosby introduced Mrs Hickman, the head teacher, Miss Berry the art teacher and a smiling very good looking man as Mr Tyler Stratham the organiser of the competition. Over 6 feet, very good looking with fair hair, dark brown eyes, broad shouldered but lean torso, he was immaculately dressed in a fawn bespoke suit, dark brown silk shirt, matching patterned tie and highly polished dark brown shoes,

Mrs Hickman told Abbey, 'you are very welcome Miss Forrest. Mr Stratham is the organiser of this competition.' She laughed, 'I didn't want to put you off but this competition is more far reaching then I revealed to you. Mr Stratham will fill in.' He was laughing.

In a beautiful cultured voice he told Abbey, 'I'm very pleased to meet you Miss Forrest, and hope that you'll be willing to go on to help judge the regional finalists and the final. I'll be explaining what the competition is for to the whole school.'

'Would you like a drink Miss Forrest?' Miss Crosby asked.

Abbey saw a tray which included orange juice. 'A small glass of orange, please.' Tyler also requested the same.

Miss Berry and Miss Crosby then led Abbey and Tyler to the gym room where tables were set with the paintings spread out on.

'You have until 10.15,' Miss Crosby laughed then left them.

Abbey made notes in her Blackberry as she went round. Seeing the commitment the young people had put into their submission, her nervousness left her. She began to enjoy being part of the competition having been prepared that the competition was for a seaside holiday picture.

Tyler asked for her chosen and spread these out on a separate table leaving her. Scrutinizing these four laterally she chose two. Miss Berry joined her and agreed with her choice then Tyler came back. After discussing he suggested they put these two of these forward. They had a quick coffee and freshened up meeting again in the gym. Miss Crosby was waiting for them with a lady she introduced as Mrs Parton the Member of Parliament for the area.

'Time to go,' Miss Crosby laughed.

Going into the large hall Abbey was amazed to see two cameramen set up to film with reporters and cameramen from the press, also a hall full of parents and children.

Beginning with a prayer time and welcome Mrs Hickman said, 'I introduce Miss Abby Forrest who lives locally. Perhaps you don't know her as she only finished university last year gaining degrees to help her dada run his hotels. Miss Forrest also gained a Masters Degree with Honours in Art for oil painting and watercolours. We asked her to be a judge as she is impartial.' She beckoned Abbey forward who hadn't anticipated this.

'Good morning.' Everyone replied. In her beautiful clear voice she said, 'it's been extremely difficult choosing and there are two winners. Please don't be despondent if you haven't won because you are all winners for working hard to enter. You all have a gift of creativity which I hope you will nurture. I'm disappointed we had no male submissions.' Great laughter broke out, Abbey laughed. 'Some of our most famous painters are men.' Laughter again broke out at this. Tyler was admiring Abbey more and more.

Mrs Hickman said, 'thank you Miss Forrest. We're very grateful to you. Now I introduce Mr Stratham.'

'Good morning,' he said. Everyone replied again. 'I'm Tyler Stratham and our Lord Mayor suggested to me as every child isn't Olympic sports people that other gifts should be encouraged. So, he has set up for a famous well known holiday camp, which I mustn't reveal as yet,' he laughed, 'to have a picture which will be used as a logo in all their publicity for a year.' Everyone was gasping. Abbey was surprised and laughing to herself.

'This morning's two chosen paintings will go forward to the regional judging, then the finalist will be chosen from all these. The prize will be a week's VIP holiday for the winner and family, plus a donation will be given to all the schools who have entered to be used in whatever way is useful to each school.' Everyone clapped him.

Mrs Hickman came forward, 'thank you Mr Stratham. Now Mrs Parton will announce the two winners. It should have only been one but as Miss Forrest has said, they couldn't decide between the two. Mr Stratham gave his permission for both of them to go through to the regional competition.'

Mrs Parton read out the names and Mrs Hickman beckoned the girls forward. Everyone clapped. 'All the paintings are set out in the gym. Mrs Hickman invites you to view and share refreshments. Then school is out the rest of the day for the children as promised. Please watch to-day's early evening news which is covering this morning.' Clapping broke out. Miss Crosby and Miss Berry had put the winning paintings on the prepared easels. The cameramen and reporters had followed them into the gym.

The two winning girls stayed close to Abbey and she discussed with them and their parents why she had chosen their picture. Not wanting to show favouritism she asked Miss Berry if she may have a word with the girls who had submitted their design and she led her to a little group who were consoling each other.

Seeing Abbey the parents joined them and she told the girls, 'now you see what the organisers are looking for, please don't copy but set your vision on similar lines. Keep persevering but enjoy being creative. Good luck!'

Tyler joined them, 'thank you for your hard work and well done. It's been very difficult to choose the winners, so carry on creating for next year.' Abbey liked him for these words which had encouraged the girls and parents.

In a gap he led Abbey away saying, 'I appreciated your words, Miss Forrest, about enjoying art.'

'Thank you.'

He quietly asked, 'may I take you out for lunch?'

'Sorry, I'm lunching with my boy friend and my dada.'

He looked disappointed. 'I need to discuss with you the venue for judging in the regional submissions, then the final winner.'

Abbey was thinking what a pleasant personality he had and had accepted with grace her turning him down. If she hadn't met Andy she would have accepted.

'How much time do you have, Mr Stratham?'

'I've meetings in London beginning at 4. The Lord Mayor is coming to these.'

'Would you like to come to my home for lunch, meet my dada and boy friend? In this glorious weather dada and I are having a few days at home, flexi working mornings.'

'I'd love to come, thank you Miss Forrest.'

'Is a chicken salad and fresh strawberry cheesecake with ice cream or custard?'

'I feel hungry already. Yes please. My car will take us.'

Abbey knew her dada would be in the morning's meeting but this was an unusual day so rang him. 'Dada, I've invited Mr Stratham, the organiser of the competition to lunch to-day.'

Tyler heard his reply. 'I'll let Birdie know, darling.'

'Thank you dada, Mr Stratham would like our menu. Please ask Birdie to tell Brian and Todd I won't need them to fetch me home.' She rang off and texted Andy about this extra guest. Tyler knew then she had a bodyguard as he had thought.

The press cameramen requested more informal photographs. After obliging them and saying goodbye, Tyler began to lead her to a luxury car where a man jumped out. Abbey guessed he was a bodyguard.

Mrs Hickman looked puzzled as she anticipated him staying with them and going to a restaurant, but this hadn't been arranged. She and others had noticed how Tyler had been admiring Abbey.

'Miss Forrest has kindly invited me for a quick lunch to meet her dada and see her oil portrait of him before I go back to London for meetings with the Lord Mayor.'

'I understand. Thank you again both of you.'

'I'll be in touch shortly,' he smilingly promised her.

Tyler handed her into the car and watched in admiration as she got in with her finishing school grace.

Travelling Tyler asked her, 'please call me Tyler in informal occasions, but we need to be formal in professional occasions. May I call you Abbey?'

'No problem.'

'What other oil paintings have you done?'

She didn't mention her mummy's portrait in her bedroom or Smillie's as this was her dada's birthday surprise. She just told him she had painted her Grandparents in Switzerland from photographs and two other.

'Your boy friend, have you known him long?'

'No, not long.'

'So it isn't anything serious?'

'I hope so. I love him.'

'I wish it was me,' he told her. 'I've never met a lady who has such an enthusiasm and love for art. Please don't be offended but you can't blame a man for trying. I promise I'll never embarrass you. Friends, ok?' She had to laugh.

'Friends,' she promised. He really meant it. He had women friends but they were just for sex. He had never met anyone like Abbey who shared his love of art.

'Mrs Hickman mentioned with your university degrees you help your dada in his hotel business.'

'Yes.'

They arrived at the gates.

Andy had arrived early to have a word with Grant before Abbey came home. Enjoying a small whiskey and water Grant told Andy, 'I do appreciate our time together before dinner, Andy.'

'Yes, Grant, so do I, man talk.'

Andy shared with him how he had built his Cottage in the Cotswolds from a small derelict building working alongside one of his architects. How he had laboured and designed with the architect using as much wood from his trees as possible. He described the large lake behind the Cottage. Grant was filled with happiness getting to know Andy more and more and knowing his affinity with Abbey. He didn't want to die, he wanted to see them married and their children, but.

Before Abbey returned, Andy said, 'With you having next week as a holiday, I would love you and Abbey to see my Cottage, Grant. It's a lovely run down through scenic countryside. We could use one of my hotel cars.'

'This sounds brilliant Andy, thank you. When are you suggesting?' He laughed, 'we are busy on Thursday!'

'I'll work round any other day that suits you and Abbey, Grant.'

'What about Monday if this is ok with Abbey?'

'Brilliant.'

'We'll sort this out, thanks Andy.'

Andy was full of joy at the prospect of Abbey and Grant seeing his Cottage knowing when they saw it, they would, especially Abbey, fully know him. Describing it more fully and showing Grant photographs in his Blackberry saying he wanted it to be a surprise for Abbey, they saw a car coming through the gates.

Meant To Meet

'Abbey will love your Cottage, Andy,' Grant quickly told him.

Hearing the car the day guard dogs jumped up. Grant strictly said, 'stay' and they lay back down. Andy went to meet Abbey. He saw a tall very well dressed good looking man helping her out. The car left. Tyler had told them the time to collect him.

Abbey smilingly greeted Andy. He took her bouquet telling her, 'you look very beautiful Abbey.' She made the introductions and they shook hands. Tyler knew who Andy was from photographs and television.

Grant made him feel very welcome. Tyler asked him, 'may I remove my jacket, sir?'

Grant assured him they wanted him to feel comfortable in the hot weather. Brian had come to show him a spare en-suite to freshen up in.

During lunch he told Grant and Andy, 'I'm hoping Miss Forrest will be one of the judges of the regional finals and then help decide on the winner.'

'You'd enjoy this, Abbey,' Andy told her.

'I would. I've thoroughly enjoyed this morning. Encouraging art in schools is so worthwhile. I accept your invitation with pleasure, Tyler.'

'The final winner will be recorded at the BBC television studios. Our Lord Mayor will announce the winner. He is quite excited at this project he suggested.' He explained so Grant and Andy would appreciate the seriousness of this project.

'The prize will be a week's VIP holiday for the winner and family, plus a donation from the holiday camp will be given to all the schools who have entered to be used in whatever way is useful to each school.

'The painting will then be used to publicise a very well known holiday camp logo for a year. Tee shirts, caps, bags and so on will be produced and all proceeds from these will go to a very worthwhile charity. The Lord Mayor will also announce this.' Grant congratulated him, 'that's good Tyler, well done.'

'Yes, well done,' Andy echoed.

'It will be repeated next year and possibly forever,' he laughed.

'This will keep you involved in your love of art, Abbey,' Andy told her.

'Yes, there will also be other occasions,' Tyler laughed again. He was enjoying himself, and they all liked him.

Grant asked, 'are you an artist Tyler?'

'I love to sketch and paint watercolours. My parents own art shops worldwide. I'm a partner and will take over. I've a sister but she is happily married with a brood of children,' he laughed.

Andy knew that Tyler was admiring Abbey and a pang went through him. Knowing her love of art, she had an affinity with Tyler.

'I've to leave, unfortunately for me, in half an hour,' Tyler told them. 'May I see your portrait sir?'

Abbey admired him for showing respect to her dada with this request.

Leading him into the sitting room and waiting whilst Tyler stood gazing up at it, then he went closer. 'This is so wonderful Abbey, so lifelike. Warmest congratulations. From a photograph you said?'

'Yes, I painted it for my degree. When I brought it home I was able to put a few touches in with my dada sitting for me.'

'I could look at this all day. Apologies, time to go.'
'You haven't had coffee,' Abbey reminded him.
'I'll have one at the meeting, thank you Abbey. Thank you for the gorgeous food.'

Andy escorted him to the ensuite he had used.

Seeing his car arriving Tyler shook Grant's hand thanking him again. Andy walked with him.

'I asked Abbey to lunch or dine with me and she replied that she had a boyfriend. She loves you.'

Waves of happiness went through Andy.

'I'm not giving up,' Tyler told him.

'I don't blame you. But I'd kill you.'

'That's good enough for me, Andy. I now know that you are serious about her, she's gorgeous. You are one lucky man. Thankfully we're going to be friends.'

Laughing together they shook hands.

Tyler got into the car and as Andy waved him off. Tyler got out his mobile and let the television studio know to broadcast that Miss Forrest had consented to help judge the regional paintings and the winner.

Grant had gone for his afternoon rest. Andy sat down looking at Abbey very mischievously, 'so, I'm your boyfriend then?'

Blushing scarlet, she said, 'I'm hoping so.'

'Well the thing is, boyfriends and girlfriends kiss.'

'You are cheeky Andy.'

'Yes and I'm one very lucky man. Tyler has an undying love for you and isn't giving up.'

'What did you say to him?'

'I told him I'd kill him. We parted the best of friends, especially after he told me he had lost hope after you told him you loved me.'

'Honestly, I'm beginning to wish I hadn't gone this morning.'

'Ah, but you did and I'm very thankful, I know where I stand now. We'd better get engaged to warn others off. Come on, let's change and go to our garden.'

She laughed, 'our garden?'

'Our garden,' he firmly stated.

Meeting up, walked hand in hand to their private place.

He fetched his spade and began to dig whilst Abbey made holes for the plants from the greenhouse. She felt him watching her. Still bent she looked up at him. He was leaning on the spade wiping perspiration from his face. 'Will the kiss happen this week, next week?'

She went to him offering her face. It was a gentle kiss but the taste of him on her lips warmed her deeply and sent her head spinning at the same time. Andy broke the kiss and she felt bereft, as if she had lost something very precious. She moaned at the loss.

'It's the same for me darling. This is why we need to marry soon.' He had disciplined himself from drawing her close to him. Still holding her shoulders and loving the feel of her skin, Abbey was thrilled with the heat of his hands on her. Putting more distance between them he said, 'come on darling, gardening!'

'Yes, I understand Andy.' They worked in silence each with their thoughts. Viola brought their jug of fresh orange juice. 'Thank you Viola, this is most welcome,' he smiled at her.

'It's a pleasure, sir,' shyly smiling at him.

To not embarrass Abbey and knowing he had to tread carefully, they sat and Andy encouraged her to talk about her morning. He then told her, 'I invited your dada if he would like to go to my Cottage for the day and he suggested next Monday, Abbey. Will you please come?'

'Whilst we are casually working next week, this can be arranged thank you Andy. It'll be a wonderful change for dada and I look forward very much to this.' She questioned him but he told her he wanted her to see it. She thought it must be something special as he was so excited with them going.

Grant and Andy were thrilled with the abbreviated news presentation of the morning. Abbey had filmed so well. The cameras had captured her lovely face and showed her beautiful mouth as she laughed. When Abbey was shown he hit the pause button for them to have a closer look. Abbey protested, 'it's not about me.'

'Yes, we know Abbey, and you've projected this by keeping in the background. Your short encouraging speech was vital and will be much appreciated by the children and relatives of those who didn't win.' Grant agreed also congratulating her. Andy recorded it for Grant's parents and would copy one for Grant and himself. He had briefly texted his brothers to watch this news programme with their wives. He was so proud of her. 'You'll be asked to judge others, Abbey,' Andy prepared her.

The media caught up on this competition with the involvement of the Lord Mayor and was widely broadcast. He was interviewed explaining what it was and how he wanted to promote creative skills in school children. Tyler Stratham filled in with more. The leading newspapers also interviewed them and enquired about Miss Forrest. Tyler told them of her Masters Degree with Honours in oil painting and watercolours and had been and would be, as an impartial judge, very useful to them.

Andy was dreading him leaking out her knowing him at this point in their relationship as the media and press would give them no peace. Tyler didn't and Andy's admiration for this trust shot up. As Abbey had stated the competition wasn't about her, so Tyler was also a professional. Not knowing his private addresses he couldn't contact him to thank him and knew it would be inappropriate for Abbey to ask Mrs Hickman, but would wait until Tyler contacted Abbey with the next step in this competition. Tyler himself wanted to send Abbey a set of oils but knew that she would be embarrassed.

Andy's brothers texted him with admiration for Abbey and she received cards of congratulations that her talent was being used in this way from her Switzerland boarding school, finishing school and university principals and art teachers. Her Grandparents told her how proud they were of her. With being educated in Switzerland so she would be near them, they knew how hard she had worked.

Early the following morning Abbey received from her Grandparents a solid bamboo box with a selection of artists' oils, a range of watercolour paints and set of brushes for both. These were from a Yorkshire manufacturer. Abbey was thrilled as she was getting ready for new. When she rang her Grandmama answered, 'How are you and Grandpapa,' she enquired.

'We are ok darling. How are you?'

'Very well thank you Grandmama. I'm absolutely thrilled to receive your present. Brilliant timing, I'm almost out of paints and need new brushes. The new range of watercolours to mix is gorgeous.'

'Well,' Tanya laughed, 'you have Adrienne to thank for these. She looked on-line and found a supplier in Yorkshire.' They exchanged loving words and Tanya assured her she would thank Granddada on her behalf. Putting her hand set mobile down Abbey cried missing her Grandparents and thinking of all the love they had lavished on her.

The pattern of Andy coming before lunch for the remainder of the week continued. He and Abbey drew closer and closer.

Whilst eating the high tea on Sunday, Abbey was very concerned how ill her dada looked. He asked to be excused to go back to bed. Abbey and Andy helped him upstairs. 'May I help you in any way, Grant?' Andy lovingly asked him.

'Thank you Andy,' he replied in a weak voice. 'I'll get straight into bed. Ask Brian to come up. You both finish your meal,' smiling at them.

Abbey kissed him, 'I'll pop in soon.' He nodded.

Going down she said, 'I'm sending for the doctor, Andy.'

'Yes, he needs to come. Am I in the way, Abbey?'

'If you're able, please stay for a while.'

Abbey rang telling Birdie what she had done. Birdie and Brian went up to Grant.

Grant's private doctor came quickly. He didn't mind being called out on a Sunday knowing how serious Grant's heart failure was. Abbey and Andy waited on the patio to meet him as he came down from Grant, he was looking concerned.

'Your dada is very tired. I've ordered a nurse to stay with him during the night, Miss Forrest. Don't worry, it's the hot weather.' Discreetly looking at Andy and shaking his head. 'Your dada would like to see you.'

Uncertain what to do but seeing Abbey needed to concentrate on her dada, said, 'I'll get off Abbey. Please ring me if I can help in any way. I'll be in touch.' He put his number in her mobile for her to speed dial. 'Thank you again Abbey, this has been another of the best days of my life.'

'I've enjoyed it very much, Andy.' He could see that she was distracted. She hurried indoors. As he stood hesitating Birdie came to him looking very anxious. He gave her his number and she promised to ring him. 'I don't want to leave you, Miss Bird, but Abbey is naturally distracted. If I leave and do some work this will free me time tomorrow if Abbey or you need me.'

'We will need your support, sir.' She of course knew of how serious Grant's illness was and he had told her Andy knew but not Abbey. 'Brian suggests he and Todd take you back to your hotel.'

'Thank them for this but Brian may be needed here. I've a car coming. We'll not be able to go to my Cottage, Miss Bird.'

'No sir, not to-morrow. Prayerfully will later.'

'Yes indeed, Miss Bird.' They looked at each other in seriousness, aware Grant may not have much time left.

Hurrying into her dada, he was propped up in bed and Brian was giving him medicine. The fan was whirring near the bed. 'I'll wait outside, Miss Abbey.' She nodded her thanks.

'Don't worry darling, I'll be well enough to go to Andy's Cottage to-morrow. This weather doesn't agree with me as you know.' He fell asleep. She went to the door and she and Brian made Grant comfortable but still propped up. Her dada had never carried excess weight but Abbey had noticed he was going even thinner lately with not eating as well. She was disturbed to see his cheeks were so sunk in and his shoulder bones protruding.

Andy's car came and Oscar fetched the dogs. Travelling Andy rang his housekeeper Dot, 'to-morrow unfortunately is postponed Dot. Mr Forrest is very ill.'

'I'm so sorry Andy. Prayerfully he'll be well soon, probably is the extremely hot weather. I know how much you were looking forward to bringing them.' They chatted until he reached his hotel.

Sitting silent and praying, Birdie came quietly back to the bedroom. 'Come on, darling, your dada will sleep now.' Abbey reluctantly left after kissing her dada. He didn't move. Brian stayed with him.

'Shall I run you a bath, darling?' Birdie asked her.

'Thank you, Birdie, but I'll wait until the nurse comes.'

'I'll let you know and bring you a hot milky drink.' She promised.

'Thank you, darling Birdie.'

After a short while Birdie came back with a small flask. 'The nurse has arrived, darling. Shall I run your bath now?'

'You've done enough, darling Birdie. Thank you but I'll do it.' Abbey kissed her on the cheek as she often did.

Chapter Eight

Abbey was unable to sleep being worried about her dada but didn't interfere as the nurse was with him. The nurse thought Mr Forrest should have prepared Abbey how ill he was, but his life expectancy was for at least another two or three months.

Just after 6 am as Abbey was swimming her lengths she saw a movement, Birdie was signalling to her. She swam to the side. Birdie held a large towel. 'Come out, darling.'

She vaulted over the side and Birdie put the towel round her. 'Your dada isn't well, darling.' Abbey picked up her robe and put in on over her wet swimsuit and ran barefoot to his room. Propped up in bed seeing Abbey come he waved the nurse out of the room.

In a very frail voice he asked, 'Listen carefully my precious, I haven't much time now.'

'What do you mean dada? Not much time?'

'My heart has been failing darling, but I thought I'd a few more months.'

Abbey was horrified. 'Why didn't you tell me, darling dada?'

'I didn't want you to be worried,' signalling for a drink of water.

She held it to his lips holding him up. He nodded when he had had enough.

'Do you like Andy?'

'Yes, dada, I do.'

'Marry him, darling. You'll be happy with him. He'll take care of you.'

'Has he said he wants to marry me, dada?'

'Yes, precious. He'll help you run our hotels. He doesn't want you for your money with him being a millionaire. Don't overburden yourself with our hotels, sell Bow and Clough. You'll have plenty of money.' He nodded again towards the glass of water. She helped him again take a drink.

'Dada, please don't die, fight it. What shall I do without you? I love Andy and will marry him, and prayerfully have children. Please hang in to see your grandchildren.'

With absolute horror she saw he had gone. Weeping uncontrollably the nurse came back followed by Birdie; they detached her hands and took her to her room. The doctor arrived and instructed the nurse to give her the mild sedative he anticipated Abbey would need. He thought again that Mr Foster had been wrong not to warn Abbey, but they really had thought he had more time.

Birdie suggested to Abbey, 'Mr Byrne needs to know. He'd be hurt if you didn't contact him. Shall I ring?'

'Please darling. I've no idea what to do.'

'Your dada has left papers for you to inform all who needs to know. Wait for the solicitor.'

'You knew he was dying?'

'Yes darling, but not expected until another two months or so. I'll run you a bath and then ring Mr Byrne.'

Andy was shocked, 'I'll be with you under the hour, Birdie.' He hadn't asked her permission to so name her, but guessed that she was in the picture.

'Thank you, sir.'

Birdie warned him Abbey was sedated and led him into the morning room where Abbey looked absolutely shocked out of her mind. Andy was amazed to see her hair full of curls and waves. He looked at Birdie questioningly touching his head. She mouthed "natural" and touched her lips. He nodded.

The funeral people arrived. Andy urged Abbey outside to the stables whilst they took Grant's body away. She spoke with the staff and accepted their condolences but wasn't functioning, then went in for breakfast. At Andy's gentle urging she drank sweet coffee but couldn't eat. The solicitor arrived with his PA and they had a fresh pot of coffee in the office.

After their coffee, the solicitor brought out his file with Grant's requests. Abbey opened hers and shared this with Andy. They compared notes and who individually they would contact. Mr Bell promised that he would help as much as possible.

The key management, Grant's PA Lorraine and Abbey's PA Lara arrived and they began to look through the papers Grant had left for each one of them.

Andy thought it appropriate to leave them in privacy. Abbey walked him to his car.

'Try and rest this afternoon, Abbey. I don't want to leave you, but it's appropriate at this moment in time. When may I come back?'

'Are you free this evening?'

'Yes, and whenever you need me.'

She knew she would need him. 'Come for dinner. Have a ride first?'

'Brilliant.' He kissed her hand. 'See you at 5. Love your hair.' He stood looking at her as tears were welling up again. He wanted to take her into his arms to comfort her. 'See you at 5,' he repeated. She waved him off.

Feeling very lonely but appreciating his innate manners in leaving whilst they sorted out private papers, she went back thinking "whatever would I do without him?" She pulled up short at this unexpected thought. Remembering he had said he loved her hair she was glad as she hadn't now the high maintenance time to spend ages straightening it. She was then annoyed at herself for this shallow thought whilst she was in shock over her beloved dada's sudden death, but knew she wanted to please Andy knowing he was her future, her hope.

Abbey knowing the time would be convenient rang her Grandparents in Switzerland, her Granddada now needing a more powerful machine to help him breathe. Abbey had chosen the Switzerland Finishing School continuing being near them. She adored them as they did her.

Sebastian answered. 'Hello Granddada, how are you?'

'Still coughing, darling,' he laughed. He always made light of his illness.

'How's Grandmama?' He didn't answer but urgently asked 'is anything wrong Abbey? You sound subdued.'

'Granddada, dada has died.' She was sobbing.

'Oh my precious I'm so sorry, what a shock for you.'

'What do you mean "a shock for me," Granddada? Did everyone know but me he was dying?'

He heard anger in her voice for the first time in her life. He was coughing again and trying to stop, covering the phone as always.

He gasped, 'now, now, sweetheart, your dada prepared us, but his heart should have been good for at least another two months or longer. He was going to tell you nearer the time, precious. There was no secrecy. Your dada as all of us wanted the very best for you. You know that, surely?'

'Forgive me Granddada, I didn't mean to be disrespectful.'

She could hear him violently coughing, distressed she pleaded, 'let me ring you later, Granddada.'

'Please bear with me darling. I'm so frustrated that I can't travel to be with you, precious. Please ring us anytime sweetheart, wake us up if necessary.'

'I will Granddada.'

He was at a loss as what to say to her so advised, 'go and rest darling. You'll have a lot to do. Is Birdie with you?'

'I asked her to leave me whilst I rang you. She's coming back.'

He was gasping again, 'our solicitor, Matthias, will come to help Mr Bell and you, precious. This was set up for him to come and stay with Mr Bell.'

'Thank you, Granddada.'

'I'll go and tell your Grandmama, my sweetheart.'

'Please ask her not to make herself ill and ring me.'

'I will darling.' He put the phone down thinking that in the midst of the shock and trauma of Grant's sudden death, she still was thinking of others. He sighed.

He later rang her asking, 'Is it convenient for us to talk, darling?'

'Of course Granddada, anytime is convenient for you.'

'I have to prepare you, you are our heiress; you know this. When your Grandmama and I die your dada would have had full control of Gresley and Cobden.'

'Yes, Granddada, I know of this.'

'Good.' Knowing Grant had been training her for this last year after completing university he had been confident Grant would have prepared her for this. 'These, then would come to you.' His breath was laboured. Abbey was very anxious about him again. She could hear Adrienne his PA speaking to him and giving him a drink.

'Will you accept our giving you our 50% now, precious?' Abbey was stunned.

'I couldn't ask you before as your dada didn't want you to have to think of this responsibility just yet. However,' he broke off coughing again, 'whilst Matthias and Mr Bell are sorting your papers out, these needs could be incorporated. Excuse me darling,' she could hear Adrienne giving him another drink.

'I need to tell you, but Adrienne will fax all this information through to you. Matthias, of course, is fully in the picture. Adrienne will speak to you, darling,' he gasped.

Adrienne spoke, 'Hello Miss Forrest, my condolences on your dada's death. Please let me know if there is anything I can do to help you.'

Abbey thanked her.

'I'm speaking now for your Granddada, and we regret you have to hear this just now. Your Grandparents could now do without any work. The efficient managers and key people you know do a sterling job but your Grandparents still have to be personally involved and make decisions.

'The papers relating to your taking over the hotels are signed up with your dada's signatures in view of his illness. Matthias has all this to hand.

'May Matthias and I release your dada's obituary and words to the effect after getting your Grandparent's approval? The hotel guests and staff need to know stability with your dada's sudden death. We need to release the news now that you are taking over full control of the hotels on your Grandparent's request. Your hotels suppliers and others involved need this re-assurance also.'

'Whatever you think is relevant, Adrienne. I'll ask Mr Bell to do likewise.'

'I'll fax you our suggested input in a very short while.

'Very important, Miss Abbey is that your Grandparents need to let the manager's and key people know first before the news is released to the newspapers and media.'

Abbey was very thankful she had refused further sedation; she needed a clear head to cope. 'Will you and Matthias also attend to this, please Adrienne? I'm very grateful for your efficiency and sound sense.'

'It's part of our job. Here's your Granddada, Miss Abbey. I'll be in touch very shortly.'

Abbey was glad see had named her so as always had done.

Sebastian was violently coughing.

'Please darling, don't overtire your self. Let me ring you later when you've rested. Of course, I'll take full control. Adrienne is co-ordinating with me. I'm very grateful.'

'Sweetheart, let me say this.' He paused, then said, 'you're young and beautiful, Abbey. You've worked hard all your education life then learning the business. You love to paint, enjoy this.' His breath was again laboured. 'Sell the four hotels, Abbey. Whitwell Wood will be enough for you to manage and use your business skills. You'll marry darling and have beautiful children, but be very careful precious.' He was coughing again. 'You are intelligent and full of common sense, but there are devious men about. Talk to your Grandmama and me.'

'I will, darling, I will. I'm very worried about you Granddada. Please, please rest now.'

'And you, my Abbey.'

Blowing kisses over the phone she then was sobbing again knowing with certainty her Granddada was nearing the end of his life. Sobbing again weariness overcame her and she lay down on the bed fully clothed and fell asleep immediately. She woke feeling disorientated wondering where she was. Then remembering the horror of her dada dying and how ill her Granddada was, wept again then showered and went down. Mr Bell and everyone had left.

Adrienne had faxed all the information and that she, Matthias and Mr Bell had sorted everything needed at this moment. Abbey faxed her approval and grateful thanks.

Sitting on the patio the dogs were unsettled sensing the unrest in the house, Abbey began to realise just how many people and business' were going to be affected by her dada's death. She also realised what a wonderful professional team she had supporting her in Switzerland and here,

Weeping again thinking of her dada's love for her with ensuring everything ran smoothly for her after his death, also her Grandparent's love also with their meticulous preparations.

Abbey despite having never met her maternal grandparents out of respect thought she ought to telegraph them in Bermuda, giving her telephone and computer addresses. She rang her Grandparents for advice and Tanya answered.

After enquiries, loving greetings and weeping together, Abbey said, 'I feel I ought to let my mummy's parents know, Grandmama.'

'No,' she answered firmly. 'Don't concern yourself with them, darling.'

'I'd love to know about mummy as she grew up, Grandmama.' She was crying again.

'Now darling, don't upset yourself.'

Abbey heard her Granddada's voice and the telephone went silent. Abbey knew her Grandmama had covered the mouthpiece. Her Granddada came on. 'Darling, your Grandmama spoke hastily. If you have the grace to inform Mr and Mrs Harvey, do so.'

Meant To Meet

'Thank you Granddada, but is Grandmama happy with this?'

Tanya came back on, 'forgive me precious, I spoke without thinking. Do what you think is right. You are very sensible and intelligent, but don't let them upset you. Tell me if they do.'

'I will thank you, Grandmama. I'll forbid them to come, but know in my heart they won't suggest this.' They blew their kisses over the phone. Abbey could hear her Granddada coughing violently. She put the phone down so they would settle and rang Mr Bell. He answered sounding distracted.

'Sorry to interrupt you Mr Bell, Abbey Forrest here.'

'Yes, Miss Forrest. Adrienne has just rung me.'

'Thank you Mr Bell, but what I need at the minute is my maternal Grandparents addresses. I feel I should let them know. My Grandparents have left this with me.'

He went silent. 'Are you quite sure of this, Miss Forrest. Wouldn't you prefer me to let them know?'

'Thank you, but no. I'm forbidding them to come.' He gave her the addresses and she sent the International telegram, hand delivered for same day.

Feeling very much alone longed to see Andy. The dogs excitedly jumped up and she couldn't believe her eyes as Andy in casual wear was running towards her. 'I've been longing for you to be here with me,' she told him.

His heart leapt, he'd wondered if he would be intruding. 'I couldn't settle wanting to be with you. I'll need to deal with e-mails in a little while.' His heart ached seeing her eyes swollen with crying.

'Have I been too forward with you, Andy?'

'You'd never be anything but gracious, Abbey. You've made me so happy.' She blushed and he was enchanted. 'I love you Abbey. I've never said that before to anyone.'

'I adore you Andy.'

He gently kissed her. 'I know you're a virgin but you're safe with me, Abbey. We'll enjoy getting to know each other more. Perhaps it's inappropriate at this moment in time, but are you willing to marry me soon?'

'I'd love to marry you soon, Andy. The moment I met you I knew that my life would never be the same again.'

'When I met you the world and everything stopped. I couldn't wait for the time to pass until that Sunday when I could be with you again, and this has been daily.' He didn't, of course, tell her about the nights when thoughts of her kept him from sleeping.

She prepared him, 'I may get a call any minute. I've telegraphed my maternal Grandparents. Did my dada tell you of them?'

He was amazed. 'Never, I thought they were dead.'

'No, they live in Bermuda and are owners of a luxury hotel. I've never met them.'

'Never met them, your Grandparents?' he asked incredulously. 'They've let you grow up without knowing you?'

With tears in her eyes she nodded. 'They disowned mummy because she married dada. They thought he wasn't good enough for her. Did he tell you how mummy died?'

'I heard of this, Abbey.' He was still shocked about her maternal Grandparent's neglect.

'I really don't want anything to do with them but out of respect, I've telegraphed them but I'm regretting it now. I thank God you've come Andy.'

'I understand your doubts, Abbey, but you're doing the Christian thing. You'll never have anything on your conscience. Be firm with them. I'm here with you.'

'Thank you Andy, my head is all over the place. I rang my Grandparent's for advice. At first Grandmama forbade me to, but Granddada made her change her mind.'

'Abbey you are 24 years old, intelligent, full of compassion and integrity, you now have the responsibility of running this home and your business. You aren't an airhead but I know how you adore your Grandparents and highly respect them as they will know. If you are the means of helping them forgive and have peace, go for it darling. What would your dada have done if it was you who had died?'

'Oh Andy thank you for this, he would have let them know. He did when mummy died, but they just ignored him. I'm only letting them know to forbid them to come.'

She sat looking at him being filled with confidence.

'I'll not stand any nonsense from them. I don't need them. They could have helped dada and me when mummy died, he wouldn't have had such a strain on his heart if they had supported him.'

'Abbey, stop right there; dismiss these negative nasty thoughts. This isn't you. Rise above it, your dada did.'

'Sorry Andy.'

Pete and Birdie came with the afternoon tea trolley. 'We're a little early Miss Abbey, but thought you would appreciate a drink as Viola said you had missed your earlier one.'

'Brilliant timing thank you Birdie, I was asleep.'

'That will have been more beneficial than a glass of orange,' she smiled lovingly at her and then Andy. 'We're very pleased to see you sir.' He had with his innate manners as always stood when she approached.

'Ring if you require anything further, Miss Abbey.' She smilingly thanked them and they left.

After enjoying their cup of tea, the sandwiches were untouched. Viola fetched the trolley they had loaded.

Abbey's mobile hand set phone rang; looking seriously at Andy she picked it up. A female voice immediately said briskly, 'apologies Abbey, we can't possibly come. I'm not strong enough to stand in your cold climate at the side of the grave.' She hadn't even greeted her.

'Hello, Grandmother.'

'Please Abbey, call me Didi.'

Abbey rolled her eyes at Andy. 'Didi, we are going through an extremely hot spell here. I didn't invite or want you or Grandfather to come. With the manners my dada taught me I'm only letting you know about his death before you read it. I never mentioned inviting you to come.' She began to cry.

Didi heard a man's voice comforting her. 'You've people with you, Abbey?'

'Andy Byrne is with me.'

'You're very lucky to have Andy Byrne with you. Is he your lover?'

Abbey gasped and grabbed hold of his hand holding it tightly firmly saying through her teeth, 'Andy isn't my lover, yet. We're going to marry in a few weeks, and then he will be.'

Andy was filled with happiness at her words.

'Let me organise your wedding here, darling.'

Abbey was muttering under her breath. Andy couldn't decipher her words, but knew they were not complimentary to Didi.

'Thank you Didi, but no,' she again firmly stated. 'In respect of dada dying, we'll have a quiet ceremony.'

'Let me know, darling, and we'll come.'

She shouted in a loud voice, 'No, definitely, NO. You wouldn't come to your own daughter's funeral; I will not allow you to come to my wedding.'

Andy could see that she was very angry. He was angry at her being made upset, especially on the day her dada had died. Trying to take the phone from her to switch off he was amazed how strong she was holding on to it. He waited. He heard Didi and a man's voice talking also angrily, then Didi crying.

'Now look what you've done Abbey. You've caused your Granddaddy to shout at me. In all my married life he's never done this before.'

Abbey and Andy heard a man's clear voice saying, 'that's the problem. I've been a nerd. I should have put my foot down years ago.'

He came on the phone, 'Abbey, precious, your Grandddaddy here. Please don't be upset. I'm so proud of you and how hard you've worked gaining your degrees and achievements. Didi is also.'

'How do you know about these?' she shouted.

'Our solicitor made enquiries for me at your schools and university. I'm sorry I've been afraid of keeping in touch with you and Grant. I was worried Didi would leave me. She's a pain at times but I adore her. She's so beautiful, I'm so lucky. Please don't ring off. Here she is.'

'Abbey precious, please forgive me. I was a terrible mummy to Faye. I wasn't cut out for motherhood. Darling, I must confess I didn't want your mummy to marry your dada. He wasn't exciting enough for her, she could have married anyone.'

'Didi, stop right there.' Andy was concerned how white she had gone. Her knuckles holding her mobile hand set were clenched. 'I've been told and have photographs of dada and mummy and they were so in love. Don't you dare pull my dada down; he was the best man in the world. He only kept living for me. Birdie has told me he was suicidal with grief after mummy was killed.

'Also, *Didi*,' she emphasized, 'Birdie has also told me that many ladies wanted dada to marry them before he married mummy and after her death, and not for his wealth. He has grieved for mummy all these years and been faithful to her memory.

'You've let me grow up not knowing anything about my mummy's life before she married dada.'

At that she did let Andy take the phone as he asked for Didi's surname. In a voice of authority said, 'Mrs Harvey, Andy Byrne here. Abbey is in deep shock and bereavement for her beloved dada. She hadn't known about his heart failing. I'll not allow you to discredit him and I'll not allow you to be so rude to Abbey. I'm disgusted with you and your husband. Abbey needed her mummy, especially in her teenage years. Grant needed Faye. You could have helped. Abbey knows nothing of her mummy only what her dada, his parents and Miss Bird could tell her. Leave us alone now as you have left Abbey alone all her life.'

'Please, Mr Byrne, don't say that. Abbey is our heiress, this hotel and everything we have will be hers.'

'I can assure you Mrs Harvey that Abbey doesn't need anything from either of you.'

Russell came back on. 'Hello there Mr Byrne, I'm so sorry for all this upset. Let's be calm. Forgive me for being a weakling, please learn from me. Take authority Andy. May I call you Andy?'

'Yes sir.

'Russell.'

'Andy, now before you and Abbey ring off, you both love to ride yes?'

'Yes, Russell, we do.'

'May we buy you a couple of thoroughbreds as part of your wedding present?'

'Thank you but Abbey has her horse and I ride the other she has. Prayerfully after marrying we'll begin our family so Abbey won't be riding whilst pregnant.'

'I envy you Andy. So would you like a luxury family car?'

'Abbey doesn't need expensive gifts; she isn't that kind of young lady. What she needs, especially at this time in her bereavement is love and respect for her beloved dada,' he emphasized

'I understand Andy, please forgive me.' He was thinking of Didi always wanting the most expensive jewellery, the most expensive haute couture clothes she only wore once then discarded. All the wasted money spent on their Penthouse and cars with Didi quickly being dissatisfied with everything. The wasted money entertaining people for lunches and dinners, Didi trying to outdo everyone else as her friends also did.

'Will you please send me a photograph of Abbey?' He gave Andy his mobile number. 'Didi wants a word.' They heard him say firmly, 'a few seconds, and behave.'

'I'm sorry Andy that I've upset Abbey. Can you possibly come soon for a couple of days or as long as you are able.'

'Thank you, I doubt it,' he said politely but firmly. They said bye. Andy had to laugh. Abbey was looking in him in amazement, 'Sorry, darling, but Russell has now for the first time in their marriage taken authority. Let's have a glass of white and I'll tell you what he's suggested for a wedding present.'

'I apologise for you hearing this, Andy, but I'm so very thankful you're here. I would have been more angry and unforgiving with them.'

'I'm very thankful that I was here for you, darling. Your Grandparents are a part of our future, if you so decide.'

'Thank you Andy. Yes, I'm now relieved I was restrained. I feel that I've not let mummy or dada down. What a shame though I didn't contact them before dada died.'

'You have to let the past go now, darling. It's not as though they live next door!'

'Good heavens, no.' she had to laugh. Andy was re-assured whilst in the trauma she was mature enough to handle it. He also knew that she was putting on a good face, hiding her heartache of losing her beloved dada to keep everyone's spirit's up, but knew she would have to break soon.

After freshening up they met on the patio and Andy had the wine ready. As they sipped he said. 'Russell suggested buying both of us a thoroughbred each.

'When I refused this offer he offered a luxury car. I also refused this, Abbey. Then Didi invited us to visit them. I told her I doubted this. Did I overstep the mark?'

Her heart swelled with emotion. 'No, my dearest, I'm so proud of you. Thank you for defending me. They'll both have learned from you. I adore you Andy and I can't wait to be married.'

He groaned, 'neither can I, precious.'

Sitting in silence again with the dogs contentedly lay at their feet. Both were so thankful they could share times of silence with each other.

He laughed, 'have you any more relatives world-wide?'

'Not as I know of, darling.'

'I admire you very much for how you dealt with Didi,' he sincerely told her. 'We need to let go of the past, darling. Our children must have the opportunity of knowing them.'

'I hear what you are saying, but I honestly think it's you, your wealth and the status you hold with your hotels that she can boast about to her friends. I think she wouldn't have bothered with me.'

He was once more amazed at her discernment, but not surprised having grown up without a mother or siblings and always caring and supporting her dada. He guessed she was right.

'Yes, I understand this, Abbey, but if I'm instrumental of reconciliation and your dada being honoured, I'll do everything to bring this about. I think you know that I'm not a "Russell."'

'I couldn't respect you if you were, my darling, but it looks as though he's recognized his weakness. We all have them.'

'Yes,' laughed Andy, 'and you're my biggest.'

'I'm so sorry dada didn't see your Cottage, Andy.'

'I told him about it when we had our times together before dinner, and showed him photographs. He was very interested.'

'May I see the photographs?'

'I would rather you wait, darling.'

Abby understood then why he had shown her dada. He had known the short time scale her dada had been given. A wave of love went through her. 'I'm so thankful he knew, darling.'

Abbey's mobile hand set phone rang, 'Excuse me Andy, its Grandmama.'

Tanya immediately said after greeting her, 'have you spoken to your Grandparents, Abbey?'

'Yes, darling, but have forbidden them to come.'

'Please forgive me for being negative, my precious. Your Granddada and I are thankful that you were able to contact them. I tried to get through to you but your phone was engaged, so I hoped that you were speaking to them.'

'Yes, I was, darling.'

'We're very proud of you.'

Abbey began to cry, she couldn't help it. Andy knowing how emotional it must have been for her speaking to Didi and Russell took hold of her hand

and squeezed it. He took the phone off her, 'Andy here Mrs Forrest. I'm so sorry Mr Forrest has died. He was a good friend and mentor to me.'

'Yes, he often spoke of you Andy. Is Abbey ok?'

'We'll go and do some gardening, Mrs Forrest.'

'Well done, Andy.' He handed the phone back to Abbey.

'Go and enjoy your gardening, darling. Speak later.'

'Thank you Grandmama. Love to Granddada. Speak to him later. Thank you both very much for my present. There are new colours I'll enjoy using.' As always they blew kisses over the phone.

'I must attend to my e-mails, darling,' Andy told her. 'Please excuse me?'

'Carry on Andy. I'll do the same.

Moving away to make his calls the dogs followed him. When he saw Abbey had finished suggested, 'shall we have a stroll to our garden, precious?'

'Let's do that, darling. Whatever would I do without you?' she asked him as she had mentally thought this numerous times.

'This applies for me, my sweetheart. I can't bear to be away from you. I daily adore you more and more and every day I learn from you. We've a good sound foundation for our marriage.'

'Wait until Didi knows we both love to garden and grow food.'

'She probably thinks food drops out of the sky.'

Standing up and the dogs jumped up with them. Walking to their garden she told him, 'Andy, dada didn't see my birthday present.'

He took hold of her hand, 'no darling, this is a shame. But it will be used and we will have it for memories.'

'Yes, we will. Would you like to see it?'

'I would please, precious, I was wondering this morning if you'd be painting.'

'I'll begin another. My Grandparents have sent me a set of oil paints and new vibrant watercolours with brushes for both.'

Going to her art room she showed him the framed Smillie. He stood looking at it and had to hold back his tears. Grant would have adored this. She then showed him her Grandparent's present. 'Do you want to do some painting, darling?'

'Not at the moment, thank you.' They went to the garden where they sat talking under the sun parasol.

'Pardon me asking darling, is your mummy buried or was she cremated?'

'It was a burial, Andy. Dada bought a large private plot for himself to be with her also his parents, and there is a space for me if I don't marry.'

'You won't need that, darling.'

'Dada planted a weeping willow tree to shade the area. He had a seat put there also.'

'Would you like me to take you there, darling?'

'Not at the moment, thank you Andy.

He was pleased knowing she was emotional enough for now.

He sent Russell the photograph of Abbey in her garden also with Grant both laughing he had taken on the first Sunday before Grant had died, with a copy of the television video of Abbey at the school's art competition. Russell put the photographs into his computer enlarging and printed them out. He couldn't tear his eyes away from the visions of his granddaughter and he couldn't control his weeping. After freshening up he went to find Didi to show her the photographs and video. She cried and Russell waited.

'She's so beautiful. I've never seen more classical features. Grant looked ill. We've been stupid fools, haven't we, darling?'

Sighing heavily he agreed, 'we certainly have,' He was also thinking he had been a bigger fool to let himself be ruled by her to keep his marriage and peace.

Enjoying a glass of wine Russell said, 'this is a new beginning for us, darling. Are you able to let go of your wrong thoughts of Grant?'

'Yes, I'm so ashamed and full of remorse at neglecting Abbey as she grew up motherless.'

'Well, we can't go back. I now will make all the decisions,' he firmly said.

'Thank you, darling, I welcome this.'

She felt as though she had been given a new lease of life. It felt good having Russell taking authority. She couldn't wait to share this with her friends. "Friends?" she thought. How many sincere friends had she? They, including her, were always in competition to be the best dressed, to have the best jewellery, to have all the attention, always competing with each other. She decided she needed to change and encourage them also to be more down to earth and be happy and content.

'I'll go for a soak now, Russell. Come to my bed tonight, darling. I'll text you when I'm ready.'

'Do you really promise me this, Didi?'

'I do, my darling, I do and every night from here on. This is a new start for us and I'm going to be a loving wife to you. Forgive me for always being selfish.' Previously Russell would have assured her she wasn't despite knowing she was, but remained silent this time.

With his ever innate manners he escorted her to the top of the stairs, then went down to his office and sat at his desk lost in thoughts. All the lunches and dinners they had attended or provided he'd never enjoyed one and had been frustrated at the wasted time. The husbands and wives were always sniping with each other. He knew the men had mistresses or one night stands, they boasted about them to him. He guessed the wives also had lovers.

That was one thing he was proud of being sure Didi hadn't. She dealt with flirting or suggestions with dignity. He was thankful that he also hadn't taken lovers. He could easily have with Didi not giving him any comfort. He knew his PA Marianne was in love with him although she hid it; he had been tempted many times but controlled himself. Now he was thankful. He then got out the two photograph albums of Faye from being born up to her defiance about marrying Grant. He looked through them regretting again how they had neglected Abbey. He decided to discreetly let Andy have them to give to Abbey at an appropriate time.

Didi lay back in her favourite fragrant bubbles and sobbed as never before, she was amazed at this, she never cried. What had she achieved in her life? A beautiful daughter she had turned her back on. Her granddaughter she had also neglected through her pettiness and false pride not wanting Faye to marry Grant because he wasn't glamorous and of her world, blaming him when Faye was killed. What was her world, what had she to show? Everything had been fleeting. Russell had been the husband she hadn't married for love but because he was rich and he wouldn't dare defy her. If she said black was white he'd agreed.

Meant To Meet

What could she do now to make it up to Abbey? From her tone of voice she knew she had to tread carefully. No one had defied her or spoken to her as Abbey had. She was filled with admiration for her. She pulled up short as the memory of Faye defending Grant came back. She had shouted at her just as Abbey had.

Then having the thought she could soften Abbey through showing a new care for Grant. She would send money to a London hospital which had a heart unit. She began to feel more settled having now a plan. She quickly got out and dried and applied her beauty routine then went to find Russell to tell him of this new suggestion. She pulled up short, no, she would not tell him, but would ask his advice.

Finding him lightly said, 'please don't have a heart attack Russell but I need your advice.' He was amazed, this was a first. After she had shared he sincerely agreed and praised her for this loving thought thinking, "better late than never."

'Would you like to go out this evening darling,' he asked, 'or have you anything arranged?'

'No. Only the usual greeting our guests.'

'I'll take you out to dinner. Wear your most glamorous. We've something to celebrate.' He managed to book a table at a local prestigious restaurant and greatly enjoyed taking control with the *maître d'* and waiters. People who knew them recognized a new Russell and Didi and were curious.

Deirdre, Didi's closest companion, was sat open mouthed as Didi and Russell walked in holding hands as young lovers. Didi was glowing. Holding her phone under the table she secretly texted the "gang."

After Russell had taken authority ordering the wines and the food a young man appeared and gave Didi a bouquet of beautiful red roses. Didi thanked Russell and when the deliverer had left he told her, 'I'll take you to-morrow and buy you jewellery.'

'Thank you, my darling, but I've more than enough. These roses are very acceptable.'

He nearly had a heart attack at her words.

Before the dessert Didi deliberately went to the powder rooms knowing Deirdre would follow. She did.

'Darling, tell me quickly. What are you taking?'

'Nothing, Deirdre, I've fallen in love with my husband.'

She stood shocked.

'Russell is now taking authority. We're at a new beginning of our lives.' Jealousy tore through Deirdre. Her husband unknown to Didi had taken his latest mistress for a holiday. 'Congratulations darling. Let's hope it lasts.'

'Thank you for your sincere good wishes, Deirdre.' Knowing how bitchy she was and hoped the opposite. Didi was thankful of recognising the shallowness she also had lived by.

'I'm so jealous, Didi, Jason has taken Elfrida on holiday. He has no respect for me.'

'Darling, I'm so sorry, I didn't know.'

'You knew he had mistresses?'

'Well, yes, darling. When he comes back home he has to see a change in you as I'm changing for Russell. I wonder if Russell has had mistresses.'

'I can assure you Didi, I doubt he has. I know certain ladies who have approached him and he told them you are his only one.'

Didi's heart swelled with emotion and pride.

'Did you, Deirdre?'

Shamefaced she admitted, 'I was one of them.'

'I need to get back to him, darling.'

Returning to their tables, Russell as always with his good manners stood as Didi approached. Smiling he said, 'I thought you had left me, darling.' She kissed him on his lips.

'No never, I've had a heart to heart with Deirdre. I'm very proud of you, my darling husband. Thank you.'

He understood what she was referring to. 'You've been and are and will be, my only one precious,' he gruffly told her.

They sat holding hands. 'Are you bothered about dessert, Russell?'

'No.'

He beckoned the *maitre d'* and asked for the bill. Home they went.

Didi had her usual bedtime routine but Gaye, her personal maid, knew she was different. She was smiling; she was happy and good tempered. 'Get my most glamorous nightdress and peignoir set out, please Gaye.'

When Didi was ready Gaye left her and met Russell coming on the corridor towards Didi's door. She knew then and was happy for them, especially Mr Harvey. Also she hoped that Didi now wouldn't be as difficult as she had been.

The next morning Russell reluctantly left Didi in bed to sort some urgent office work out with Marianne.

Didi sitting up in bed enjoying her morning cup of tea rang Deirdre, 'sorry darling, I can't meet up with you. I've urgent preparations to make. Russell and I are going to London for an overnight stay.'

'You're going to a special show?'

'No Deirdre.' She knew that she had to tell her. 'I'm going to confess something that I'm not proud of.'

Deirdre was filled with excitement thinking she would have the "gang's" attention during their usual afternoon tea.

'Russell and I have a granddaughter.'

'You've only just found this out?' she asked in amazement.

'No Deirdre, I've known for 24 years.'

'You've known for 24 years you have a granddaughter?' Deirdre repeated.

'Will you please listen whilst I tell you, darling? This isn't easy for me.'

'Sorry Didi, I'll keep silent.' Didi was thinking this would be a miracle.

'I didn't want my daughter to marry Grant Forrest. I thought he wasn't good enough for her and not outgoing enough.'

'He was marrying her for her money?'

'Deirdre please, no. Russell and I came here to buy our hotel.

'When Faye was killed I blamed Grant for this. I've been a stupid fool, Deirdre, but Russell and I are going to make it up with Abbey. Grant has died and Abbey is allowing us to go to his funeral.' She felt guilty at this lie.

'Allowing you, darling?'

'Yes, she was and possibly still is, very angry with us for our behaviour with her dada. She adored him and is heartbroken over his sudden death. It was heart failure.'

'Good grief Didi, I had no idea that you have a granddaughter.'

'She has a Masters Degree with Honours in Business Management and other business degrees, languages, a wonderful painter in oils, an accomplished pianist and horsewoman. She's so beautiful, Deirdre, her features are much more classical than mine or Faye's.'

'Wow. Sorry Didi, carry on.'

'She'll run the hotels. Her paternal Grandparents live in Switzerland through ill heath. Russell and I have to make our peace with them also.'

'Will she be able to manage all these hotels?'

'Yes, she will have trusted staff. Andy Byrne is now a close friend and is supporting her,' she proudly told her.

'Andy Byrne, the multi millionaire hotel owner?' Deirdre shrieked.

'Yes, in fact they are in love and will marry.'

'This is better than any film, darling. Will Andy and Abbey be coming here?'

'Yes, in a while.' Again she thought she had to stop lying.

'I must go now, darling. Bye for now. Keep in touch when you are able. Love to Russell.'

'Deirdre, please don't reveal about Abbey and Andy getting married. The paparazzi will haunt them. Andy and Abbey will be very cross with me. Let Abbey have respect and quiet for her bereavement. I'll know you've revealed as you are the only one I'll tell about this as yet. I'm so proud of her. If you don't reveal I'll invite you to dinner when they visit. If you do, I'll cut you out of my life. I shouldn't have told you this yet.'

'I won't, I promise on my heart darling, reveal this. May I tell the gang about your granddaughter?'

'Yes. Ask them not to disturb me. As I said I'm spending time with Russell to-day, but I'll come to-morrow afternoon and fill you all in." They blew kisses over the phone.

Didi groaned. She regretted telling her about Andy and Abbey. She regretted lying. Russell would be cross with her, but was sure Deirdre would adhere. 'I must control my gossiping and boasting tongue,' she told herself.

Then laughing, thought "well, I've something to boast about. I doubt the gang can match this!"

Deirdre was excited as when her husband Jason returned she would tell him she was Didi's personal confidante and about this new connection with Andy Byrne. This would make her more attractive to him. She then pulled her thoughts short. "What the hell am I thinking of? He is shallow. How many times has he humiliated me in front of my friends? How many middle aged rich mistresses has he had who, like me, have pampered to his gambling and drinking? He's with one now and staying not far away, adding to my humiliation."

She went on thinking being wealthy with old money how he had lived off her. She felt bilious, "no, no way am I having him involved in any way with Didi's granddaughter and Andy." She didn't even want them to know her association with him.

Remembering how he had robbed her of her self-esteem, how unhappy he had constantly made her and she had always put a good face on so Didi and her female "gang" wouldn't know. How she had always tried to buy his love, she began to sob.

Filled with a new determination she pushed the bell for Tina, her personal maid. 'I need you to help me, Tina.'

"Anything ma'am, you know this.' She loved Deirdre and hated Jason who had several times tried to fondle her until she'd kneed him where it really hurt. He hadn't attempted again. She and her husband Berwick the butler had been with Deirdre for over thirty years when she lived in a luxury apartment, coming with her when she bought "Wood view" after marrying Jason just over five years ago. They would have left but stuck it out not leaving Deirdre with him.

'I'm turning Mr Shepherd out, Tina.'

She clapped vigorously, 'oh Mrs Shepherd, I could kiss you.'

'I'm going back to my maiden name. We need your husband, Tina, please ring him.'

He was cleaning the silver but rushed to Deirdre, 'you need me, madam?'

'Yes Berwick, have you any empty boxes?'

He was astounded. 'Plenty ma'am, what can I do?'

'Take them into Mr Shepherd's bedroom. I'm getting rid of him and sending all his clothes to the charity shop.'

'Pardon me, madam, I am delighted you're turning him out but, knowing you and your heart, will you regret not letting him have his clothes?'

He and Tina stood looking at her as she considered this. 'Maybe I'm being a bit harsh. Ok. Fetch the boxes please. His suits are in covers so we only need to carry these down as they are.'

He and Tina went for the boxes. Deirdre went up to the suite opening all the windows.

They quickly packed and the three of them began to carry down to the Gatehouse, much to the caretaker's amazement.

'Mr Shepherd will collect these, Binksby.' Berwick winked at him. He got the message.

'When he comes do you want me to escort him, ma'am?'

'We'll be with madam,' Berwick firmly said.

'This is something I need to do on my own, thank you all for your kindness. I'll be living here with you.' They were relieved.

After completing she rang Jason knowing he was nearby adding to her further humiliation. 'Please come immediately. I've some exciting news.'

'What is it, pet?'

In a teasing note said, 'wait and see.'

She poured a gin and tonic and sat down waiting for him, her mobile nearby.

As anticipated he didn't keep her waiting long. Rushing in red in face, 'what is it pet?'

She stood up with her mobile, 'I'm not your pet and I'm throwing you out. Your belongings are in the Gatehouse. Take them and go, be thankful I'm not burning them. Leave my car here and never return.'

'You can't mean this. You love me.'

'Go,' she shouted.

He was frightened of this new Deirdre. 'Please, Deirdre let me have another chance, don't be hasty.'

'You have had more than your share of chances.'

His recent mistress had told him he was getting old, flabby and past it, and she wasn't the only one who had said this. She had cut their time short but feeling humiliated he had stayed at the hotel and the irony of it was, that he had begun to think of Deirdre and that she wouldn't turn her back on him. She would welcome him with open arms as she always had. She wouldn't look at him with disgust. Now he had nothing and without Deirdre's money, no one would be interested in him

'How can I transport my belongings?' He was also thinking he had no-where to go without Deirdre's allowance.

'Get one of your mistresses to fetch them,' she again shouted.

He came with his fist raised and his face was viscious.

'You touch me and I'll speed dial Russell Harvey. His security will be here in a few minutes.'

Dropping his fist, Berwick and Tina came into the room, they had been stood at the door listening.

'Well,' Jason said, 'you can always ring me when you have come to your senses.' The three of them burst out laughing. He left.

'He'll not dare come back or interfere with you now he knows Mr Harvey is protecting you.'

Tina saw Deirdre had gone very white under her make-up. 'Sit down, darling. Ask Mrs Faith to come with a pot of tea for the four of us, please Berwick.' He rushed off.

Tina sat with her holding her hand. 'He frightened me, Tina.'

'He never will again, ma'am. Has he hit you before?'

'No, never, but I've never opposed him.'

'What are doing this afternoon, going to bed?'

'No, Tina, I'm meeting my gang as usual. His going is secret just for now.'

'Yes, darling, I'll tell Binksby.'

Tina stayed with her and the housekeeper, Mrs Faith came with Berwick carrying the tray.

'Good riddance, ma'am,' the housekeeper said. Berwick had quickly put her in the picture.

Deirdre invited them to sit down, Mrs Faith poured the tea. 'Will you please arrange for Mr Shepherd's furniture to be taken away, Berwick?'

'I will, ma'am.' He left them to arrange this.

'Then will you get your extra cleaners in Mrs Faith, to strip the room bare and thoroughly clean it?'

'I'll do anything for you, ma'am, you know this.'

Deirdre then asked her, 'will you arrange for these two suites to be redecorated and refurbished?'

'I will, Miss Worsley.'

'I'll go to Paris for a couple of months.'

'Yes, ma'am, this is a good idea. You've plenty of friends there.'

'Am I going with you ma'am?' Tina asked.

'Will Berwick allow this?'

'He'll not allow you to go on your own. He'll be a great help for Mrs Faith.'

'Thank you, darlings,' smiling through tears at them both.

Tina seeing Deirdre was back in control, suggested, 'I'll prepare your bath, ma'am.'

'Thank you Tina, and then wash and attend to my hair. I want to get rid of his smell.'

When she was ready she thought, "I'll set up a hat business." Having always been creative had designed her hats. "I'll make Didi a hat for the funeral and then suggest I make her hat for the wedding."

She texted Didi, "I know you're busy helping Russell so please don't reply until you have time. Having enough humiliation I've made Jason leave. I'm going to set up my own hat making business. May I make you your funeral hat Didi?"

When Didi read this she was filled with thankfulness. Deirdre covered up Jason's infidelities but she knew how humiliated she had been. Didi replied back, "Good for you, Deirdre. Let him go and don't respond to his begging to come back. Realize it's your money he wants darling, however hard this is. But you already know being so intelligent. Please begin designing my hat, a simple style. I'll send a mannequin. We have a top class security team serving the hotel and they will be at your disposal. You are now our beloved sister and my confidante. Go for it, darling, be strong. You deserve to be happy as I now am. XX"

Deirdre briefly mentioned to the gang as she had Didi's permission about Abbey and the funeral. They were all agog as she had been. She then, to distract them, told them she was setting up her hat making business, beginning with making Didi a hat for the funeral service and was going to Paris for a while.

They all immediately gave her an order for their glamorous straw sun hats they had made in Paris and Italy.

Chapter Nine

Abbey received a bouquet of the gorgeous perfumed cream roses with pink streaks. Thinking they were from Andy she was amazed when she read the card, "To my darling granddaughter, from your very proud Grandpapa Russell. Be happy, precious."

When Andy came he was very pleased at Russell's loving gesture. 'We need to encourage them to come to the funeral darling, if for just overnight. I've been thinking they could stay with me in the Penthouse, Have I to speak to Russell?'

'Please do, darling.'

Andy knowing a convenient time rang Russell's mobile. He briskly answered immediately, 'Russell Harvey.'

'Andy Byrne. Have you a few minutes Russell?'

'As long as you like, Andy' he replied.

'Abbey wants a word.'

'Thank you Grandpapa for the gorgeous roses. I love them. Andy now wants to speak to you.'

'I'm suggesting Russell that you and Didi come to Grant's funeral even if just overnight. Stay with me in my Penthouse in my London hotel.'

'Andy, we accept with gratitude. We've been sorting out a hotel to stay in so Abbey can be quiet preparing for her very traumatic day. We willingly will come and stay overnight with you and leave after the service.'

'Would you like to stay for the lunch Russell? I'll ask Abbey if I may arrange this in one of my colleagues' restaurants.'

'We'll then leave you before the will reading.'

Andy discerned that Russell was re-assuring him they wouldn't impose on their time. He liked that.

'Let me know the time you'll be arriving at Heathrow and I with one of my hotel cars will meet you. Afterwards a car with a member of my security team will take you back to the airport escorting you both safely back on board.'

'Thank you Andy, well done. I'll be in touch very shortly to finalise the arrangements. Give our love to Abbey.' He rang off.

'I'm so proud of you, Andy, thank you. I suggest I invite the Vicar out of respect to meet them.'

'That would be spot on Abbey. Good lateral thinking. Will you join us for dinner?'

'No darling. Please let me have a quiet time with Grandmama.'

'If this is what you want, darling, so is it.'

Andy rang Russell back and told him what Abbey had suggested. 'With Abbey needing a quiet dinner and early night, where would you and Didi like to dine?'

'I suggest in your Penthouse, Andy. Didi will be tired after travelling and the emotions of the afternoon.'

'No problem, Russell. You'll have a valet and Didi will have the number one personal maid to attend to you from arriving to leaving.'

'Good man, Andy, thank you. I very much look forward to meeting you as well as Abbey. Are you with Abbey?'

'Not at the moment, Russell.'

'Didi is fearful she'll be too emotional seeing Faye's grave. We ask if she may stay in the car for the burial.'

'With it being a cremation at Grant's request, his ashes will be buried the next day. Just a few will attend this.'

Russell went quiet, then in a choked voice said, 'I need to see Faye's grave, Andy.'

Andy was sorting this out in his thoughts, and suggested, 'what about if I come to the airport with you and we call en route?'

'Thank you Andy. Abbey will need you. But for us to go en route, do you think the vicar will escort us?'

'I'm positive he will. He's cleared the day for us.'

Russell began to cry. Andy sensitively rang off.

Andy telephoned Mr Bell and Birdie suggesting that he put a security agent from the team he used in his hotels in the gatehouse for the night hours after the ex-policeman security on the gates went home after the afternoon shift at 10 pm. He would leave at 6 am when the day ex-policeman security came on. Mr Bell welcomed this and also Birdie. Andy suggested to them both that Abbey didn't know. Holly House had one of the most secure alarm systems made, but Mr Bell and the house staff welcomed the night security whilst they were feeling vulnerable after Grant's sudden death.

Meant To Meet

Birdie passed this on to Oscar and that the night security men would need to meet the two Rottweillers who roamed the grounds during the night. They were enclosed during the day.

Todd and Abbey's chauffeur Brian also approved this. Brian and his wife Debbie lived in the flat built over the garage. When not needed he cleaned the cars and kept the patio slabs running round the house and windows clean. Debbie was a cleaner in the house.

Grant's Jack Russell, Smillie, lay outside his bedroom door. Abbey had given him his bowl of food but it was still untouched. The vet advised, 'just continue giving him plenty of water and encourage him to go walking with you.'

Before breakfast Abbey told Birdie, 'there was a light in the gatehouse, Birdie. The dogs were settled so I knew there wasn't a cause for concern.'

'No, Miss Abbey, no concern. There will be a light on each night. Mr Byrne asked my and Mr Bell's permission to have one of his security team there during the night whilst we are feeling vulnerable. He asked that we didn't mention this to you, but now you'll be wondering why there is a light on. He's aware that inscrutable people will be hoping to photograph him being here at night with you and disturb the dogs, but with this not happening they will soon move on.'

'Wow, he's a star, isn't he?'

'He is. You are still not sleeping, Miss Abbey?'

'Not as yet, darling Birdie.'

'Please take the sleeping tablets the doctor prescribed. You need your rest.'

'If I don't sleep soon, I'll consider them, Birdie. I'm sure I'll get back into the routine soon. I'll ring Mrs Woodhead, Birdie, to see if she can run me a dress up for the funeral.'

'No, Miss Abbey.'

'No?'

'No. You need to dress more couture now. You are the mistress of this home and owner of hotels. Also you've Mr Byrne to think of.'

Abbey sat looking at her and understanding dawned.

'Of course, thank you Birdie, I hadn't thought. I'll contact a boutique for now and then get in touch with an haute couture seamstress.'

She looked online and found an exclusive boutique not far away and booked an afternoon appointment with the manager whilst she should be having her afternoon rest with still not being able to sleep.

Brian and Todd took her and Ms Sherwood escorted her into a private room conversing in French. She measured Abbey and told her, 'you are wonderful to dress Miss Forrest.' She showed Abbey a few exclusive black dresses but being too fussy, they didn't appeal to her.

'I know what you would like, Miss Forrest, more classic, yes. We've a new line being delivered to one of our Paris boutiques. Pardon me Miss Forrest, I'll fetch my laptop. Are you comfortable?'

'Thank you, yes, but I haven't much time to-day.'

'I understand, madam. Will you have a glass of wine?'

'Please, a small red.'

A young lady brought this and then took Abbey to the powder rooms and waited to escort her back to

Ms Sherwood who had four dresses in her laptop to show her.

'These haven't been seen yet, Miss Forrest.'

Abbey asked her to zoom in on the second and then see the back. Ms Sherwood did and showed Abbey from several views. The more Abbey saw of it the more she liked. A knee length classic black silk with chiffon three quarter length sleeves.

'This one definitely please, Ms Sherwood.'

'I'll have them send the four here or we could bring to your home if you prefer.'

'This will be a great help, thank you.'

Ms Sherwood knew as she had seen the death of her father in the newspapers and television.

'We'll love to help you, you've a marvellous figure but I know you don't want to flaunt it.'

'Exactly, thank you Ms Sherwood for this understanding.'

She then asked, 'may we help you further, Miss Forrest.'

'I need a hat and handbag. Perhaps gloves.'

Ms Sherwood took Abbey and introduced her to an assistant who took her into the hat department. Abbey liked an Italian straw hat with brim curved over her face and tried it on. 'Until I try it with the dress I can't really decide, can I?'

'No, madam, we'll bring it and two or three more I think you'll like with the dresses.' Ms Sherwood had quickly put her in the picture of Abbey's requirements. 'We'll bring gloves and tights or hold up stockings?'

'Hold up stockings please in this hot weather.'

Mrs Slinn said, 'now shoes or sandals.'

Abbey looked at her watch. 'I have suitable shoes. I must get back now. I've a meeting.'

Ms Sherwood was waiting, 'Paris are delivering to-morrow, Miss Forrest, when may we bring them?'

'I'm supposed to rest for a short time in the afternoons as I'm not sleeping.'

They sympathised but assured her she would get back into the routine in time.

'Can you please come to-morrow afternoon at 2.30?'

'It will be a pleasure to help you, madam.'

Abbey began to tell them her address.'

'We know, Miss Forrest,' Ms Sherwood smilingly told her.

She walked to the door with her and Brian pulled up.

Todd held his arm as she got in with her elegant Finishing School training.

Abbey sank back and heaved a big sigh of relief. She knew Andy would like the second dress, but needed to see how it fitted.

Mrs Slinn and Ms Sherwood stood watching her and then waved goodbye.

'What a lovely cultured young lady, Jayne.'

'Yes.'

'Definitely she's still a virgin.'

'She's in contact with Andy Byrne. Doubt she'll be a virgin for long with him.'

'I think that you're most wrong. She has grown up without a mother or siblings.' She had this information from on-line. 'She has a mind of her own, and you wait, she'll only buy what she likes and is comfortable in.'

'Yes. Miss Forrest didn't ask the prices.'

'She admitted her head is all over the place just now. She has the most wonderful figure, Jayne. Her breasts- wow- no bra, just a nipple protector.'

'Mr Byrne will love her breasts.'

'You are awful Jayne. We'd better have a coffee and then do some work. I wonder if Mr Byrne will be there when we go.'

'Hopefully, he will.' They both laughed.

Abbey didn't tell Andy about visiting the boutique. She wanted him to be proud of her as she also did in memory of her dada.

The newspapers and gossip magazines were printing untruths about Abbey. Andy was determined to put a stop to this. Reporters were waiting for him as they shadowed him and also Abbey who just smiled at them and moved on.

Firing questions at him he stood tall and with authority, warning them. 'Stop pestering Miss Forrest and stop printing incorrect stories about her or you'll all be in serious trouble with me.

'Miss Forrest is in deep bereavement losing her beloved father. She didn't know the seriousness of his failing heart and the prognoses his time scale was. He asked everyone in the know not to reveal this being months away. His untimely sudden death took everyone with surprise. Please realise how this has affected her.'

Apologies were called out and Andy thanked them.

A male voice called out, 'you are Miss Forrest's companion, sir?'

In a firm voice he replied, 'I'm being a friend to her. Miss Forrest's mother died shortly after giving birth so she has grown up with no siblings.

'Miss Forrest is a very highly intelligent young lady who has always worked hard at her education and gained Honours in her degrees she took to enable her to help her father in their hotel business. Since leaving university for the last year, this is what she has been doing. Please respect her. She's a very refined special young lady.'

'You admire her, sir?' he was then asked.

'I do, very much so. Miss Forrest is a credit to each one of us. I'm in awe of her hotel business knowledge. She didn't have to work so hard being educated as her father's only child and her grandparent's only grandchild. I admire her for how she has applied herself with dignity, never causing her father any problems and always supporting him. One doesn't get Honours degrees with wasting time pursuing pleasures.'

More questions were fired at him. Andy held his hand up and walking away heard thanks of appreciation for his time and putting them in the picture. All of them were aware that they now had a new line to follow as Miss Forrest emerged from obscurity.

A female called out, 'Are you going to marry Miss Forrest, Mr Byrne?'

'I very much hope so.'

Gasps were heard as this was brilliant news for them and their work. He then left and excited chatter broke out at this unexpected revelation.

Walking away Andy hoped he hadn't said anything untoward about Abbey; he knew she trusted him but should he have mentioned marriage? He got through his work as quickly as possible and not having lunch. Abbey was expecting him at 5 but he went earlier to catch her before the evening newspapers were delivered

Working at the patio table under the awning, the dogs were laid in the shade when they all jumped up and ran off. Smillie stayed with her as always. She was amazed to see Andy in one of his business suits running up to her, it was only just after 3 o'clock.

'Is anything wrong, Andy?'

'No. I wanted to be with you.' He sat down.

Abbey saw he looked very white and sensed his uneasiness. Despondency filled her as she thought, "he has met or been with a woman." She looked steadily at him. 'You are looking guilty Andy. Do you want to talk to me?'

'Yes please darling. I feel I've been indiscreet with the reporters.' She waited. 'I told them that you're going to marry me.'

She laughed in relief. 'Oh Andy, I was fearful you'd been with or met another woman.'

He was shocked. 'Good gracious Abbey this will never happen. When I've the promise of a life of happiness with the most beautiful wonderful young lady I could ever meet.'

'I could kiss you, darling.'

'Please feel free,' he laughed with joy.

She jumped up and kissed him on his lips sealing her love and commitment to him. He was very aroused so sat still whilst he controlled himself. 'Thank you, precious,' he huskily told her. 'I now know the secret to get you to kiss me. I'll come looking guilty.'

'Please don't darling. You nearly caused me to have a heart attack. You're looking pale, have you eaten?'

'No, I've been rushing around so I could get to you.'

'Come on, I'll soon rustle you a plate up. Would you like a steak or salad and cold meat?'

'Salad you've grown and cold meat will be ideal, please precious.'

Birdie had a rest in the afternoons and Pete had three hours off. Viola was in the kitchen and was surprised to see Abbey and Andy come in.

'Mr Byrne has missed lunch Viola. I'll get him a salad.'

'May I, Miss Forrest and bring it out?'

'Thank you Viola but you've enough to do. No problem for me,' smiling at her. Viola left them.

After washing their hands, Andy sat and for quickness Abbey made him a beaker of decaffeinated coffee granules with milk and put it into the microwave. He sat drinking it and watching her as she made an omelette, grating parmesan cheese and chopping fresh spinach from the herb pot into it.

As he ate, he told her, 'this is the most delicious omelette I've ever eaten, it's so fluffy.'

'I always whisk the whites first. Would you like another?'

'Are you having one?'

'I had my lunch.' Not telling him she had eaten very little again.

'This is very good of you, Abbey.'

She lightly teased him, 'I can't have you fading away! Anytime, it's a pleasure.'

His colour had come back she was thankful to see, and efficiently made him another.

Whilst he ate this she opened the fridge and got out a bowl of prepared salad and sliced him roast ham from the bone. She worked economically and deftly, slicing him three slices of Pete's home made granary bread spreading with butter.

'Would you like mustard with your ham, Andy?'
'Yes, please.'

She quickly mixed him a little from powder and he ate with enjoyment. She was happy that he always enjoyed his food as she usually did and like her, wasn't a "picky" eater.

'This is the very best meal of my life, Abbey, thank you. You've no idea how appealing and sexy it is to have you preparing me a meal.' She poured them both a glass of water.

'Are you hinting that you want me to do this full-time?' she mischievously asked him. He laughed. Knowing he had a good appetite and he was a big man, asked, 'would you like some more, Andy?'

'It's delicious and tempting, but no thanks. I'll wait for my sandwiches at tea time.'

She laughed at this then seriously told him, 'It would kill me Andy, if you had another woman before we marry or afterwards. I'd rather you stay with me now than that happen.'

'Darling,' he broke in, 'this is the best invitation of my life. Thank you I long to be with you BUT not before we marry. I'm not having your reputation and character smeared in any way. I can go for months without sex.

'YOU,' he emphasized, 'keep me awake at night and haunt my days but knowing I've your promise that we'll marry soon, I'll cope.'

'Keep you awake at night and haunt your days?'

'As we're going to marry, darling, and you're now more relaxed with me?'

'Yes, I am, my darling.'

'I'll tell you. You and also your beautiful breasts, you don't wear a bra?'

Blushing and laughing, she told him, 'no, not always.'
'I've never seen your nipples.'
'You are cheeky, Andy. I wondered why you were always looking. Yes we'll marry soon, darling, and then you'll see them. I wear a nipple protector.'
'A nipple protector, whatever is that?'
'So I don't get sore.'
'Oh.'
She realised that he was more innocent than she had thought. Waves of love poured through her.
'I do love you, my precious Andy.'
'I adore you, my gorgeous Abbey,' gently kissing her.
He washed the dishes and Abbey dried. Viola came back and said, 'there is the dishwasher, ma'am, sir.'
'Yes, but we're enjoying doing them this way, Viola. There aren't many.'
She looked at them as they'd grown two heads. She hated washing and drying so left them to it.
Abbey wrote a note for Pete for what she had taken. He was used to this when she was too late for lunch.
'Please excuse me. I'll get out of my uniform.' He mischievously promised, 'I'll brush my teeth!'
Abbey approved this. He had wonderful strong teeth. She'd seen them when he laughed. Grabbing two apples from the bowl she went outside to wait for him, checking up on her e-mails and texts.
Andy quickly returned, 'I've interrupted your work, darling.'
'May I just send some urgent e-mails?'
'Carry on, precious.'
Her fingers flew over the laptop keys. Bringing his chair up close to her, Andy watched in admiration.
'You're a quick typist, darling.'

'I think it helps being a pianist. Do you type, Andy?'

'With two fingers,' he laughed. 'I voice send.'

'I use that technology, darling.'

Sitting close to her reading what she was typing he was very impressed with her hotel expertise.

Andy switched his mobile back on. As always he had several urgent matters to attend to.

'Will you excuse me, precious?'

'Don't be long,' she laughed.

He moved away, walking and replying to his calls. Abbey continued working.

Birdie came as always after they had enjoyed their 5 pm cup of tea and sandwiches, to enquire if they needed anything further. She was very pleased to see how happy they both looked.

'Birdie, Andy is the most wonderful man. I love him to bits.' He was laughing.

'I'm very thankful, Miss Abbey. We all think the world of him.' Andy as always wheeled the trolley for her to the kitchen door.

She told him, 'I'm very thankful Miss Abbey has you, sir. I don't know what she would have done and all of us also. God is good. We didn't want Mr Forrest to die, but he would be happy to know you and Miss Abbey are in love. What a shame he isn't here to share in your happiness.'

'It certainly is, Birdie. If there's anything I can do, you promise me to let me know. Ring me anytime, night or day.' They had reached the door.

'Thank you, sir.'

He ran back to Abbey, she was reading the morning's revelation in the evening newspapers. Andy began reading dreading what they had put.

Abbey waited until he had finished and congratulated him. 'Thank you darling, this is spot on.' Exchanging the papers both were thankful how sensitive the reporters had been keeping to Andy's words.

'They won't leave us alone now, darling, but it won't be forever. Come on Abbey, the dogs are restless for their walk.'

He was right. Curiosity went wild with everyone wanting to know who had captured his heart. Also they needed to get to know more of Miss Forrest.

'What are you doing to-morrow, Abbey?'

'I need to go into the office, just for the morning, then continue working here whilst I'm sorting things out with the managers, Lorraine, Lara, Mr Bell and whoever.'

'Good girl. I need to do some serious work to leave me free to spend afternoons with you next week.'

'I'll appreciate you being with me.' She kissed him. 'There's a lot of personal correspondence I must reply to, will you help me?'

'You don't have to ask, my precious. Then we must start thinking of our engagement now the news is in the papers.'

'Yes. Just a brief announcement to the public that this is being celebrated low key and a quiet wedding in about two months. Gossip will go round that I'm pregnant,' she laughed.

'I wish. What would you like to do to celebrate our engagement, darling?'

'I haven't thought this far.'

'Sorry darling, forgive me. You need to meet my family. Would you like to have lunch at Marlon and Sabrina's, invite my parents come over and Stuart and Louis join us. Perhaps all the kids have the day off to meet you?'

'That would be lovely, please Andy. Then perhaps we could all walk in the wood and get to know each other. As long as it isn't pouring with rain!' she laughed.

'Believe me, sweetheart, they'll all enjoy walking in the rain as we do, but they haven't got a wood,' he laughed. 'Beautiful countryside and a special walk on their private land at the side of a river.'

'I haven't been in contact with young people, Andy. I don't know their language.'

'Neither do I, darling, only the odd symbol or whatever they call it. Don't worry, they'll adore you. They're good kids. Don't let them embarrass you when they no doubt will fire questions at you. I'll help you.'

'Thank you. It sounds as though it's going to be very interesting,' she laughed. 'I didn't think it possible Andy, but I love you more and more each day.'

'Same here, my precious,' he huskily answered her.

The next afternoon Andy came in time to share a pot of tea and sandwiches with Abbey before walking with the dogs. She told him the funeral was arranged for next Monday 11 am. He asked 'Will you allow me to book a restaurant for the lunch, Abbey?'

'Will I be expected to hold it here?'

'No. The ones mentioned in your dada's will need to come back here with you. Also Birdie and the staff are working hard enough providing refreshments and meals for your helpers.

'Yes. Forgive me, Andy, I wasn't thinking.'

'Have you the lunch numbers yet?'

'I'll arrange this to-morrow with Mr Bell. Most likely dada will have prepared a list. I don't want anyone to feel excluded.'

'Let me know. I'll prepare my friend. His restaurants are closed Mondays, but he'll work round this on this occasion.'

'This will be big help Andy. Thank you, but is it fair to ask?'

'Yes, he'll be honoured to do this for you, and the staff is always appreciative of extra money.'

She stood looking at him. 'I honestly don't know what I would do without you.'

'Good,' he grunted.'

She shared several matters with him and then told him of her Grandparents Swiss solicitor, Matthias coming and staying with Mr Bell. 'My Grandparents are giving me full control of Gresley and Cobden, Andy.'

'I expected them doing this. A sensible idea all round.'

'Granddada suggested I think about selling these and Ireton and Linacre Andy. He says I'll have enough on with Whitwell Wood.'

'Your Granddada is very wise, Abbey.'

'He wants me to not be overburdened. As dada was dying he told me to sell Ireton and Linacre. He also said he didn't want me to be overburdened.'

'I agree wholeheartedly, but there's no rush. You've enough to deal with just now.'

'No rush with the excellent staff being such a good help, they and the guests need to feel secure at this point in time. People are questioning. There isn't any need to make any quick decisions for a while.'

'I very much admire your lateral thinking, my darling. Well done. Yes, everyone needs stability.'

Abbey continued sharing with him the arrangements being made for the funeral.

Meant To Meet

Grant had made a list of who to invite to the service, lunch, and then be available for the reading of the will. Abbey had sobbed again at this loving concern for her he had again organised to make everything run as smoothly for her as possible.

After confirming with Sebastian, Tanya and Andy, Lorraine and Lara sent out the formal and informal invitations. Abbey invited Lorraine to be the office manager with a PA, which she willingly accepted.

Hundreds of condolence cards and letters of appreciation arrived along with flowers. Grant had been very highly respected. The press, media and local magazines gave him a glowing eulogy.

The next afternoon Abbey had made a hair appointment and manicure, Reporters and cameras were waiting for her at the gates. Andy had warned her they would be. Todd got out and Abbey opened her window.

'Good afternoon Miss Forrest,' a male said. 'Please accept our condolences on the death of your father.'

'Thank you.' She couldn't help the tears welling up in her eyes.

'Congratulations on keeping the hotels ma'am.'

'My dada and Grandparents have always valued our guests, and I'll continue to do so.'

'We hope that you'll be very happily married to Mr Byrne,' a female said.

'Thank you. I don't know what I would do without him.' She smiled, waved to them and closed the window and Todd got back in.

They had taken their photographs and appreciated her being well mannered enough to acknowledge them.

One male said, 'I didn't know how beautiful she is. I can understand Andy falling in love with her. He's a lucky man.'

Reaching the salon Todd helping her out told her, 'We are waiting here, Miss Forrest, on Mr Byrne's instructions. You will be pursued by the press.'

Abbey had prepared Tim she needed a new style and was bringing a picture. When she arrived he told her, 'the press will now be following you, Miss Forrest. We could come to your home if this is a problem.'

'Thank you Tim, but I can't lock myself away. I know how to cope with them and it will be only short term.'

Tim admired her even more for this. He was interested in her picture. 'I'll enjoy creating this.'

'Now I haven't time to constantly straighten my hair Tim, I need you to keep it short and well thinned out as this picture. I'll have to come more often or accept your kind offer to come to my home.'

She was amazed when he had finished. Her eyes looked even bigger and her bones were more pronounced. It was also an easier style for her. She hoped Andy would like it. He did.

The leading newspaper editor contacted Abbey's university and was willingly given a glowing report of her achievements, how hard she had worked and how popular she had been. He was put through to the Art tutor who told him about her Art degree in oils and how she could have made a career from this. He mentioned 'Miss Forrest completed at home the most wonderful portrait of her father. He looks as though he is going to step out of it. This must be a great comfort to her now.'

Meant To Meet

This was a real scoop and all this was included in the evening and the next morning's papers.

Andy texted, "I'm in the area, darling. May I come? If you're busy I'll be able to sort a few things out at the patio table."

Abbey texted back, "Never ask permission, you're always very welcome." She carried on working until the dogs jumped up, it was Andy.

After kissing her and fussing the dogs he sat down.

'Would you like a glass of wine, darling?' she asked.

'Thank you but I'll wait for our cuppa. I've something to discuss with you. I know you don't want to lose the links connected with your dada and Grandparents' hotels, precious. All the hard work they, especially your dada, has put into running them. Everyone in the business knows how "hands on" he was.'

'Yes, he always worked very hard with 100% commitment,' she agreed.

He went silent. Abbey waited discerning he was about to say something very serious.

'We'll discuss this fully later after the funeral, darling, but I'm suggesting I sell my Dubai and Jersey hotels, and buy Gresley, Cobden, Ireton and Linacre from you. When we're married and hopefully starting our family, you realistically with running our home will have enough on running Whitwell Wood. I want you to continue using your business expertise you worked so hard for.

'I'll build the family hotel in Poole as I promised. I've all the plans from the Jersey hotel, so this will be easy. Keep my Kent and London hotels.'

Abbey was looking at him with all the love she had for him pouring from her.

'You're willing to do all this for me and my family?'

'Abbey, I'll do anything for you. Don't you know this by now?'

'I do know, Andy. You've carefully thought this out.'

'Yes I have, my precious.' He didn't tell her the hours of sleep he had lost sussing out.

'Will you tell my Granddada, darling? He and Grandmama will be so happy to know the hotels will be in your hands.'

'Ok darling, with pleasure.'

'You've taken a great weight from my shoulders, Andy. Everyone will be uplifted at your news.'

'We need to set up a meeting with the key staff. Invite Mr Bell out of respect. In confidence for the time being but the guests need stability as you mentioned, my precious.'

Viola was wheeling the tea trolley to them.

'Thank you, Viola, this is very welcome,' smiling at her.

'It's a pleasure sir, ma'am.' They tucked in.

Sebastian, Tanya, Matthias and Adrienne were thrilled at Andy's news as was Mr Bell. Adrienne on Sebastian's request, arranged for a box of the finest champagne to be sent to Abbey and Andy for a celebration glass for when Andy had told the key staff.

On arrival Abbey gave out the identification badges and when everyone had come they sat round the dining table. The managers didn't record for their secretaries this time on Abbey's instruction. Knowing it was a special meeting with Andy being with them were fearful of the outcome knowing realistically running five hotels would be too much for Miss Forrest.

Andy introduced himself and after the table had given their name and occupation, said, 'after much thought and discussion with Miss Forrest and her approval, I'm buying and will run Gresley, Cobden, Ireton and Linacre.' They all clapped in relief.

'Miss Forrest and I are suggesting as these hotels are closed January, we extend this to include February the most quiet months, for decorating and re-furbishing in line with what the faithful guests have been comfortable with. I'll sell my hotels in Dubai and Jersey to be available here. Miss Forrest will now reveal her plans for Whitwell Wood.'

Thanking him, she then looking at Royston Bergman, her senior manager, Stephen Gambles, Ian Harris, Sam Atkins, in her clear voice asked, 'I'm hoping you and your deputies will continue working with me running Whitwell Wood.' Assuring her they would be honoured and the deputies were hoping to be retained.

Thanking them she next said, 'I need you Lorraine to be my office manager and you Lara to be my PA in Whitwell Wood. Do you agree to this?'

'Just Whitwell Wood, Miss Forrest?' Lorraine queried.

'Yes. I'm grateful for your help during this period, but without dada it would long term be too much work for you. I'll be leaning heavily on you to help me.'

'I'll do everything I can,' Lorraine assured her.

Lara echoed, 'I also, Miss Forrest.'

She thanked them and looked at Andy.

He took over and asked Brandon, 'are you willing to continue managing Gresley, Mr Skyler with your deputy?'

'Yes sir, with pleasure,'

He asked Jack Mitchell the manager of Cobden the same question and he assured him he would, as would the deputy. Gavin Laing the manager of Ireton and Dean Irving manager of Linacre also willingly accepted and for their deputies.

Gavin told him, 'we're very grateful we are being kept on, sir. We've been fearful.'

'Yes, I understand. This is why we're having this meeting to re-assure you. We all need stability and the guests also.

'I'll be advertising for a male office manager, but will be using my faithful PA, Chase Meyer. He's a good man; you'll meet him soon.'

Lorraine questioned, 'when are you revealing this to the public, sir?'

'The end of next week will be appropriate, with respect to Miss Forrest. I'll bring this in after coffee.'

Abbey said, 'we need to let the February guests know before it goes out public. Please prepare me a list of our year round regulars and I'll prepare a personal letter explaining what's happening and Mr Byrne won't be increasing the cost. I've the technology for this in my computer. We need to do this to-morrow, please Lara.'

'Yes Miss Forrest. I've all the address labels set up in my computer.'

'Good,' Abbey smiled at her.

'You'll receive your salary as usual,' Andy told his managers. After thanking him, he said, 'I'll need to meet with you all to keep me updated.'

Abbey then said, 'we'll need to let the staff know their wages will continue in this time. May I leave this with you Lorraine, but not mentioning the take over?'

'Yes, with pleasure ma'am. Will the cleaners be needed?'

'The company I contract will put their staff into each hotel and have their cleaners,' Andy explained. 'I'll need everyone to re-start work the week beginning 26th February preparing for the opening on the Saturday. I suggest we meet on say Thursday 22nd with your deputies, restaurant managers, front office managers and housekeepers.'

'The venue for this will be, sir?' Lorraine asked.

'May I leave it with you to arrange this?'

'Of course I'll do this, Mr Byrne.'

They put all this in their diary. 'I'll ensure everyone knows, sir,' Brandon promised.

'Will Lara and I be needed, Miss Forrest.'

'Yes, please, as to-day. I regret that Whitwell Wood won't be having two months paid holiday, but you'll have the three days after New Year's Day!'

Everyone laughed.

'Right, to be fair and to celebrate everyone at Whitwell Wood will receive a bonus.'

'That isn't necessary sir,' Royston Bergman protested.

'Thank you, Mr Bergman,' Abbey broke in, 'let's go for this, courtesy of my dada. Make it a Christmas bonus?'

'Good idea Miss Forrest.' Royston agreed. 'Thank you sir, ma'am,'

Abbey rang the bell signalling Birdie and Viola to bring the coffee. Andy and Abbey poured, Birdie and Viola served. They continued conversing until Andy and

Abbey were sure everyone had no further questions for the time being.

Pete, Birdie and Viola brought bottles of champagne and glasses. Abbey and Andy poured and when everyone had been served, Mr Bell stood up. 'I'll be putting the announcement in the leading London newspapers of Mr Byrne buying the hotels.

'Miss Forrest has requested I include the names of the hotels are forests in North Derbyshire where her ancestors six generations back were born and lived. Her ancestors Rupert Hindley and Percy Markham had been colliery workers. Her Great Grandfather Clive Forrest bought his first hotel and named it Gresley Wood and his son, Sebastian Forrest later bought another naming it Cobden Wood. Her dada then continued with Bow, Clough, Ireton, Linacre and Whitwell Wood.' The staff expressed their surprise and delight of this connection. After a pause Mr Bell continued.

'I will also reveal Mr Byrne and Miss Forrest are getting engaged and will marry on Monday July 6th in St. John's Church, Windsor. Please raise your glasses.' Everyone stood up cheering and Mr Bell, laughing, proposed, 'To Miss Forrest and Mr Byrne's future happiness.' They all toasted and delightedly congratulated them secretly anticipating this. Abbey was blushing and Andy looked as though he was going to burst with happiness.

The staff had noted through body language how much in love they were, and how they had listened to each other. How Mr Byrne had given her space when he had finished speaking for her comments. The managers knew working with Mr Byrne was going to be different from working with Mr Forrest, but they were eager for

Meant To Meet

the challenge. Before going back to work Abbey gave each one an envelope with contained a generous bonus with a thank you note for the extra work they had done and were doing.

Alone Abbey told Andy, 'I'm very proud of you darling, a very constructive meeting. You covered the relevant matters so efficiently. It's a good job you've a meeting this afternoon, your sex appeal is very attractive. I'm also very pleased you have male staff.'

'Yes, always. I never mix business with pleasure. Now for you, I would break that rule. I'm pleased that you have a female PA. You are very dishy and the men folk were thinking this.'

She laughed dismissingly, 'let's freshen up. I'm starving.'

'Yes, so am I, but not for food,' he teased.

During lunch they discussed the hotels then Abbey with no commitments decided to take time out to do some more secret painting to Andy's portrait.

Andy gave Abbey the albums Russell had sent by secure mail recording her mummy's life and she loved them. It was the first time she felt she was close to her. She cried when the photographs stopped after she had met her dada, but knew now that she was being healed.

When the media and press sent out Mr Bell's announcements Andy and Abbey received numerous congratulations and good wishes. Abbey also received personal letters from the hotel guests saying how much they had appreciated her father's personal supervision and friendship and would be greatly missed. They added their good wishes for both her and Mr Byrne.

Didi had Abbey a shoulder handbag made of the finest leather in colours of the rainbow making layers of small pleats. When she showed Deirdre she excitedly asked, 'may I make her a fascinator matching the colours in silks?'

'Please do, darling.'

She took photographs from different angles. 'I'll show you my design for your approval, Didi. My fingers are itching to do produce this.'

Deirdre now had a new lease of life.

Abbey loved the handbag Didi also had sent by secure mail. She didn't mention the fascinator as she didn't want Abbey to think that she was overwhelming her.

Andy's family knew Abbey must be a very special young lady and looked forward to meeting her and welcoming her into their family.

Andy warned them, 'she's a very refined virgin, so don't embarrass her. She's very precious to me, my soul mate. Abbey is highly intelligent and took the same degrees I did at university. She's a proficient artist in oils and water colours. A skilled horsewoman and pianist, but she's no prude and has a wonderful sense of humour, very loving and compassionate.

Abbey asked me to mention she's having no bridesmaids or page boys with the wedding being low key.'

'That's very sensible of her, Andy,' Sabrina agreed.

'Abbey's in deep mourning for her beloved dada and now carries the hotels business.

Stuart said, 'wow, so she's not marrying you for your money?'

Meant To Meet

'Certainly not, I'm very, very fortunate that she loves me and we have great compatibility.'

Abbey dressed casually in jeans and a capped shoulder blouse covered with colourful viola flowers, and walking shoes.

The family were all waiting as Andy helped her out of the car. Although in jeans she still got out gracefully. Both laughing Andy proudly introduced her and Abbey immediately felt at ease.

Going first to see the horses in their stables Olivia and Skye held Abbey's hands, she could have cried. Louis recognising her fearlessness as Abbey letting each horse smell her hand and then stroking their head she was thrilled with the horses and had a longing to ride. After freshening up they went for a substantial meal.

Harvey asked, 'Abbey, are you going to marry Uncle Andy?'

'Well,' she teased, 'I'm thinking about that.'

They all laughed knowing she was teasing.

'Will you have a lot of children?' Harvey then asked

Sabrina told him, 'stop pestering Abbey. Let her enjoy her lunch.

Looking crestfallen Abbey felt sympathy for him so glancing and winking at Sabrina answered, 'if they're horrid as you four, perhaps not.'

They all burst out laughing at this.

'Now eat your lunch or you will not be able to go walking with Abbey,' Marlon firmly told them.

The adults sensitively conversed with her. Being highly intelligent themselves they recognised her culture and intelligence. Andy had forbade them to mention Haven Cottage the adults had visited, he was so eager for it to be a surprise for Abbey. His parents and brothers were realising how wonderful it was for Andy marrying a young lady with an affinity with him in hotels.

Abbey enjoyed the day with Andy's family who made her feel relaxed; she liked them very much as they did her. Her heart warmed at the rapport between the children and Andy.

They discussed the low key wedding. Andy's elder brother Marlon was to be the best man. Stuart happily agreed to be the usher. Abbey had asked Russell to give her away and he was thrilled with this.

Travelling home with Andy she silently began to weep. He closed the inner window and held her hand with insight knowing they were tears of healing. It must have been emotional for her meeting his family at this point in time without her dada and growing up without siblings.

'You'll never be lonely again, my Abbey' he huskily told her.

'I hadn't realised how lonely I must have been until I met you and you talked about your childhood darling. Being an only child busy being educated, I had a sense of loss with no siblings.'

'I've also been lonely, Abbey. Yes, I had my bothers and both parents but with them being in the solicitor business apart from sports, we weren't on the same wave length.'

Understanding dawned in her. 'You have me now, my darling.'

'Yes, thank God,' he replied. 'I feel complete now, my precious.'

'It's the same for me, my Andy. I've just fully realized for the first time how dada must have ached with loneliness after my mummy died. How unselfish he was thinking always of my happiness and my not being lonely.' They held hands tighter, silently communicating their love for each other.

'Have you any work to do, darling?' she asked.

'It will wait until later, what would you like to do?'

'Have a ride.'

'Brilliant.'

Abbey rang Oscar asking him to saddle up. When they reached the stables he had the horses ready.

'Thank you Oscar, we appreciate this but didn't want to impose on you.'

'Anything I can help you with, Miss Abbey, just let me know.'

Both thanking him they mounted and set off.

Chapter Ten

Arriving at Switzerland the chauffeur and bodyguard were waiting and Abbey was eager to see her beloved Grandparents. Her Grandmama had asked if she and Andy wanted the same room. 'No, Grandmama, I'm still a virgin and will be so until I marry him.' Her Grandmama was very proud of them both and also relieved. After cuddling them she introduced Andy who was amazed how much her Grandfather was an older version of Grant. Abbey had brought Faye's photograph albums for them to see.

Tanya led Andy to the oil portrait Abbey of her and Sebastian, he was again aware of how talented she was. Tanya told them, 'any furniture, anything you both would like in your new life please make a note of and we'll transport to you. We have unused presents of dinner, tea and dinner services; crystal, cooking pans and lots of other items.'

'We'll have these please, Grandmama. As you will appreciate, Andy and I will need to entertain.'

'Yes, darling, you will. You know for years we have lived quietly but happy and content with each other.'

'Thank you Mrs Forrest,' Andy said. 'We'll love to use your presents and enjoy taking care of them. I'm so thankful that you and Mr Forrest have a happy and contended marriage. I'm confident Abbey and I will follow your example.'

Smiling lovingly at him Tanya said, 'Andy, please call us Grandmama and Granddada as Abbey does.'

Andy and Abbey knew that he was accepted.

'There, I knew you would both love Andy.'

'He's a fine young man,' Sebastian said. Tanya agreed.

'Grant always gave you a glowing report of your hotels business, Andy. He greatly appreciated your company and being a golf partner.'

'I miss him very much, Granddada. He was my mentor and I learned a lot from him. Despite I didn't see him in the time when I was too busy to be in London, I always knew he was there for me.'

He was holding Abbey's hand and the four of them cried thinking about Grant, and that he had gone from them.

Sitting comfortably Sebastian asked, 'will you spend time here when this home is yours?'

'We have discussed this Granddada, and with running our hotels, hoping to have children, we ask your permission if we may sell it and in memory of you both, have a convalescent home be built for young children with breathing difficulties. We could also help fund it.'

Sebastian and Tanya clapped their hands startling Abbey and Andy. 'Shall we have a drink?' Sebastian asked. After agreeing, Tanya and Abbey had a gin and tonic, Andy a whiskey and Sebastian freshly squeezed oranges.

Tanya took over to help Sebastian who was coughing and gasping. 'We were going to share with you when you should have come last week for a few days holiday. We're moving into newly built accommodation quite near, which will provide for your Granddada's medical needs in a relaxed homely setting. It isn't a hospital or anything like that.

'This home is too big and inconvenient for us now and, although kept spotlessly clean, with the furniture and furnishings there are dust mites and whatever in the air causing your Granddada more stress.

'We had thought now you have completed your education but helping your dada, you would spend holidays here.'

'Until I met Andy, I hadn't even thought of any of this.'

'Our faithful house staff is older now of course, but willing out of love keeps this home going. But they really will be thankful to be able to retire.'

Abbey jumped up and cuddled her, then Sebastian. 'Why haven't you said, my darlings?'

'Well,' Sebastian laughed, 'we're saying now we know your plans.'

'May we see literature of the sheltered accommodation sir?' Andy asked.

'I'll get it later,' Tanya offered.

Whilst Sebastian went for his regular treatment, Tanya took Abbey and Andy into Sebastian's and her office. Andy fell in love with the carved furniture, which he recognized as solid English oak. He ran his hand round the edge of the polished solid carved desk.

'Andy loves wood, Grandmama.'

Tanya's face lit up, 'would you like all this furniture Andy?'

Looking at Abbey in surprise she smilingly nodded. 'I'd be very honoured, Grandmama,' Andy excitedly told her. The matching furniture was exquisite. The green leather desk top was worn but he could easily have this replaced. He had arranged with Abbey that he could work from Holly House with the latest upmarket technology for part of the day, fitting in with her routine so they could spend as much together as possible. Abbey was going to use the study with not needing as much technology.

'When you have time go through the house and choose anything you want. There are lots of unopened gifts we received going back to our Silver Wedding then our Golden. Dinner and tea services, table settings, crystal, kitchen equipment, you will see for yourselves. The crates and boxes are marked and how they should be transported. I remember a porcelain set because when I saw it I knew you would love this, Abbey. It has a design of horses.' Abbey gave a shriek of excitement. She couldn't wait to see this.

Andy was looking at the watercolours on the walls. 'Abbey did these, Andy. Do you want them?'

'Yes please, Grandmama,' he answered smiling lovingly at her.

'Make a list and we'll have everything transported to you.'

They thanked her.

'I'm feeling much better with you two being here and Granddada and I are now released from the burden of this big house.'

Andy was so thankful for the love that existed between Abbey and her Grandparents, and they had been here for her whilst she was growing up.

'If there is anything big or small, I can help you with, please let me know day or night.'

'Thank you Andy, but we are content now knowing you are supporting Abbey.'

'Yes, indeed.'

'May I see the photographs you have mummy and dada's wedding, please Grandmama, and the photographs dada sent you when he first met mummy?'

Tanya brought the small album and they sat at the desk looking at the few wedding photographs different to what her dada had. 'What a shame her parent's didn't come.'

Tanya looked annoyed,' yes darling, don't fret over them.' She looked at Andy with disgust on her face and began to cry, Abbey also. Andy felt it was polite to leave them in privacy.

He found Sebastian reading the newspaper. Andy explained that Abbey and Grandmama were looking at the wedding photographs.

'Would you like a drink, Andy?'

'If you're having one, please sir.'

'It's about time for my drop of whiskey,' he laughed then coughed violently. He pressed the bell on the table.

Helena the housekeeper came smiling at them both 'let me guess, whiskey.'

'Yes, please Helena, without water.'

She wagged her finger at him, 'yours with water sir.'

Meant To Meet

A maid brought a decanter with a small amount in, water and two glasses and left.

Congratulations Andy, on building up your hotel business. Your parents must be very proud of you.'

'I hope so Granddada, but they wanted me to go into my Grandfather and their family solicitor and attorney business with my brothers. I wasn't being awkward but it never appealed to me. From a young age I was interested in buildings. I thought my career would be construction building. Am I tiring you, Granddada?'

'No, please carry on Andy. I just hope my coughing doesn't disturb you.'

'No sir.' This wasn't quite true as Andy was filled with compassion for him recognising he was nearing the end of his life.

He then briefly told him about his gap year before going to university and how he began with his first run down hotel.

'I'm proud of you, Andy.'

'Thank you, sir. I tell you when prayerfully Abbey and I have a family and when our children get to the age when they decide on their career, even if I'm disappointed they aren't coming into the hotel business, I wouldn't put any pressure on them and I know Abbey will be the same. If, of course, we thought they were going the wrong way, we would talk with them.'

Sebastian was listening intently and recognising what a good man Andy was, full of integrity as Grant had always said. Being shrewd, had known Grant must have invited Andy to lunch as a devious plot to introduce him to Abbey.

'Do you want me to leave you, sir?'

'No Andy. I'm more than happy talking with you and getting to know you. Everybody tiptoes round me expecting me to die any second,' he laughed which started off his coughing again. Andy gave him a drink of water.

'You are good for years yet, sir.' He knew this wasn't true.

'Abbey told us you have a cottage in the Cotswolds.'

'Yes sir, I'm keeping it a secret for when we are married.'

'I suspect it's more than a small cottage, Andy.'

'Yes Granddada. I bought it as a derelict cottage six years ago and re-built enlarging it. I designed it to use the trees from my wood. I love wood, the smell, the feel, walking or riding through a wood in the rain or afterwards and breathing in the perfumes of the wet wood.'

Sebastian was remembering when he enjoyed exactly the same.

He showed Sebastian photographs in his mobile. He asked Andy to pass him the magnifying glass he used for small print.

'This is wonderful Andy. Abbey will love this. Do you have horses?'

Andy showed him a picture of the stables and horses; he was just showing him part of the wood when he heard Tanya and Abbey coming. 'Excuse me sir, show you later,' and quickly switched off and put in in his pocket. Sebastian smiled at him.

After kissing her Granddada and Andy, Abbey sat down.

'You have a fine man here, Abbey. Look after him.'

'I will Granddada, I adore everything about him.'

'Yes, we're so proud of you Andy and are so thankful our beloved Abbey has you,' Tanya told him.

'I still can't believe Abbey loves me, Grandmama. God has certainly blessed me.'

Tanya told her husband, 'Andy loves your office furniture.'

'Please have it all Andy. This will make me so happy now knowing your love of wood. Also anything else you like. I brought it from my parent's home when my father retired. No woodworm anywhere, Andy, I have all the wood regularly inspected.'

'Thank you, Granddada,' Andy said, 'I'll take great care of everything.'

The nurse came and smilingly took Sebastian for further treatment and his rest. Tanya also went for her rest, leaving them on their own.

'Granddada is very much worse Andy.' She looked very worried.

Andy, to distract her, suggested, 'do you want to go and see your horses' china?'

'Love to darling, our china,' she emphasized. They went hand in hand and were amazed at the number of unopened crates and boxes all marked with the contents and transport instructions.

'We won't need any wedding presents,' Andy laughed.

Abbey agreed. 'Would it be appropriate to request small amount gift vouchers?'

'I think people will be relieved. I know I would,' he laughed.

She found the six piece china tea and dinner set and carefully lifting out a cup she loved it, Andy did also.

She had seen other horse designs but this was a classic. They both loved the shape and the comfortable handle.

'Here's a matching coffee set, Abbey.'

'We will use these sets daily, darling.'

'Yes sweetheart.'

'Do you think your Grandparents would let me set up Spyke so we can see them and they us as we speak?'

'What a brilliant idea, Andy, thank you. Please suggest this.'

They however declined. Sebastian explained, 'it would be too much of a strain for us.' He didn't want them to see him coughing and deteriorating further as he knew he was, but warmly thanked him for the thought.

Later whilst Abbey was having a cup of tea with Tanya, Sebastian was resting and Andy was dealing with e-mails. Tanya told Abbey, 'as you know darling, I don't want to leave your Granddada but I'll come to your dada's funeral. He insists I be with you.'

Abbey was so relieved, 'thank you darling Grandmama, Granddada is right. I need you to be with me. As you know Andy is taking care of Didi and Grandpapa's arrangements, so may he reserves your seat and meets you in one of his hotel cars from the plane?'

'This will be brilliant, Abbey. I suggest Matthias travel with me, it's arranged that he will stay with your solicitor so they are able to discuss matters.'

Abbey knew this but kept silent.

'Andy will book his seat also. You'll stay with me, of course, Grandmama. Do you agree to meet Didi and Grandpapa for afternoon tea? I could invite Rev Heardley to come to take us through the services. It would be etiquette to also invite Matthias and Mr Bell.'

'Yes, Abbey, spot on to use this opportunity. Well done. I'm sorry I can't help you more.'

'You and Granddada have helped me all my life, darling. That is the most important.

'Everyone is pulling together, Grandmama. Dada and my PA's and the managers are keeping things rolling without much help from me at this time. Dada has trained them well. The vital thing is our family are reconciled.'

'Yes sweetheart, you've a forgiving heart, but it would have been better if they had been reconciled with your dada.'

'Are you going to be upset when you meet them, darling?'

'I promise you that I won't cause any concern.'

'Just think Grandmama, I haven't invited them to Holly House for the night. You and I will have time together.'

'We will, my precious. Don't you fret; everything will be in the highest taste.'

'It will as befits dada.' She broke off crying, Tanya was also.

An en-suite room at Holly House near Abbey was prepared for Tanya.

Andy with one of his hotel security team was waiting for Russell and Didi at the airport. After greetings Didi said, 'it's warmer than I anticipated, Andy.'

'Do you regret packing your fur coat, darling,' Russell teased her. Andy and he knew this was a traumatic time for her. Andy couldn't warm to her remembering how she had neglected Faye, Grant and Abbey, but he was polite.

She was delighted with Andy, his respectful manner, immaculate appearance and recognising his air of authority. Russell also was.

Enjoying the journey and conversing about Abbey, Andy managed to make himself feel at ease. He took them to his hotel Penthouse where they left their luggage with their allocated personal maid and valet for their stay.

After a glass of wine, Didi and Russell freshened up in the before unused second large luxury suite. Didi loved it and thanked Andy for the gorgeous flower arrangements. He had made arrangements for the hairdresser and spa treatment for Didi the following morning.

Arriving at Holly House Abbey was waiting outside for them. She hugged Didi then Russell, they were all crying. Smillie was getting anxious so Andy comforted him.

'You are very beautiful,' Didi told her.

Birdie came to greet them and she was very cool but polite. 'Are you ready for a drink, Miss Abbey?'

Looking at Didi, Russell and Andy she asked, 'would you like a glass of wine?'

They said, 'yes, please, white.' Birdie went to arrange this.

Abbey took Didi up to her ensuite and Andy as arranged took Russell to Grant's bathroom. Didi gasped when she saw Faye's portrait she had done and cried. Abbey gave her a few seconds and then said, 'do you think Grandpapa would like to see it?'

'He would darling, yes please.'

Abbey left her gazing at the portrait and standing on the corridor saw Andy waiting for Russell. He came out and Abbey invited him to see her mummy's portrait.

Russell eagerly accepted Abbey's invitation and she led the way, Andy waited on the corridor. 'Aren't you coming, Andy?' Russell asked.

'Well, no.'

'Please come, darling,' Abbey invited him.

'Andy hasn't seen the portrait, Abbey?'

Blushing, she said, 'no.'

Andy nudged Russell to keep silent and not embarrass virgin Abbey.

Russell rushed to the portrait and standing in awe began crying. Andy was very uncomfortable looking at the single bed and imagining Abbey in it. He knew he had to escape. He quietly left them and went downstairs, Russell joined him giving Didi and Abbey time alone.

'It's very good of you Andy, allowing us to stay in your Penthouse. We understand Abbey isn't prepared for us to stay here and it may have been a strain for us and her in this moment of time.'

'The Penthouse is just my London base Russell. My family and I congregate at my brother's in Gloustershire. Your suite has never been used. Although I don't live here yet, this is my home Russell, also my cottage in the Cotswolds.'

'I imagine it isn't a small cottage.'

'No, but I want to surprise and please Abbey. It isn't accessible on the media. Everyone respects my privacy. I love to escape there Russell. You and Didi will be very welcome later on.'

'Thank you Andy. Have you taken any women to your Penthouse, Andy?'

'No Russell, nor my Cottage. I have had women. Not many as I've been too busy and am selective. Abbey knows but I tell you Russell, Abbey is now my only one and will be forever.'

'I had women Andy. It's expected of us but Didi has been my one and only since I met her. I tell you Andy I've had reason since marrying Didi to have other women, but now thanks to you and Abbey, I'm now back in Didi's bed, so it has all been worthwhile. I've always adored her. It's good to have you to talk with, Andy.'

'Thank you, Russell, same here. Here come the girls.'

Abbey and Didi came in arm in arm still tearful, but at one with each other.

Tanya and Matthias arrived and the security man carefully handed Tanya out then her luggage. Birdie came and greeted them and Tanya cuddled her. Brian took her luggage upstairs to the ensuite room prepared for her.

Russell held his hand out to Tanya and she accepted it. 'I'm so sorry for your loss, Mrs Forrest.'

'Thank you,' she answered with dignity.

Russell brought Didi forward and they shook hands, but didn't speak.

Tanya introduced Matthias.

Abbey took Tanya to freshen up and Brian as arranged took Matthias to a spare en-suite.

Reverend Heardly arrived and was introduced. Andy had put him in the picture of the circumstances of the estranged relationship between Grant and his in-laws. Mr Bell came and after introductions he and Matthias had a few private words.

Meant To Meet

Pete and Viola supervised by Birdie wheeled the trolley to the patio table. The weather was even hot enough for Didi with a jacket on!

They had a very constructive meeting discussing the service and Tanya added to Grant's epitaph. Rev Heardly asked if he may pray. They all willingly agreed and afterwards each one of them felt stronger and more peaceful.

Andy suggested they had a glass of red wine. He had bought the finest full bodied. They all relaxed and then Rev Heardly left them.

Russell, Andy and Abbey had a short stroll to see Abbey's horse, Tanya and Didi stayed sitting and conversing. Abbey was so proud of her Grandmama's graciousness and Didi had relaxed. Andy's car and security came to take them back to the hotel where he, Didi and Russell were having dinner in his Penthouse dining room suggested by Russell before an early night.

The press and media were waiting for Rev Heardly. Anything Andy Byrne was involved with they were interested in and now they had the excitement of his friendship with Abbey and her emerging having the position of hotels owner and also a very beautiful intelligent young lady heiress.

One reporter asked the vicar, 'is Mr Byrne escorting Miss Forrest?'

'No, her maternal Grandfather is.'

'This is the first we have heard of him. Is he local?' All the journalists were recording excited at this new revelation. Each of them knew there would be a scoop for them behind this secrecy.

'No, he and Miss Forrest's Grandmother own a hotel in Bermuda. Unfortunately, Miss Forrest's paternal

Granddada is too ill to travel from Switzerland, but her Grandmama is briefly attending. Mr Byrne may give you more information in a few days time. Please be discreet.' Walking away he was hoping that he hadn't been indiscreet.

Andy and Abbey had designed the glossy card cover of the service programme with a photograph of the oil portrait of Grant on the front and on the back a photograph of Faye and Grant on their wedding day. Andy and the printers had made a wonderful production of bringing the photographs up to life.

Russell walked between Abbey and Tanya arm in arm behind Grant's coffin followed by Didi and Andy, then Biddy and Brian, Mr Bell and Matthias for this short service. Andy and Abbey were going to have time alone when the will had been read and everyone had left.

As the coffin was disappearing and the curtains closed Abbey screamed out, 'dada.' She was sobbing uncontrollably. Russell quickly moved for Andy to sit with her. He held Didi who also was discreetly crying. Birdie gave Abbey a hip flask and she drank a little. She was still overwrought. Tanya, Andy, Birdie and everyone who had been in contact with Abbey wasn't surprised at her emotions overflowing. She had kept her feelings hidden but now she had to let go.

Andy spoke quietly to Abbey giving her time to feel composed. Rev Heardly gave them a few minutes. The crematorium was silent apart from people crying. As the vicar began to walk out everyone stood and Abbey took hold of Andy and Tanya's arm leaning heavily on Andy, her hat brim covering her bent face. Tears were rolling down his and Tanya's cheeks as were the majority of the guests. Everyone, seeing Andy's tenderness to Abbey knew that he loved her. They all went quietly and reverently to St John's Church.

After much thought, Abbey had arranged for the secure art transporters to put her dada's portrait in St John's church for the Celebration service. Andy had suggested her portraits of Faye and Smillie should stand each side of him. After carefully thinking she agreed. They had been an important part of his life. These were guarded by members of Andy hotel security team and the church wardens. Microphones were set up outside and no filming or photographs allowed inside, but Abbey had promised the media and newspaper cameramen they could record the portraits after the funeral was over.

The sun streamed through the stained glass windows on to the three portraits displayed in the middle of the aisle leading up to the choir stalls. The experts from the local art museum had done these and arranged two spotlights shining down on them. Everyone was grateful for Abbey's graciousness allowing these to be displayed in memory of her beloved dada.

Rev Heardley in his message began with, 'you must all, especially Miss Forrest, have been and still are thinking "it wasn't fair for Mr Forrest to die at only 55 years." He paused. "It wasn't fair for Mr Forrest's wife Faye to be killed whilst so young and eight months pregnant, the child she and Mr Forrest were so looking forward to, the beginning of their large family. It wasn't fair that Miss Abbey had to grow up motherless and without siblings. It wasn't fair for Mr and Mrs Harvey

Hazel Helliwell

to lose their beautiful daughter. It wasn't fair for Mr Forrest's father to be injured whilst a young man and has consequently suffered greatly with his damaged lungs and other complications rendering him impossible to have more children.

It wasn't fair that Miss Abbey had painted this beautiful picture of her dada's beloved dog Smillie and he died four days before his birthday, so didn't see it.' He stood looking at this portrait.

'How many times in my ministry do people say to me daily, 'It isn't fair?

'No, in all the terrible things that happen in the world, all the sufferings and sickness, the abuse ad violence especially to vulnerable people and children, it isn't fair.'

He paused. 'I have no answer. Only that God made a perfect world for us, but evil came in when Eve was disobedient and ate the apple.

'I haven't any answers only that we remember how Jesus, the Son of God suffered and died so each one of us, if we choose to believe and trust in him to have eternal life of peace and joy. In all the tragedies we have took at the Cross and remember.

'We know with all certainty that Mr Forrest is now in the safe place. But it's the ones who are left who loved him, especially his daughter growing up with a strong bond of love between her dada and herself. Mr Forrest's parents, how will they cope?

'We can only pray, support and trust they will take their strength and hope from the Word of God and all his promises.

"It wasn't fair. It isn't fair." But if we keep asking the reason why, we could go crazy. Amen.'

Meant To Meet

There was a silence whilst these words sank in. Then the choir quietly stood and sang the anthem Abbey had chosen. She silently wept with her head bent clinging to Andy's hands.

The sensitive beautiful service continued with two of Grant's favourite hymns and bible readings. The long standing senior manager of Grant's first hotel and Mr Bell gave sincere eulogies. Both had broken down whilst speaking. Mr Bell ended saying how constantly Mr Forrest had spoken of his beloved daughter, Miss Abbey, how proud he had been of her and how he couldn't possibly have a more loving thoughtful daughter. He had to stop as tears fell again.

After a few moments Rev Heardley led the prayers and the service concluded with the final hymn Grant had chosen.

Abbey and Tanya went to thank the choir master, choir and organist and then stood as everyone came out. Andy moved to one side as Abbey, Tanya and Rev Heardly with Russell and Didi greeted people. Abbey and Tanya thanked each one for coming. Andy was so proud of her dignity and bearing and she was so thankful for her Finishing School training.

The cars from the private hire Andy's hotels used were waiting so they and the invited guests began to set off for Ricardo's restaurant. Rev Heardley had quickly disrobed.

As everyone was leaving, Abbey and Andy were walking to their car a very well dressed man came with Mr Bell who introduced him as his new junior partner with his full qualifications being achieved. Mr Bell moved on with Tanya and Matthias.

Josh said, 'my parents have a riding school and own race horses, Miss Forrest. My mother asks if you would come on Sunday for lunch and ride before or afterwards.' Andy stood tall; he knew men would seek Abbey out.

'Thank you Mr Wright, but I'm spending Sunday with Mr Byrne.'

He looked deflated but said. 'The Sunday invitation stands anytime in the future, Miss Forrest.' He left.

Andy was amazed at seeing this firm Abbey and was very thankful. Grant had once told him that she was no pushover. She certainly wasn't. He silently applauded her.

In a few seconds on their own he whispered, 'you look very beautiful, Abbey. Your dada would be so proud of you.' She thanked him.

On Abbey's table were Tanya, Andy, Didi, Russell, Birdie, Rev Heardley, Mr Bell and Matthias. Lorraine and Lara had greatly helped advising who the other guests should sit with to be compatible. It was a most refined time; the food was delicious. Abbey hadn't eaten since Grant's death but she tucked into this and they enjoyed the exquisite wines. Andy had ensured everything was the top quality as befitted Grant.

At the end of the meal everyone was served with a glass of the finest champagne and Russell stood and said, 'please raise your glass to the memory of Mr Forrest.' Everyone stood up for this and then clapped. This touched Abbey, Tanya and Didi greatly.

The table congratulated Andy for organising this lunch, Tanya told him, 'Well done, Andy, it's been spot on.'

Everyone who was not involved in the will reading left, they were going back to St John's church to have a closer view of the portraits. Andy's private cars transported the few back to Holly House.

Queues non stop viewed the portraits, all marvelling at Abbey expertise.

Collection baskets were on view in the foyer with the request for donations for St John's Church funds. Abbey had requested there be no collection during her dada's service. People had been very generous. Russell had discreetly given Rev Heardley an envelope containing a cheque on leaving him at the airport.

As Abbey and Andy walked with Didi and Russell to the hotel car with their luggage in to take back to the airport, Andy introduced the bodyguard who was escorting them on to the plane. Rev Heardley was going with them to see Faye's grave as arranged. He was thankful for this as Russell and Didi had been able to have a few private minutes with him. Abbey kissed her Grandparents and went back for the will reading. She had asked Andy to be with her.

Rev Heardley had promised the media and press that Mr Harvey would have a few words with them. They were all set up waiting at the gates.

'Good afternoon,' he began in his deep cultured voice. They all replied. Didi stood at his side. 'Our Granddaughter, Miss Abbey Forrest, I'm ashamed to admit didn't know us until her beloved dada died. We live in Bermuda. With her grace she contacted us with this news but didn't want us to attend.

'When our daughter Faye insisted that she was going to marry Grant Forrest, we'

Didi broke in, 'no, no, I cut all ties with her and forced my husband to go along with me. I thought Mr Forrest was too quiet and not outgoing enough for her. I'm deeply remorseful.'

Russell firmly took over again, 'However it happened and we're both deeply ashamed of this. We are the losers not knowing Abbey who is beautiful inside and out and also her dada. We can't go back but Abbey with her generous spirit allowed us after communication, to come to the funeral. We are at a new beginning but there are bridges to be built.

'What is embedded in me is when trying to buy Abbey's love with a thoroughbred horse or luxury car, Mr Byrne very firmly told me she didn't want or need gifts. All she had wanted was for her dada and her to have been shown support, respect and someone to tell her what her mummy had been like growing up.

'This was a real lesson for me and my wife. Material things are nothing compared to being loved and supported.

'I have now taken authority of our marriage.

'As Miss Forrest's Grandpapa I ask you to let her grieve for her dada and rebuild her life. Thank you.'

A female called out, 'Is Miss Forrest and Mr Byrne?' Russell, with authority cut her off and abruptly moved away, both he and Didi were crying. Everyone clapped them. The bodyguard stepped in and escorted them back in the waiting car.

Walking up to Faye's grave Russell and Didi seeing the willow tree, the seat, how well cared for the plot was began to cry uncontrollably and sank down on their knees. Rev Heardley tearfully stood apart praying for them. It finally registered with Didi how much Grant had loved their daughter. After a while Russell helped her up and they re-joined the vicar who knew how very traumatic this was for both of them, but healing had begun. Quietly they went back to the car.

Didi had the surprise of the car slowing down outside Fortnum and Mason, then Liberty, Selfridges, Harrods, The Ritz, Next they went past Buckingham Palace and Westminster Abbey. Didi was enthralled seeing these and the beautiful flower displays everywhere looking their best in the gorgeous weather. Russell greatly appreciated Andy organising this sightseeing surprise with understanding of their trauma.

Travelling home on the plane Russell told Didi, 'I'm so proud of you, darling. I know what the service and everything cost you, but you've behaved as a true lady, very dignified.'

'It was hard, Russell, but in no way was I going to lose my self control. I owed Abbey that at least. This was her and Grant's day.'

Russell was overwhelmed at this wisdom, but then he remembered that he shouldn't be as Didi had never let him down in any situation. 'Would you like to go away for a holiday darling?'

'Perhaps later, thank you darling. With our building bridges with Abbey I'd like to be here available if she needs us. I feel quite lost now.'

'Yes, I understand but Abbey and Andy need time on their own.'

'Yes, of course, they do. I need to boast about my granddaughter and also continue receiving ministry from our local church.'

'So would I darling. Something entered me in St John's church.'

They went quiet reflecting, and then Didi said, 'I would like to invite my "gang" to afternoon tea. Will you please set up a portable screen with Abbey's photographs enlarged, also some of Andy and Abbey's film judging the painting competition?'

'I will, with pleasure.'

Abbey and Andy and Mr Bell travelled with Tanya and Matthias to the airport in one of Andy's cars and bodyguard. Tanya was quiet and they respected this knowing she was anxious to get back to Sebastian, and the day had been stressful for her.

Andy had brought his casual clothes to change into to have dinner with Abbey. Returning from the airport he could see that she was absolutely exhausted. She had kept up during the day. Birdie came to see if they were ready for a pot of tea.

'Abbey, you're exhausted, you've coped wonderfully to-day. Birdie, I think I should go home and let Abbey go to bed now.'

'Yes, sir, that would be a good idea. I'll take Miss Abbey's supper up.' Abbey was too spent to argue.

'Thank you, Andy, I admit to being tired.'

'Sleep well. I'll see you in the morning. I'll go and catch up on some work.' Abbey, Andy, Birdie, Brian and Mr Bell were going to Faye's grave plot where Grant's ashes were being buried.

'Thank you for everything, Andy. We'll talk to-morrow.'

'Yes, thank you sir,' Birdie echoed, smiling lovingly at him. Birdie led Abbey indoors.

The money received from the donations was enough to have a major repair done on the church.

Requests to commission were received in Abbey's office. Lara replied to each that Miss Forrest was too busy taking over the running of the hotels, but thanked them for their enquiry.

A few days after the funeral Abbey said she needed to visit her Grandparents. 'Am I coming with you, Abbey?'

'If you can spare the time, yes please Andy. Then we need to begin planning our wedding.'

He gently gathered her into his arms keeping a distance between them. 'I won't make demands until you are ready, darling. A quiet church wedding in respect of your bereavement, lunch at Ricardo's restaurant if this is what you want.'

'That sounds good, thank you Andy.'

'When you have things settled after marrying, we could go to Haven Cottage for a few days or as long as you like. We can work from there temporarily.'

'I'd welcome this, please. Did you buy it recently?'

'No six years ago. Ok darling. That's enough for now.' He gently kissed her on her lips.

'You know I've had a few short-term women Abbey.' She looked pained. 'When I first met you it was as though the world stopped and I'd met someone I'd been searching for all my life.' He longed to take her into his arms and Abbey also longed to gather him close.

'When I met you, darling, I'd the strange feeling that my life would never be the same. I'd no idea who dada had invited for that lunch.'

To control himself he briskly said, 'ring if I can help you, otherwise see you to-morrow.'

She walked to his car with him and stood waving until he went through the gates. She felt lonely when he had gone as he did leaving her.

In the post was a letter from the local hospital thanking her for her maternal grandparents sending a very generous cheque for their heart unit in memory of their daughter and son-in-law. She cried with thankfulness after reading this and texted Andy with this good news.

Later she rang and Russell answered business like. After exchanging pleasantries, Abbey asked, 'may I ask personal questions, Grandpapa?'

'Ask away, darling,' wondering what was coming.

'Are your parents still living?'

'No, darling, just over four years ago they were killed with many others in a horrific train crash. The driver was charged with negligence.'

'What about Didi's parents?'

'They divorced, Abbey, re-married and their new partners didn't want the connection with Didi. She reminded the new partners of the first marriages. She kept in touch with her Grandparents with Christmas and birthday cards.'

A pang of resentment went through Abbey. This was more that she had done for her and her dada. Sighing, she quickly rebuked these thoughts. As Andy had said, "the past was behind them."

'Oh dear, I'm sorry, Grandpapa.'

'Yes, and both Didi and I are only children. Your great Grandfather died just over six years ago and your great Grandmother is 92 years old. '

'Thank you for telling me this. Where does my great Grandmother live?'

'In the Lake District, do you know it?'

'I've never been but I have heard of it.'

'Did my great Grandparents know about me?'

'I'm sorry precious, but I've no idea. Would you like your great Grandmother to get in touch with you?'

'I don't know, Grandpapa. It may cause complications I honestly could do without as now.' She changed the subject enquiring how Didi was.

'I wonder if you'll do me a big favour, darling.'

'Tell me what it is, Grandpapa.'

'Will you do me an oil painting of Didi in evening dress from a photograph? I'll pay you.'

'Thank you. Let me have the photograph.'

'It will be a wonderful surprise for her.'

They chatted for a further few minutes.

Putting her phone down Abbey sighed deeply thinking, "what a mess my family is. What a shame." She was beginning to feel quite despondent but knew she would be able to discuss this with Andy.

After listening as he always did, he said, 'you've enough on darling. Keep going and see what happens, you haven't anything to feel guilty about.' He was beginning to feel angry again how she'd been treated by her blood relations.

A reporter from the most popular gossip and fashion magazine had caught up with Sonya and asked how she felt about Mr Byrne marrying Miss Forrest?'

She replied with dignity, 'I knew it was a short-term fling with Mr Byrne. Miss Forrest is a very fortunate young lady.

Chapter Eleven

Abbey arranged with Birdie for both of them to see the Master Suite. Andy was amazed when Abbey told him that she had never seen it.

It was at the end of the gallery corridor and ran the width of the house overlooking the front and the woods at the back. Biddy unlocked the carved door which matched all the others and going in they saw an empty room filled with sunshine from two large windows and a huge sparkling chandelier hung from an exquisite patterned ceiling. Highly varnished floorboards Andy was thrilled to see.

No one spoke. After a few minutes Biddy then led them through an arched opening down a corridor which housed Faye's dressing room and opened the carved wooden door leading into a feminine ensuite gorgeous bathroom. Abbey and Andy were astounded to see a free standing large cast iron bath Andy had previously laughingly requested this with Abbey. Sadness went through him as this revealed to him Grant and Faye had been a modern couple madly in love and at one with each other enjoying fun. A sliding door housed a shower unit.

The walls were beautifully tiled and the wash basin and backwash were set in marble matching the gold and white tiles.

Going back up the narrow corridor Birdie led them through the second arch into another narrow corridor housing Grant's dressing room and en suite with a male urinal, a small bath and shower unit. Andy made a mental note that the overhead spray could be improved on now in each shower. The tiling again was as new.

'It's all so fresh and clean,' Abbey exclaimed. She hadn't known what to expect having not been used for 25 years.

'Yes, Miss Abbey, the windows are opened daily and it's cleaned weekly.'

'The windows in the bathrooms,' Andy questioned, 'they are smokescreen?'

'Yes sir. See outward but not inward. Also the same quality is in the bedroom.'

Andy explained further to Abbey, 'and no UV rays can get through or heat or cold.

The bathrooms are brilliant with a few plumbing improvements.'

Birdie sensitively led them back into the bedroom. Abbey was looking round feeling very emotional seeing for the first time, her parent's rooms.

This was where her sisters and brothers would have begun their life. This was where her parent's would have been so happy in their privacy. Andy sensing her sadness squeezed her hand in understanding and held on to it.

'Seriously Abbey, will you settle in these rooms? There are plenty we can adapt.'

'I'll be proud to use these Andy. All the thought, planning and expense my parent's put into this project. I'll be happy to use them. Tell me, have you any doubts?'

'No, precious, but please don't think I'm being disrespectful,' he hesitated.

'Go on darling.'

'I would prefer not to have your mummy's portrait in here.'

'Oh darling, I was going to ask your opinion on hanging this and Smillie's in the alcoves either side of dada.'

'Brilliant. Sorry precious, I should have known your sensitivity.'

'I have a watercolour I believe you'll like to have over our bed.'

Andy groaned, then to distract his thoughts jumped up and down on the floor. 'Yes, solid floorboards, Abbey. I love wood. May we have these re-varnished and a few rugs or a carpet?'

'I prefer the boards,' she agreed.

Andy was thrilled at this. He was impatient to take her to his Cottage where she would see all the wood he had used.

Looking at Abbey he said, 'this bedroom is 26 years old and you are a vibrant young lady. I would like to re-decorate the walls.'

Birdie agreed, 'it needs modernising, sir.'

'Ok Andy. What are you suggesting?'

'I suggest decorated wall panels. I'll get samples then you can match up with curtains and bedding.

Would you rather Whitwell Wood decorators do this job, or mine?'

'Mine are closer, darling.'

Abbey was seeing a different Andy as she recognised his input into his hotels.

'We should be able to have all this prepared for when we are married, darling.'

'Yes. My dada would be so pleased that we are using these rooms. He and mummy only used it for eleven months.'

They stood looking through large bay window. Andy was thinking that Grant had not only lost his companion, he had lost being loved by an adoring wife and enjoying life together. He thanked God that Abbey had been saved. If they both had gone he knew Grant being the man he was, life wouldn't have been worth living for.

He felt Abbey's eyes on him. They gazed at each other both thinking of how they would begin their married life in this room and were filled with a great longing in this new environment. Birdie gently knocked on the door. Abbey wondered what would have happened if she hadn't come at that moment.

'Let's go and see the bed and dressing table.' Andy suggested again disciplining his thoughts.

Birdie helped them take the covers off and they were both delighted with the tasteful solid wooden bed and side cupboards matching the doors. Andy had wondered if the mattress would still be there but this had been removed. He was very thankful as this may have upset Abbey further.

'With all respect, we should have a new bed, darling. I'll match the wood.'

Birdie nodded.

'I understand, Andy.' She then had a thought, 'Birdie, would you like a new bed and furnishings?'

'It's still good but now you ask, I would like a new mattress, Miss Abbey,' she laughed. 'Your mummy bought us the very best quality.'

'You haven't changed your mattress in 26 years?' Andy asked in amazement.

'Well sir, there's been only me,' she laughed.

'Update your room darling and please ask Debbie and Brian if we may provide new for their rooms. I'll arrange to meet up with you three when you have decided and the re-decorating. We're at a new beginning.'

'Thank you, Miss Abbey.'

Birdie and Andy recognized that she was taking her new role as mistress of the house seriously. They both lovingly smiled at her. Birdie had to hold back her tears once more as Abbey was getting more and more like Faye.

Uncovering the dressing table Abbey was stood awe struck with this. Golden polished wood as the bed and wood throughout the house, Shaped mirror with leaf carved scroll supports over top of three fitted drawers, shaped base with one central drawer and standing on beautifully carved legs. She then began to sob. Andy held her but away from him until her storm had passed, speaking soothingly to her. He anticipated as they approached the Green room that she would be upset seeing this link with her mummy. Birdie suggesting she arranged a tray of tea quietly left them He sat Abbey down on the matching stool.

Birdie and Brian brought the tray and they looked at Andy nodding in understanding. 'Thank you both for taking such good care of all this. I feel so close to my mummy imagining her sat here preparing to go out.'

Brian said, 'pardon us Miss Abbey.' She looked at them through her tears and they were both also weeping. Jumping up she gathered Birdie in her arms and they wept together. Andy was weeping also with them, he was just beginning to realise the reality of their loss at Faye's young life and now Grant's untimely death.

Giving them a few minutes he then suggested, 'have you time for a glass of wine, or are you driving, Brian?' Abbey looked at him in gratitude.

'No sir, only if you and Miss Abbey want taking somewhere.'

Abbey shook her head. She was beginning to realise the position she held, mistress of the home but also there were Birdie and Brian's emotional grieving needs to be met.

Brian took more covers off revealing a beautiful quality settee with deep cushions. 'Your parent's used to sit in front of the bedroom window overlooking the wood, Miss Abbey.' Through her tears she nodded.

'These are wonderful rooms. Thank you both for taking such care. We're very lucky.'

'You both deserve the best.' They quietly left.

Andy then suggested, 'let's go back into the bathrooms, darling.' Looking in both and the beautiful tiling on the walls, the bidet, he said, 'this is as modern as to-day, precious. Minor up to date improvements could be put in.'

With her knowledge of the modern hotel Whitwell Wood she knew exactly what he was suggesting. 'We'll contact the plumber and decorator, darling.'

'Come on my sweetheart, that's enough for you for now.' Going out to the patio and Brian and Birdie joined them with the bottle of wine.

After they had enjoyed a glass the four of them sat in silence reflecting. Abbey's phone rang; she raised her eyebrows, "should she answer it?" Andy nodded. Birdie and Brian left thanking them for this break. It was Lara with a request. Abbey quickly dealt with it. More mature understanding came into Abbey's brain of the responsibility she also carried for her hotel business and staff. She gave a prayer of thanks to God that she had Andy who would identify with her needs and help her.

'What would you like to do now, darling?'

'I think a walk in the wood.' The dogs jumped at that. Smillie had begun with Andy's coaxing to join them. Whilst walking they discussed what changes they could make in the en suites.

'I love the dressing table Andy. It's so comfortable to be sat at. I would have used it before if I had seen it.'

'Never mind darling, you will be using it soon.' They continued discussing what needed doing in the rooms and made the arrangements.

Andy recognised the new maturity in Abbey but didn't mention it.

After meeting with Pete to discuss the weeks' menu's then as usual, had a discussion with Birdie, Abbey suggested, 'will you need an extra cleaning lady Birdie, when Mr Byrne and I are married?'

'We are well covered, Miss Abbey, it will be only as cleaning your dada's rooms and yours and with Mr Byrne continuing to use his valet service for his clothes.'

'Let me know, darling Birdie, if you have any problems.'

'You can be sure of that, precious.'

Abbey having known Birdie all her life cuddled her.

Andy and Abbey arranged a meeting with Rev Heardley and Andy asked him if he would marry them on Monday 6th July 12 pm. He, asking looking in his diary, said that would be possible, He didn't tell them Monday was his day off.

'In view of Abbey's bereavement we would like to keep this low key but reverent,' Andy then told him.

'Of course, Andy, I wouldn't expect anything less of you. In view of people wanting to see you married, will you consider the larger St John's and make use of the choir? We all owe you and your family a huge gratitude for the donations from Mr Forrest's funeral service.'

'This may be too traumatic for Abbey. But thank you for the thought and I'll ask her.'

After hesitating but appreciating what Rev Heardley and the community wanted for their wedding venue, she agreed. 'Good girl, Abbey, your dada would be so proud of you.' They made an appointment to meet Rev Heardley for the following week.

'Will you be able to lunch with us, Rev Heardley?'

'Yes please. Will Mr and Mrs Harvey be returning home after the lunch?'

'Yes vicar.'

'Is it possible for me to travel with them to the airport again?'

'I'll arrange this,' Andy promised. He and Abbey knew how much stronger Didi and Russell had felt after their conversation with him travelling to the airport after Grant's funeral. But obviously Rev Heardley knew there was unfinished business.

Andy set the wheels in motion. He had asked Ricardo if they may lunch on this particular day if the date fitted in with the church. With being closed Mondays which had been a factor in their choosing that day, Ricardo was only too pleased with this honour, and the staff was eager to work knowing they would receive another good bonus as they had after Mr Forrest's funeral.

'We're off to a good start, darling,' Andy told Abbey.

Next was letting Grandmama, Didi, Russell and Andy's family know.

Making an appointment at the boutique for her dress, Ms Spencer made arrangements for the senior haute couture lady in Paris to come to Holly House. Abbey had her exact requirements ready. Classic pure white silk calf length, three quarter sleeves and a pill box hat made of the same material with silk white flowers on one side matching her bouquet. She also asked for an evening dress for her wedding eve dinner.

Abbey asked her Grandmama where she would like to go for the wedding eve dinner, she immediately said, 'The Ritz Hotel, please. This has so many happy memories of your Granddada and my wedding eve dinner.' Abbey invited Didi, Russell and Mr Bell who all accepted with joy, Andy invited his parents, brothers and sisters-in-law. The meal was set for 7 pm for an early bed.

Andy and Abbey had arranged to have three days free and went first to Gresley Wood hotel then Cobden Wood. Arriving at Gresley compared to newly built Whitwell Wood, Abbey knew that it looked a little shabby. Royston Bergman the senior manager and Sam Atkins, Lorraine and Lara came outside to greet them. Royston introduced Andy to the deputy managers, front desk managers and the housekeepers. Abbey was so proud how respectful he was as always.

Royston had passed on to everyone Mr Byrne would meet everyone in time. He had stated the domestic staff and everyone helping the hotels to function efficiently daily was as important as anyone. This was received with approval and relief knowing how Mr Forrest had cared for them.

Abbey was presented with a bouquet. Lorraine had arranged this with the instruction that Miss Forrest didn't like anything ostentatious.

Going on to the Ireton and Linacre hotels where the same procedure was carried out, but this time they had coffee in the head office where the other managers met them and Brandon had set up a portable screen to show Andy every part of. Another small bouquet was presented to Abbey.

With Whitwell Wood being built to house their faithful patrons from Bow and Clough also had a restaurant open to the public to lunch with prior bookings. Abbey wore her pale lilac with the edelweiss flowers for the visit to Whitwell.

After introductions and greetings in reception, the *maître d'* and sommelier led them to their table. Walking through the diners who stood up as Abbey approached and greeted Andy but with their culture and good manners didn't detain them. Royston brought the head chef to be introduced.

The same format was carried through with them having coffee together with the key staff in the head office where on screen Andy saw every part of the hotel, which had his admiration and approval. He discerned Grant had used the top architects and designers to create an up to date hotel befitting Abbey. It was another good constructive meeting and they all really appreciated this informal time. Abbey was presented with a beautiful white orchid in a clear glass dome. 'Thank you very much. This is so gorgeous; you have matched my dress again.'

Travelling on Friday to English Oak Andy filled her in more and arriving Abbey looked at it in awe. Going into the luxurious marble foyer with a sweeping two-sided staircase with a fountain as a centrepiece she stopped short gazing around in wonder. Waving her arms she told Andy, 'this is so wonderful, Andy, I'm so proud of you.' She was looking at him with all the love for him she had, the world disappeared as they looked into each other's eyes and kissed.

Laughter brought them back down to earth and they saw they were surrounding by a crowd who clapped a blushing Abbey and bemused Andy. The *maître d'* and sommelier came forward. Abbey smiled and they went into the dining room where their table was in an open alcove. The hotel was open to lunch as Whitwell was but also evening bookings. Abbey was looking round with interest. Andy had shown her pictures in his mobile of the suites and gym and spa facilities, but seeing it first hand was overwhelming. She hadn't seen his Penthouse.

Enjoying the lunch and a little wine, they conversed but were aware of people passing deliberately to have a look at Abbey, curious to see the young lady who had captured Andy's heart, but with their breeding didn't interrupt.

Andy had anticipated this so had arranged for her to meet English Oak managers Darius Bourne, senior manager, Scott Hudson, Levine Shepherd, Josh Hall, Len Haynes, office manager and Chase Meyer his PA in the area at the top of the staircase with deep leather sofas and armchairs placed in intimate formations to give privacy to guests as they socialised over a drink. After introductions Abbey recognised their respect and admiration for Andy, two young waiters served them coffee.

Andy led them to his private lift in the bank of lifts to his penthouse. Going in Abbey was filled with dismay. Beautifully furnished and decorated, but it was soulless, no photographs or anything. She didn't know Andy had a framed photograph of her at the side of his bed. She had the urge to say to him, 'get your clothes and come to Holly House.' Knowing this would be inappropriate she also knew he only used this as a base for sleeping and catching up in his laptop and using the hotel's gym.

Discussing English Oak and encouraging Abbey to talk about her hotels they recognized what a good command and understanding she had of hotel workings.

Chase asked, 'you love sports, Miss Forrest?'

'I do, and riding, walking or running in the countryside with the dogs.'

'Now you do these with Mr Byrne?'

'Yes, I'm very happy he's likeminded,' smiling at him. He was looking at her in adoration.

Chase persisted, 'you swim together?'

Abbey blushed scarlet. Andy frowned at him. 'We will when we are married.'

Andy could see they were suppressing their amusement at her keeping him waiting. Abbey also picked this up and began to laugh. Joining in they visibly relaxed with her. Seeing how much in love they were and their compatibility were re-assured, having the highest regard for Andy and would do anything to ease his work load.

'We'll do everything we can to free Mr Byrne to spend time with you, Miss Forrest.' Darius promised.

'Thank you. I appreciate this and I deeply appreciate how you freed Andy when my dada died. I don't know what I would have done without him.'

'It was a pleasure,' Chase told her.

'Chase is one of my squash partners, darling,' Andy told her.

'Have you been able to play lately, Andy? Perhaps you leave too late at 9 pm. Please don't give up your squash, darling.'

'Well, I have a good work out and swim twelve lengths night and morning,' he laughed. 'Then you have me digging.'

'Digging?' the three asked in amazement.

'I've a tiny plot in the garden with a small greenhouse. I like to grow salad ingredients.'

She could see that she had amused them again and they were discreetly looking at their watches. She knew they needed to get back to work. Unknown to her, Andy had suggested the timing for this first time meeting her.

Going down in the lift, Chase mischievously asked, 'are you going to do some gardening, Mr Byrne?' He was always formal in work situations.

'Are we, darling,' he asked Abbey.

'Good idea.'

'We envy you, Mr Byrne,' Darius told him. 'We would like to continue this afternoon. We are so happy to have met you Miss Forrest, and wish you both everything good for your future.'

In reception Abbey told them, 'I have really enjoyed this time with you, and am looking forward to meeting with you soon.'

Royston, beaming, gave her a dozen apricot roses. 'Thank you, I love these. You have matched my dress,' she teased.

Walking out with them, the car was waiting. Watching her gracefully getting into the car, Len said, 'isn't she a star? What a wonderful wife and companion she will be to Andy. I'm thankful she has a sense of humour and is so down to earth. I feel quite lost now. I would have loved to have gone with them. Oh well, better get some work done.'

Going back in discussing the time with Abbey, Scott said, 'they are just right for each other, aren't they?'

Darius and Chase agreed. Darius then told them, 'I could hardly believe it when she said she liked growing salad ingredients. She's a millionaire. Wow. I can see this is part of her personality which attracted Andy. Down to earth, pardon the pun thinking of Andy digging. If only there were more young ladies like her.'

'Yes. She has an air of purity about her. Also, beauty and brains,' Levine came in with.

They agreed.

'I wonder if she knows about Andy's former women,' Chase asked knowing of them.

'Definitely Andy will have told her. I discerned they communicated together. He wouldn't want her to find out from someone else.'

'I discerned,' Josh said, 'that she's no push over and likes straight talking. Andy's future is safe in her hands, she's a business lady. She wouldn't have worked so hard getting her degrees if she was going to fritter her life away. I look forward to getting to know her more; she's like a breath of fresh air. I've never seen anything more attractive than when she blushed. Oh well, back to work boys, we've an added incentive now.'

Travelling home Abbey couldn't stop admiring the beautiful apricot roses. 'Darling, this is the colour I would like for a rose bush in our garden.'

'Yes, I agree, they're gorgeous.'

Meeting up in reception the next lunch time, Andy's managers and Chase were very impressed with Whitwell Wood and realised the responsibility Abbey was carrying. But now knew that she was more than "up to it."

As for English Oak films and photographs in mobiles were passed round the table and everyone enjoyed themselves.

After enjoying their gorgeous lunch Andy's colleagues left for Abbey and Andy to have a coffee time and fellowship with Lorraine, Lara, Jeffrey and Stephen.

Abbey and Andy told them also how much they had appreciated their sacrificing their time over the last few weeks.

Lorraine told them, 'it's a pleasure, sir, and ma'am. I speak for all of us. We are so happy to help and this will continue so please ask.'

Abbey then said, 'I'm giving each of you a bonus in recognition of your helping us,'

'No, Miss Forrest, a, this isn't necessary. We have loved helping you and this will carry on and b; your dada gave us a generous legacy.'

Andy said, 'Thank you, but my key people have accepted a bonus and Miss Forrest and I will treat you all the same.'

Thanking them they carried on discussing in the relaxed atmosphere, very happy that Abbey had Andy supporting her and themselves also.

Wednesday afternoon before the wedding, Tanya rang Abbey. 'Darling, I'm so sorry my pet, but I can't leave your Granddada to attend your wedding. I haven't told him yet, but you know how he isn't at all well in this hot weather period. Please, please understand. Will it be possible for Andy to have it filmed for us?'

Abbey was so disappointed but she'd had doubts as knowing her Granddada was deteriorating rapidly and was praying he would live to see his first great grandchild at least.

'I'm so sorry my darling Grandmama, but I understand and Andy will also. Certainly we'll film for you. You mustn't be worried about us. I'm so thankful knowing your love for each other has lasted all these years, I'm confident Andy and I will be the same and I would in no way leave him if he was ill. I'll ring later, darling.' Tanya had sounded tired. Abbey prayed for her and her Granddada. She knew her Grandmama coming to the funeral must have upset her. When Andy came and she shared this with him, he was so sorry. She told him what she had said to her Grandmama that if he was ill she wouldn't leave him. He made arrangements for the wedding to be filmed.

Didi knowing Andy wasn't with Abbey rang her. 'Have you a few minutes darling?'

'Yes, Didi, is anything wrong?'

'No, Abbey. I thought you may like a little chat before you marry.'

Abbey had to choke back her laughter thinking "Oh well, better late than never." 'Thank you Didi, I know about the birds and the bees,' she teased her. 'But there is something.'

'Carry on, darling.'

'I've big nipples, Didi.'

'So have I darling, and your mummy had.'

'I wish I'd known this when I was in my teens.'

Guilt tore through Didi again at her neglect of Abbey.

'I'm so sorry, my precious, but we can't go back. We now have the future. Your Grandpapa loves them. Andy will also. Would you like your Grandpapa to have a word with you?'

Abbey almost choked again. 'Please don't tell him, Didi.'

'Of course I won't, but you've nothing to be ashamed of. You can talk with him about anything, darling. It's a family thing. Your daughters will probably be the same.'

'I do appreciate you re-assuring me, Didi. Apart from my sports bra I wear protectors.'

'Whatever are these, Abbey?'

'A GP told me about them when I was 17. They're very comfortable.'

'I didn't know about these, Abbey.'

They chatted about the wedding. Abbey phone her phone down and for the first time in her life happily lost her inferiority about her nipples, very grateful to Didi re-assuring her, even if it was late.

Didi so excited that she had helped Abbey she had to tell Russell. He laughed, 'wow, Andy is a lucky man.'

'Don't you dare say anything to Abbey, please?'

'Of course I won't, darling. Surely you know me well enough not to?'

'I do, my darling. I do, sorry.' She then felt guilty that she had broken her promise to Abbey, but she was getting more in control of her gossiping tongue.

Chapter Twelve

Andy, at Tanya's choice with her wonderful memories of times there with Sebastian, had booked a table for the wedding eve dinner at The Ritz. Andy and Abbey invited Andy's parents, his two brothers and their wives with Didi and Russell for this low key wedding with Abbey still grieving for her beloved dada. Russell insisted on paying for this.

They were all sorry Tanya wasn't coming, but understood her commitment to her ill husband. Andy promised to send photographs.

Andy came to collect Abbey. The media and press were waiting at the gates. His car went through the gates and Andy got out, then it returned to outside the gates. The security man got out and smiling at them said, 'Mr Byrne and Miss Forrest are walking down for a few words.' They all were grateful for this.

Overflowing with happiness Abbey and Andy walked hand in hand to greet them. Everyone clapped them. Andy looked magnificent in his tailored evening clothes and Abbey had never looked more beautiful in her haute couture gown of opaque floral silk chiffon in delicate shades of pale cream and lavender with a hint of pink, beautifully fitted with a ruched bodice. Diamonds sparkled from her drop ear rings and dainty necklace Andy had just given her. She had a specialist mobile phone made which would be very useful for Andy. Knowing he wouldn't want a gold pen had a light bamboo one made and inscribed with his name.

Questions were fired at them. Andy replied, 'Mr Harvey, my future Grandfather in law is treating my family and us to dinner at The Ritz. Miss Forrest's paternal Grandmama chose this venue but we deeply regret she's not now able to come this evening or for the wedding. You all know that her husband through ill health hasn't been able to travel for years, but regretfully he now isn't well enough for her to comfortably leave him. We're having a film made privately for them to view.'

Abbey looked upset. Andy took hold of her hand. Thankfully the reporters didn't mention Grant, but knew that it was a low key time in respect of his death. Abbey answered questions.

A female then asked, 'are you going to Bermuda for our honeymoon, sir?'

'No, we're staying in Britain,' Andy told them.

'Where are you going, sir?' He shook his head, then looking at his watch they went to the car. Shouts of congratulations and thanks rang out. Acknowledging them Andy helped Abbey into the car carefully folding her gown in and they set off waving. Quite a lot of them would have liked to be going with them.

'We could have asked them to kiss,' a female reporter complained.

'No, this will happen after the wedding. Miss Forrest is still a virgin. That's why they are marrying so quickly. She's definitely not pregnant.'

Arriving at The Ritz the managers, with respect to Andy and Abbey being hotel owners were waiting for them outside with the *maître d*. After welcoming he escorted them to their table. It looked glorious. Everyone at the table stood up to greet them and told Abbey how beautiful she looked.

It was an exquisite meal with the very best quality wines. None of them indulged in view of their early morning start. Abbey and Andy sat close together their thighs touching for the first time in a world of their own knowing this was the last night they would sleep alone, but were attentive and polite. Everyone understood. Russell stood and toasted them with champagne.

The press were waiting outside for them and Andy's parents escorted her home where Birdie was waiting for her.

Andy guessing a good time texted Abbey telling her how much he adored her. She texted back telling him she adored him and couldn't wait until to-morrow. Thinking she would be awake all night, fell asleep as soon as her head hit the pillow. Andy spent a short time with Didi and Russell then they retired for the early start.

Ms Spencer with Tim and his assistants came to attend to Abbey. It was a beautiful summer day. Abbey had been fearful she would begin her period as always been regular, had been hit and miss since her dada's death, but knew it was the shock of this that had upset her regularity. However, she was safe when ready. Didi and Birdie cried with joy at her pure virginal beauty. It was emotional for her knowing it wasn't her beloved dada sharing in this day, but this was the beginning of a new journey with Andy.

Russell looking very handsome was very proud to be given the honour of giving her away to Andy. Before setting off he took several photographs and sent them through to Adrienne for Tanya and Sebastian. With keeping the wedding party small, Andy had asked Marlon to be his best man and Stuart the usher.

Crowds waving and cheering this time were lining the route. The media, press and cameramen from the papers and fashion magazines were waiting outside the church.

The church looked beautiful decorated with flowers and Quentin, Marlon, Stuart and the men were very smart in their also bespoke grey lounge suits, pristine white shirts, grey tie and grey shoes. Andy looked magnificent in his bespoke grey silk suit, white silk shirt and tie, grey shoes. The children were in their new clothes and excited at their Uncle Andy getting married. The ladies looked beautiful. Didi had underplayed to not take attention away from anyone else. She and Andy's family were very happy together and the church was filled to over flowing. The choir had given up the stalls and were sat in chairs in front of the altar.

Members of the choir who were able had the day off as a holiday in respect of Abbey and her dada. Rev Heardley had recruited other singers to make up the full choir to render the anthem Abbey had chosen. She and Andy had chosen all the beautiful organ music and hymns. Microphones had been set up outside. No filming or photographs were allowed inside. Rev Heardley explained the wedding was going to be privately filmed for Miss Forrest's paternal Grandparents in Switzerland who were too ill to attend.

As the organ began playing the music Abbey had chosen, Marlon excitedly told Andy, 'Abbey's here,' Andy was choked. He turned and saw the beautiful vision of her smilingly coming down the long aisle to him. Andy's parents and sisters-in-law were weeping with joy, so thankful Andy's future was safe with Abbey adoring him.

'You look so beautiful, darling,' he told her.

'So do you,' and kissed him,

Rev Heardley joked, 'this should come afterwards.' Everyone laughed; they all knew she was still a virgin. It was a beautiful reverent service. Andy and Abbey made their vows clearly in all sincerity and truth. They sat hand in hand on two chairs covered in white cotton to listen to the anthem, both trying not to cry at the beauty of the organ and the singing.

Outside the children presented Abbey with horse shoes, and a small rolling pin!

After they had all good naturedly let the media, press and everyone have the photographs and filming they needed. Andy quietly told Abbey, 'Well done. I'm so proud of you, my precious.' It had been hard for her knowing her dada wasn't there to share in their day, also her mummy and paternal Grandparents.

Andy ensured the film was ready to send to Adrienne who would transfer it on to a large portable screen for Tanya and Sebastian. Russell had asked if he may have a copy, this was arranged also for Abbey and Andy and Andy's family.

Setting off for Ricardo's where he, the chefs and staff once more had excelled ensuring everyone enjoyed the delicious lunch and wines. Marlon gave a humourous short speech ending with 'we all look forward to Andy and Abbey's little ones and I don't mean hotels.' Everyone clapped and cheered. Flutes of champagne were handed round and Russell stood, 'Your parents would have been so proud of you Abbey and you Andy. We are including your paternal Grandparents and everyone. We wish you a happy future with plenty of little ones as Marlon has indicated. Please stand.' With glasses raised they all said, 'to Abbey and Andy.'

Quentin stood and with tears of joy in his eyes he said, 'thank you Abbey for becoming part of our family. You are very, very welcome.' They all toasted them again.

Everyone saw Abbey and Andy set off to take her bouquet to her parent's graves. Rev Heardley travelled with Didi and Russell again to the airport.

Back home Andy swung Abbey up in his arms and carried her over the threshold. Birdie and the staff were laughing and clapping. Birdie went upstairs with Abbey to help her change. Before going down Abbey rang her Grandmama. Adrienne answered. This surprised her having promised to ring when she arrived home. 'Hello Adrienne, how are my Grandparents?'

'Mr Forrest is the same, Mrs Byrne. Mrs Forrest is resting, she has a slight headache. I'm setting up the portable screen for them both to see your wedding together. They are looking forward to this. Mrs Forrest said when you rang to not bother with them and both enjoy your honeymoon.'

'Thank you Adrienne for all you have done and are doing. When we have had a few days acknowledging our gifts, we'll come.' They had received hundreds of congratulation cards; many had a gift voucher in. Abbey were grateful for these and not presents they had received and duplicated.

'I'll pass this on Mrs Byrne, thank you.' They said bye.

Abbey was concerned about her Grandmama's headache, so prayed for her. She went down to the waiting Andy and passed this message on.

Welcome rain after the long dry spell was pouring down. Enjoying a cup of tea and relaxing in the sitting room Andy said, 'well, Mrs Byrne, your dada would be very pleased with our being married.'

'Yes, he would.' Then a thought struck her. 'When you first came to lunch and we met, did my dada know then he was dying?'

'Yes darling.'

'Did he ask you to marry me?'

He had been dreading her asking this. 'Yes, he did. I could lie but I'll never lie to you, Abbey.'

She stood up facing him; her face was stricken and drained. 'You only came into my life because he invited you purposely for this?'

'Yes.'

'So, otherwise we wouldn't be married?'

'If we hadn't met, how could we be?'

'You were sleeping with Sonya and broke off your relationship after meeting me?'

'How do you know this?'

'I read it.'

'She knew it was only short term.'

He stood at her side, 'Please Abbey, don't let anything spoil what we have. I love you. I told you I've had women but I'm not promiscuous. They understood they were short term and months went by in between. Your dada had women before he married your mummy. I'm 33 years old, Abbey. I never asked one of them to be my wife. You're different. You are a star. I loved and wanted you from the moment I saw you.'

'I don't feel well; I must have begun my period. My monthly cycle has been irregular since the shock of dada's death.'

He went upstairs with her and she went into her en-suite bathroom and closed the door.

He waited until she came out. 'Do you want to lie down, darling?'

'Yes.'

He rang Birdie and went he meet her explaining Abbey wasn't feeling well having begun her period. 'I'm not surprised, sir. Her body has been upset since the shock of her bereavement. She'll settle down shortly. Let her quietly rest. I'll make her a cup of tea and put a shot of whiskey in it. That will soothe her. Oh dear, it would be to-day of all days.'

'No problem Birdie. Hopefully we've our lives in front of us.'

'She adores you, sir.'

'Thank you, Birdie. I adore Abbey and would do anything for her. All I want is for her to be happy.'

He went back in to Abbey and sat in the armchair. 'Birdie is bringing you tea and whiskey, darling.'

'Thank you, Andy,' she quietly answered.

'May I sit with you, darling?'

'I would prefer to be alone. I'll have a nap.'

'I'll take the dogs for a run then.' Amazingly for the first time Smillie jumped up and stood at his side to go with him.

'I'll see you downstairs soon.' She looked very tired and drawn. He was very worried but thankful at her promise.

After a short run he went back upstairs and gently knocked on the door and opened it slightly. She was sound asleep looking very young and pale. A wave of tenderness went through him. He sat in the armchair knowing he had to tread carefully. She stirred muttering something he didn't catch, opened her eyes and saw him.

'Forgive me if I've woken you, darling.'

'I doubt you have, Andy.' She sat up holding the sheet up and looked at her watch. They sat in silence gazing at each other. Abbey was thinking how despondent he looked and her heart melted.

'Please forgive me for hurting you, my darling. I wouldn't hurt you for the world.'

'I've been immature Andy, and I apologise. I don't know how I could have got through these last weeks without you and your help.'

'I will do anything for you, precious. I do love you.'

'Andy, come and sit here darling.'

'I'll stay here Abbey. I'm in enough agony seeing you in bed. We'll be ok, sweetheart, we get on well and like the same things. We've so much in common. I can't thank your dada enough for introducing us and I would have pursued you to the ends of the earth.'

'Yes. I love you, Andy. We were meant to meet. I'm so sorry this has happened to-day, I long to be in your arms.'

'Thank you my darling. Would you like a drink?'

'I'll have a shower and come down. Has it stopped raining?'

'Yes, the sun is back out.'

'May we have a walk?'

'Anything you want, my precious. Do you need Birdie?'

'I'm ok thank you.'

''May I use the swimming pool?'

'Andy,' Abbey spoke firmly, 'this is your home. Please don't ever ask to use anything. You are the Master.'

'Ok thank you darling. See you downstairs.' She nodded.

As he was leaving she began to think of the responsibility of being married to Andy. She began to cry again thinking how they had fallen in love at first sight, how he had supported her in the shock of her dada's sudden death, how he had defended her with Didi, how he had respected her and his wonderful sense of humour. Of the sheer love her dada had had for her, introducing her to Andy, wanting her to be loved and secure with him when he knew that he was dying.

After showering she went to find him. He was stood talking to the dogs. She ran up to him and he opened his arms, she weeping held him tight kissing him passionately as though she would never let him go.

'Hey, come on darling, please don't cry, there is nothing to be upset about. Please don't make yourself ill.' Murmuring soft words of love he held her by her shoulders away from him overcome by her closeness and her body. She had loved the feel of him.

'I'm so sorry, Andy, I long to be in your arms.'

'It won't be long now precious. I've waited all this time.'

'All this time?' she laughed. 'We've only known each other for a few weeks!'

'I feel that I've known you all my life, my darling. Would you be better sat down?'

'A stroll, please.'

Setting off with their arm wound each other, the dogs had been laid waiting eagerly set off with them. They'd been subdued sensing Andy and Abbey's upset emotions.

Walking in the wood, the dogs were chasing about all over the place. Andy suggested, 'take it easy tomorrow darling. Perhaps we could get the addresses ready for a thank you letter.'

'Yes, we need to open the other presents. I'll write a thank you letter in my writing with our signatures, then ask Lara to print these out on the special technology and paper she has and post them.' They had received loads of congratulation cards with a voucher to be used in well known stores and presents.

'Would you like to go to an art exhibition near here on Wednesday, sweet?'

'Yes please precious. Where is it?'

He told her. She was overflowing with love for him at this thoughtful invitation.

'On Thursday I need to pop into the office to thank everyone for holding the fort.'

'May I come with you?'

'Of course if you've the time, darling.'

'What about going to the Cottage on Sunday, Abbey?'

'Love to, clothes?'

'Just casuals darling. We'll be able to go riding.'

They continued discussing the wedding presents before going back for dinner.

'Are you sleeping in our suite, darling?'

'Do you mind if I stay in my rooms for now Andy? Will you sleep in our suite?'

'May I use your Grandmama's?'

'Good idea, I'll let Birdie know. Let's keep our suite until we're together. I want our first time together to be very special, Andy."

He groaned.

'I genuinely regret having my period just now, but it won't be forever Andy.'

'Thank God for that,' he said with feeling. She had to laugh and he joined in. She kissed him goodnight.

Abbey rang her grandparents, Tanya answered. 'How are you both Grandmama?'

'We are well, my pet. Don't you bother about us; you and Andy enjoy your precious few days holiday.'

'May we come next week?'

'This isn't necessary after you just getting married, darling.'

'We both need to come and see you and Granddada.'

'Thank you, darling. You know that you'll be very welcome. We love you very much and always have done and are so proud of you. We now love Andy and rest assured that you are in safe hands. Now you go back to your lovely Andy.' They blew kisses as always.

Russell texted Andy, "Thank you and Abbey for the wonderful wedding, the opportunity of meeting Tanya and for the surprise of the sight seeing tour, we were both enthralled with. I took photographs for our memories and to show Didi's "gang."

Wishing you both all the best and hoping you will be able to visit us soon to enjoy your company. Didi is longing for her "gang" to see you both. Russell."

To visit the art museum Abbey was undecided between the three silk dresses she had bought in Switzerland with her Grandparent's birthday money. Spaghetti straps pale mauve silk with sprays of edelweiss flowers and leaves, or the cream silk dress with vibrant coloured honeysuckle flowers with climbers interweaving? Deciding on the cream her dada had especially liked, and her matching wedge shoes and small shoulder handbag. Andy told her she looked very beautiful. He silently approved that she wasn't wearing a mourning dress on their honeymoon; her dada wouldn't have liked that. He looked gorgeous in a grey silk bespoke suit, pale lilac shirt and lilac and grey striped tie. His shoes were as always hand made.

People at the art museum congratulated them on their wedding and gave Abbey their condolences about her bereavement as they went around looking at the paintings. She stopped at a small watercolour of trees in their autumn glory with a stream running though and sun rays breaking through the rain. Andy knew she liked it. 'Is it for sale?' he asked an official.

'They all are sir.'

'Would you like it, Abbey?'

'Yes please.'

He was so glad she had chosen one, he'd hoped she would.

'I do appreciate you bringing me here, darling.'

'I want you to feel at home in Holly House, darling. You are the master now. Change whatever you don't like. Perhaps you'd like a bigger gym?'

He looked at her with a mischeivious look, 'I certainly need a gym desperately if I've to continue sleeping away from you.' She blushed. Abbey excused herself and went into the bathroom facilities.

Unknowingly to them someone had taken a mobile photograph of them looking into each other's eyes with love and commitment, and sent it to the newspapers.

The press had been tipped off and were waiting for them outside. 'May we have a word sir, madam?' Andy looked at her and she nodded her head.

'Congratulations, sir, madam, on your marriage. We all hope that you will both be very happy. We understand why it was low key in view of Mrs Byrne still grieving in her bereavement.

'Yes,' Andy answered.

'Are you going on honeymoon?'

'Yes, shortly. Naturally we've much sorting out to do at the moment.'

'You must have, sir, madam. Please accept our condolences on losing your father, Mrs Byrne.'

'Thank you.'

'Will you give us a few words about your ancestors, Mrs Byrne?' She looked at Andy.

'I'm very proud of my heritage. They were hard working decent people.'

'Your great, great, great Grandmother Katherine Hindley in 1897 was an unmarried mother who never revealed who the father was?'

'Yes. Right or wrong but I wouldn't have been born. They weren't born privileged as I was. I worked hard at my education to help my dada and Grandparents run our hotels, but I also worked hard in honour of my ancestors. I'm the last of the line as yet.'

They fired more questions but she walked away smiling at them. Andy also smiling said goodbye. They knew they daren't pursue or they would have him to answer to.

Brian and Todd were waiting.

'Would you like to go anywhere else, darling?' Andy asked her.

'Where would you like to go, Andy?'

'Back home precious.'

After a cup of tea, Andy asked, 'are you having a rest, darling?'

'Yes, I didn't sleep well.'

He gave her a rueful look, 'Neither did I. I'll go for a run with the dogs.'

'I'll join you in a couple of days, Andy.'

'Do your wear running shorts?'

'Usually I do.'

He groaned. 'We'd better get that gym soon.'

She laughed and he joined in.

'I look forward to running with you, precious.'

Andy had a very important meeting the next morning as a few problems had arisen. Abbey rang Brian and Todd to take her shopping. She had looked on-line and found a boutique not far away which sold beautiful sexy underwear. Knowing her period had finished, she was determined Andy wouldn't sleep alone this night.

Meant To Meet

Going through the boutique Sonya she recognised from her photographs in the magazine was heading towards her, Abbey groaned inwardly.

'Good morning.' Sonya greeted her. 'Make the most of your married life for now. Andy soon tires and moves on. You look very virginal. Perhaps it's a marriage of convenience?'

'Good morning, Ms Day. At least when Andy saw my virgin body he knew that I' am a natural blonde.' Sonya gasped. Abbey with dignity moved towards the exit but was trembling. She had anticipated she may bump into her whilst shopping, but not so soon. She felt cheap buying sexy underwear Sonya and Andy's other lovers would have worn.

Back home she asked Gerry if she may cut some roses. He helped her and she arranged them and carried the vase into the study. She was amazed to see Andy at her desk bent over his laptop. He'd been waiting for her. Seeing her he stood up and saw that she was crying.

'I'm sorry to disturb you, Andy. I didn't anticipate you being back yet.'

'I cut the meeting short. The key men can deal with the problem. I wanted to get back to you.'

She stood at the window re-arranging the roses. He sat back down and looked at her beautiful but despondent shoulders and back. 'Would you like to talk to me, Abbey?'

'I've let you and myself down, Andy.'

'How on earth have you done this? I can't believe it.'

She hesitated, and then told him, 'I met Sonya in a shop and was rude to her.' She didn't reveal. He did stand up at that and went to join her.

He held her shoulders, pulling him near him. 'I've had women, Abbey, but before I met you. I never asked a woman to be my wife.'

She turned to look at him. He saw the shadows under her eyes, the unshed tears and cursed under his breath.

'Shall we have a glass of wine outside, darling?'

'Good idea, please Andy.'

He rang Birdie.

As they were seated under the awning the dogs ran up and sat at their feet. Viola was bringing the tray. Andy took it from her and put it on the table exchanging pleasantries before she hurried back.

Birdie came enquiring if they needed anything and that lunch would be ready in twenty minutes. Abbey told her about going to the Cottage. 'It will do you both the world of good,' Birdie said.

After lunch they had both enjoyed as always Birdie returned to enquire as always if she could help further. Abbey quickly told her, 'my husband and I would like privacy in our Master Suite this afternoon, Birdie.' Andy gave a great laugh of joy.

Birdie could see that she looked excited. 'What about afternoon tea, madam?' She had difficulty not calling her Miss Abbey. Abbey hated being called madam by Birdie.

'We'll pass on that, but a bottle of champagne in the freezer box, please.'

'We'll arrange that now, madam.'

Abbey looked at Andy. He was gazing at her in awe.

'It will be so good to begin having babies in the house. You were a beautiful baby, Miss Abbey.' In her excitement she had slipped up.

'Abbey and I need a space together first, Birdie.' Nodding in agreement she joyfully went to instruct the staff.

'Give me 20 minutes, darling?' she asked Andy.

'20 minutes only.'

Running upstairs she had the quickest shower of her life. Getting out a set of the new underwear, then put it back and covered herself with a new peignoir and arrived at the Master Suite four minutes early. Andy coming into the bedroom in a bath robe and drying his hair stopped short and stood watching her. Smiling in adoration she ran to him and dropped her robe.

Chapter Thirteen

The paparazzi were waiting outside the gates for Andy and Abbey who had given their permission before setting off for the Cotswolds. Andy helped Abbey as she got out with her usual graceful Finishing School training. Stood side by side with their arm round each other and laughing, Smillie at their feet, the reporters were grateful for this informal interview.

'Will you stay together, sir, madam?' one female asked. Andy and Abbey looked shocked. 'We certainly will. We both made our vows before God and to each other, "till death do us part."

'Yes,' Abbey replied in a firm voice of authority surprising them. 'I adore Andy. When I first met him I had a strange thought that my life would never be the same again. I'd have pursued him to the ends of the earth!'

'When I first met Abbey, my world stood still.'

The paparazzi all clapped.

'In no way will we have a dull marriage,' Abbey laughed.

Meant To Meet

'Life is never dull with my wife,' Andy laughingly told them. 'We must set off now.'

'Where are you going sir? Abroad?' they fired at him. Andy tapped his nose. Thankfully they didn't know about the Cottage.

Calls of thanks rang out as they got in with Smillie and waving set off. Several females and males had pangs of jealousy at their obvious happiness.

With Brian driving and Todd the bodyguard sat with him in Andy's BMW they set off for the Cotswolds Cottage. Leaving the motorway they travelled through picturesque villages and countryside Abbey hadn't previously seen. Going through the security gates she gasped when she saw Haven Cottage. 'I expected a small country cottage,' she exclaimed. Brian, Todd and Andy laughed.

'It's a cottage compared to the homes around here, Abbey.'

'It's wonderful.' It was, set near a wood.

Andy proudly introduced her to his housekeeper Mrs Dermot, John the chef, and the staff. Mrs Dermot cuddled Andy. Abbey recognized another aspect of Andy. He was more relaxed here than she had ever seen him. She knew he loved it here, this was his home.

Mrs Dermot asked, 'may I show you the downstairs, Mrs Byrne?' Abbey looked at Andy.

'I'll go and say hello to my horse, darling.'

'Don't be long Andy, your lunch will be ready soon,' Mrs Dermot advised.

Laughing he set off.

Leading Abbey into the sitting room she gasped expecting it to be ultra modern. She fell in love with it and the Cottage in that moment. Lacquered pine oak floor boards led to the fireplace built with Cotswold stones and housing an open log fire. A large fresh flowers arrangement sat in the hearth. A television set was in the alcove on the left and an oak bookcase housed three shelves of books in the other alcove over a music centre, Abbey looked forward to seeing these books.

Two settees and four armchairs you could sink into and covered in material matching the two bay windows curtains overlooking the back. A tasteful veneered oak long coffee table held a colourful vase of flowers, the perfume wafted across the room.

'This is absolutely delightful, Mrs Dermot. I feel so much at home here. I honestly couldn't have furnished this room any better.'

'That's good, ma'am.'

She then led Abbey into the dining room again with the lacquered pine oak floor boards continuing. Another large open fire and a veneered pine oak table to seat twelve and chairs dominated the room and a matching long sideboard. A vase of flowers sat on the table. There was an empty matching large china cabinet along the wall.

'You'll be able to fill this with your choice, ma'am.'

'Yes, I will.' Abbey was thinking of the pots her Grandparents had given them.

Next Mrs Dermot led Abbey into another large room with where a scrubbed table and beautiful wooden chairs sat round it. A big Welsh dresser housed matching pots. Again there was an open log fire.

'What a wonderful breakfast room,' Abbey exclaimed. 'How many bedrooms is there, Mrs Dermot?'

'There are six ma'ams; four are en-suite.'

Abbey began to laugh. 'Wow, some "cottage" Mrs Dermot.'

'It's lovely, Mrs Byrne.'

Abbey liked being called "Mrs Byrne" but thought with her calling Andy by his Christian name it sounded a bit too formal. She would ask Andy's advice about this.

Mrs Dermot looked at her watch. 'You've just time for a quick look in the kitchen. We don't want your first meal here to be spoiled.'

'Did Andy buy this Cottage furnished?'

'No ma'am. It was derelict, but he'll tell you. Everything now is to his taste.' The swing door leading into the kitchen had four small clear windows for safety bringing food in.

A big country kitchen was revealed with a terra cotta tiled floor. John the chef was busy at the very large Aga range cooker and a gorgeous smell of food permeated the room. A small electric cooker sat at the side of it. Abbey greeted the staff. A large well scrubbed table sat in the middle and a huge Welsh dresser ran along the wall full of stoneware pots. A big black polished fireplace with logs piled at the side, herbs. Garlic, onions and cooking pots hung from the ceiling. Mrs Dermot then showed Abbey a utility room and another door which she explained led to the cellar which housed the wines. Every door was solid core veneered.

The more Abbey saw the more she fell in love with the Cottage and was very relieved that Andy had the same taste as she.

'Your husband will be waiting for you.'

'Yes.' She quickly thanked everyone who was delighted that Andy was married. 'I'm starving, I've a very good appetite, I must warn you.'

They all laughed. 'That's good ma'am,' John replied very re-assured at this. Meeting Abbey he saw a slim young lady who probably just picked at her food.

Andy was coming through the door into the hall when they met. 'I'm ravenous Dot. I had an exceptionally good breakfast, but you know me.'

'Yes sir. Also the air here creates appetite.' She left.

Abbey went and through her arms round him and passionately kissed him. 'I'm in love with your home, my darling.'

'It's our home sweetheart.'

'Yes. It's our home.'

'You have the same tastes as me. I want you to think about a swimming pool, inside?'

'Good idea for the winter as Holly House. Come on, let's eat. Afterwards we need to rest!'

He smacked her bottom. 'Do we need to eat first?'

'We have to keep our strength up, darling.'

He laughed again with joy.

'This food is gorgeous Andy. It's very tasty at Holly House, but there is something different here.'

'It's the spring water, darling.'

'Spring water?' she queried.

'Yes, from the spring,' he laughed. 'Also, everything is fresh from a local organic farm shop.'

'Perhaps we should look into this at home, Holly House,' she quickly amended.

'Yes, our London home precious.'

Brian and Todd had enjoyed a nourishing meal and after Andy and Abbey bid them goodbye, returned to Holly House until they came back for them.

Mrs Dermot met Andy and Abbey. 'Dot, my wife and I would like privacy in our room this afternoon.'

Meant To Meet

'Yes, Andy. We'll take your pots up now, knock and leave the fresh tea outside your door later.'

'Thank you, Dot.' They both smiled at her. Abbey was blushing. Mrs Dermot was delighted with her.

'I made the Master Suite which hasn't been used yet, in preparation of my one day, marrying. It's been unfurnished until recently. I hope you like the surprise. The mattress is to your preference.'

'Yes,' she teased him, 'the mattress is very important.'

He groaned.

Later Andy took Abbey and introduced her to Alec who was in charge of the stables, and his horse and the one he suggested for her. She was thrilled with the colt.

Andy and Abbey watched their wedding on the portable screen Andy had bought. 'It's so lovely seeing everyone arriving, I wouldn't have known this without this film.' She went quiet holding his hand as he and Marlon arrived and responded to the cheering crowd. Then the crowds were cheering again as her car was coming and Russell helping her out. They both listened intently to the music, watching her go up to him from the back view.

They were filmed from the front for the vows having agreed on this for her Grandparents. Abbey and Andy were both crying as they watched. Sitting listening to the anthem with their heads bowed was especially precious too. They intently watched the remainder of the service, going out for the photographs, and setting off for Ricardo's.

'Thank you darling, this was wonderful for me,' Abbey told him.

'Our children will be able to watch this.'

'Yes, and we will when we're old and grey!' she laughed. 'Didi is still beautiful, isn't she? She must have had work done on her face.'

'I doubt she has,' he answered. 'If you'd seen women as I have in the hotels that have had surgery, you'd recognise she hasn't. She has beautiful bone structure and you have even more so, darling. You'll never need surgery either.'

'I wouldn't Andy.'

'She looks good, Russell too. Credit to them darling.'

'Yes,' she agreed. 'During the service I felt strength and love coming to me from her, Andy.

They both went quiet thinking of this, Andy then asked, 'may Dot and the staff see this?'

'Certainly darling, if they want to.'

After breakfast Andy asked, 'put your walking shoes on, please darling, and bring your camera.' He was waiting downstairs and led her to a large lake at the back of the house with a wood surrounding it.

'This is wonderful, sweetheart. What a marvellous backdrop.' Her fingers were itching to begin sketching the scene.

'I hoped that you'd like it. I want you to develop it, do anything you think. I guess you'll want to paint it.'

'I'd paint it as it is after I've completed Didi's.'

'Look at the wild life.' He gave her the binoculars he had brought.

Abbey gasped. The small birds flying about were very colourful and the butterflies. Insects were hovering over the lake and diving down to the surface.

'What species are these birds, darling?' she asked him.

'Sorry Abbey, I don't know. This is the first time I've seen them close. But we'll soon find out. We can get books and look on the Internet.'

'How long have you had the Cottage, Andy?'

'I bought it six years ago, it was very run down. It took three years to re-build. All the wood is from our trees.'

'Did you have an interior designer?'

'No, darling, I did it.'

'Well done, my husband. You have the same tastes as me. I adore it nearly as much as I adore you.' She kissed him passionately fully realizing fully what he based his life on, solidity. He had said that she would fully know him when she had been to their Cottage.

With her long camera lens she captured the wildlife- the absolutely gorgeously coloured birds, butterflies and insects. Showing Andy he was amazed at their vibrant colours. 'All the times I've been here, I've never realized there was such beauty.'

She took him in her arms and kissed him. 'Have we privacy here?'

'Regretfully, no there isn't.'

'We have in our room, darling.'

'Have you brought any of your women here, Andy?'

'No precious. If you don't believe me ask Dot.'

'I believe you, darling. I'm very thankful.'

Andy also was.

She was filled with well being. Sadness over her dada began to lift at his words. She knew her dada wanted her to be happy, he had always wanted that.

The next morning sitting comfortably under the sun shade by the lake, Abbey had brought her sketching pad. Whilst enjoying their coffee Andy asked, 'you like it here, darling?'

'I love it.'

'I do. From buying the ruins, I've always felt this was my home.'

Her face fell. 'Are you not comfortable at Holly House?'

Yes, I am, sweetheart,' he swiftly assured her, 'very much so. I love it but here we are away from London, and it's different.'

'Yes I identify exactly what you mean.'

Seeing Andy fall into the deep sleep she realized how much pressure he had carried for her over the last months. They could come here for weekends and longer when possible. She would be hands on with their children as much as possible whilst they were growing up.

Sketching Andy as he lay relaxed, Smillie was also asleep. She had a photograph of Andy sat in an armchair looking at her with a mischeivious look on his face she would capture in oils and emphasize the glint in his eyes. This would be for their bedroom.

His phone peeped; he hadn't switched off waiting for a vital business call, otherwise he wasn't going to be disturbed. Waking, answered it. It was Adrienne, Sebastian and Tanya's PA. Knowing she wouldn't ring him unless there was something wrong, he said, 'excuse me darling.' Abbey nodded and continued sketching as he moved away.

'Carry on Adrienne, my wife is nearby.'

'I deeply regret, Mr Byrne,' her voice broke and she was sobbing, 'to have to tell you Mrs Byrne's Grandmama has died from a stroke and her husband on hearing the news, has died from a heart attack.' Andy was horrified; he was thinking "I must be still asleep and having a nightmare?" It was so unbelievable. Sebastian, yes, this was expected. But Tanya no way, no she hadn't been ill.

A man's accented voice broke into his thoughts, 'Mr Byrne, I'm Mr and Mrs Forrest's family doctor. What has happened is devastating but not unexpected. Mrs Forrest has had a few slight strokes recently hence she couldn't attend your wedding but forbade us to tell Mrs Byrne so as not to take away any enjoyment of marrying you. Also to be told this on top of her beloved dada dying.' He cleared his throat, Andy knew what he had just said had cost him as he also must be in shock. 'All I can say sir, is they are together. I always thought that one wouldn't live without the other.' Andy was crying as the news had sunk in.

'I'll tell Abbey, doctor. Please tell Adrienne that we'll be with you to-day.'

'Thank you sir, we will all be very grateful for this.' They said bye.

Andy was stood rooted, how on earth was he going to break this news to Abbey? He rang Dot, 'please let have a tray of tea brought to us, Dot. I've some bad news to tell Abbey. Please don't reveal this. I'll speak to you very shortly.' He then rang the airport, booked a flight and arranged for a taxi. Sighing deeply he went back to Abbey. John had brought the tea tray and left.

Andy poured her a cup. 'Have a drink, darling.'

'What's going on Andy? Has something happened?'

'Yes, precious.' He began to cry but controlled himself for her sake. 'Your Grandmama and Granddada have died.'

'Died?' she shrieked, 'in an accident?'

'Your Grandmama died from a stroke and on hearing the news your Granddada suffered a fatal heart attack.'

Abbey sat shocked, 'I can't take this in.'

'Drink your tea darling we've a lot to do.' He drank his cup in one. Abbey didn't touch hers.

'I've booked a flight. Go and pack an overnight bag for us both.' She jumped up. He knew he had to keep her busy. He rang Birdie, she also was shocked. 'We're going to Switzerland this afternoon Birdie, Smillie is staying here being so well settled. We'll return to Holly House from Switzerland, possibly to-morrow. I'll let you know immediately we know. Ring you later Birdie.' He rang off. He went to find Dot but she'd gone up with Abbey.

He hurried to see Alec and put him in the picture then asked, 'will you please look after Smillie? He appears to have settled here. This break will help him forget his master.'

'He'll never forget sir, but he's happy here. I'll continue taking good care of him.'

'Thank you, I must go.' He bent and stroked Smillie then ran to the Cottage.

Travelling in the car the deaths hit Abbey and she began to sob. As Andy cuddled her, she asked, 'why didn't they tell me Grandmama was suffering strokes? I'm getting fed up being treated like a child. First not knowing dada was dying, now Grandmama.'

He closed the privacy window. 'No, no, darling, don't upset your self. You need to be strong. As your dada's fatal heart attack, Grandmama's final stroke was unexpected also. Darling, they didn't want to upset our wedding.'

'Of course, darling, forgive me.'

'There is nothing to forgive. Let's be happy that they're together.'

'Yes,' she sighed. 'I'm very thankful they met you. I must let Grandpapa know.'

'Yes, it would be better coming from you, darling.'

She rang Russell's private mobile. He answered promptly in a business like tone. 'Grandpapa, Abbey here. How are you and Didi?'

'We are well, thank you Abbey. How are you both?'

'Grandpapa, I've terrible news. Granddada and Grandmama have both died.'

'Both died?' he questioned in horror.

'Yes. Unknown to me Grandmama has been having slight strokes. That is why she didn't come to our wedding. She had a major one and died. The shock caused Granddada to have a heart attack and he immediately died. Andy and I are on the plane going to Switzerland.'

'Darling, do you want us to come over?'

'Not yet, thank you, we'll have a lot of sorting out to do both ends.'

'Of course darling, let me know if I can help in any way, please.'

'I will thank you Grandpapa. Love to Didi. We'll be in touch soon.'

Russell went to find Didi and told her the news.

'Why didn't she speak to me?'

'She's on the plane with Andy of course. They're going to keep in touch with us.'

'Let me speak with her, darling.'

'Of course I will, but please understand they've loads to do.'

They discussed how this would affect Abbey whilst still grieving for her dada.

With Andy being on his honeymoon there were no appointments made, which made the situation easier. He rang his PA and put him in the picture.

Abbey rang Lara and told her. She was shocked and asked 'is there anything I can do, Mrs Byrne.'

'Yes, please Lara, tell Lorraine, Dylan and Mr Bell my solicitor. Apologise for my not letting them know, but we're on the plane now to Switzerland and that I'll be communicating with you in my busyness. I'll let you know the situation to-morrow.'

Lara was very honoured with this responsibility and vowed that she would do everything she could to make Abbey's business life easier.

Their air hostess coming to enquire if they required anything saw them both crying. Knowing Andy Byrne as a regular customer on their airlines, she was amazed. 'Pardon me sir, madam; is there anything I can bring you, tea, coffee or something stronger?'

'Thank you, we'll be grateful for a pot of tea,' Andy answered.

She stood hesitating wondering if something had gone wrong with their marriage.

'We've received the horrific news that my wife's paternal Grandparents have both suddenly died through ill health. Please be discreet.'

'I will sir, madam. Please let me know if I can help in any way.'

They both thanked her. She hurried to arrange the tea thinking, "how terrible this happening when they had just gone on their honeymoon." With the new interest in Abbey and ongoing interest in Andy, the media had broadcast this.

Abbey was grateful for her cup of tea. Andy would have liked a whiskey, but later.

'I hope that we'll not be separated tonight, darling. I need you with me.'

'I need to be with you, my precious. We'll be together. Grandmama had ensuite rooms prepared for us visiting them after we married.' Thinking of this planning and all the love her Grandparents had showered on her all her life, she wept again. 'I always received such love from them both all my life Andy, I adored them both. I can't thank you enough for all you are doing. Whatever what I do without you? '

'We're in this together, my darling. I'm so grateful for you loving and marrying me, I'll do anything for you.' They sat quietly holding hands.

Didi arranged afternoon tea in the hotel and then took the "gang" up to her sitting room where Russell had had a portable screen set up. When they were settled he put a photograph of Abbey at her dada's funeral. They recognised her dress was haute couture.

'The hat suits her,' Deirdre commented.

'Yes, it's a shame it hides her eyes, but this was chosen deliberately for that,' Didi answered.

Russell then put a full face photograph of her. They all exclaimed at her beautiful face with the exquisite bone structure.

Russell next put his copy of the wedding film on. Not a sound was heard whilst they watched this, apart from "oohs" as Andy was shown and then again when Abbey got out of the car.

When it had finished Polly said, 'what a beautiful granddaughter. I can't believe you didn't know her.'

Russell sternly said, 'that's in the past Polly, we're not going over that. It's a new beginning for each one of us.' Didi was proud of him for defending her. She looked at him with gratitude. The "gang" knew now they had to be careful what they said.

Deirdre quickly came in with, 'You said it was going to be a quiet wedding, Didi.'

'Yes, and it was in view of Abbey being in bereavement for her beloved dada.'

Angela asked, 'is she pregnant?'

Russell again answered, 'no, Didi and I are very proud that our granddaughter was a virgin, and they married quickly as they are so much in love and needed to be together.'

He next asked, 'what about a glass of champagne to celebrate this wedding?'

They all agreed with this. They were all quite jealous of the new relationship between Russell and Didi.

Deirdre was still feeling raw over her split with Jason but knew that she had made the right choice.

After discussions with Abbey, Andy, Matthias and Mr Bell, Adrienne sent a bulletin to the leading Switzerland and London newspapers reporting the deaths, promising more details later.

Thankfully as Grant had his funeral organised, so had Sebastian and Tanya making sure it would easier for her. She and Andy with Matthias and Adrienne carried out all the instructions and requests. Tanya had chosen the hymns and bible readings. Abbey had the oil painting she had done of them put in front of the altar. It was a beautiful service in the little church they had worshipped God in. Abbey, in the hot season, wore her dress and hat she had bought for her dada's funeral service.

Adrienne had invited Sebastian and Tanya's chosen to the lunch Andy organised in a local restaurant. After the short speeches everyone not involved in the will reading left after Abbey had spoken to each one of them.

Returning to Lake View and settling in the sitting room. As expected Abbey was the main benefactor. Matthias read, 'Mr and Mrs Forrest thank their beloved granddaughter for all her love and care throughout her life.' He read out the legacies they had left to the staff, church and their chosen charities. After all this business was dealt with they had a glass of wine, or beverage with sandwiches and cakes. Abbey and Andy returned to Holly House with the ashes to be buried alongside Grant and Faye. They were going to buy a rose bush in memory of them in their little garden plot at the side of Faye's and Grants.

Adrienne sent the acknowledgement letters to everyone who had sent cards and flowers in Switzerland and London.

Abbey rang Adrienne. 'I can't thank you enough, Adrienne, for all the care and help you gave my Grandparents.'

'It's been a pleasure, Mrs Byrne.'

'Have you made any plans?'

'Yes. I'm going, with the legacy your Grandparents left me, to travel and see the world.'

'That's lovely, Adrienne. Are you going with a friend?'

'No, I want to please myself as much as possible going with tours, which are wonderful. From past experience one has to be careful not to get tied up with other passenger's wants, but at times it's good to have company. Does that make sense?' she laughed.

'It does, Adrienne, I'd do the same. If you're anywhere near me please get touch. And if you're looking for a new position I'll have something to offer you. My PA is leaving in about three years to begin a family. You'd be very useful to me Adrienne, and your managerial skills would be used.'

Lara had let Abbey know that she and her fiancée were getting married next summer and when they had enough money to buy a home, begin their family. Lara assured Abbey she would hopefully work when pregnant with the first child. Abbey knew she would be a hard act to follow.

'Thank you, Mrs Byrne for your trust. At this moment in time I'm thinking of applying for a managerial position in the new convalescent home for children you will be building. With seeing Mr Forrest's sufferings and also Mrs Forrest's, I think I would be useful.'

'That's wonderful. God Bless you darling. Please keep in touch with me after I've settled up. Andy and I will return to you in a couple of days.' With Andy and Abbey having no appointments they thought it wise to use this time.

'Is there anything in the house you would like, Adrienne?'

'May I think about this? Thank you.'

'Of course you may. Take your time.'

To cheer her up Abbey lightly said, 'I'm taking my Grandparents oil painting!' Adrienne did laugh at this.

'You are a wonderful lady, Adrienne. Anything I or Andy can help you with, let us know. Please accept my gratitude again for all you have done for my Grandparents and me as I grew up.'

'You were a beautiful girl, ma'am. I pray you will have daughters who are just like you.'

'Thank you, but please pray for some boys as well.'

Abbey then rang Helena conversing in German. 'How are you, Helena?'

'I'm bearing up, ma'am. What a terrible shock especially for you.'

'Yes, it was. Thank you for everything you have done Helena, is there anything I can help you with?'

'I'm taking each day as it comes, ma'am.'

'Is there anything you would like from the house?'

'Thank you for this. I'll have a think.'

'What are your plans, Helena?'

'With the legacy your Grandparents have given me Mrs Byrne and my savings, my husband and I are retiring. We have plenty of hobbies and our family.'

'That's good, Helena. I want to personally thank you for all the care you have shown to my Grandparents and my self as I grew up.'

Helena started to cry. Abbey nearly crying herself but trying to control her tears waited.

'Thank you Mrs Byrne. I still think of you as Miss Abbey. I feel much better for talking with you. I'll go and get on.'

'Please accept my gratitude for everything, Helena. My husband and I will be with you in a couple of days.'

Abbey then wrote a letter to the doctors and nursing staff thanking them for all their care and support to her beloved Grandparents. She was sat thinking what else she had to do when Andy appeared. 'Ok darling?' he asked.

'I think I'm getting there precious.' She told him what she had done and he lovingly congratulated her. They went for a walk in the wood.

Matthias sent the announcement to all the leading newspapers in Switzerland and London. "Mrs Andy Byrne is putting her Grandparent's home, "Lake View" in Switzerland up for sale. She had their approval with the proceeds to have a convalescent home for eight children suffering lung damage and breathing difficulties to be built in Switzerland. This will be funded by Mr and Mrs Byrne and her maternal Grandparents in honour of Mr and Mrs Sebastian Forrest.

Please respect Mrs Byrne's privacy as she mourns the sudden deaths of her Grandparents following the early death of her beloved father."

Sebastian and Tanya's office furniture was delivered and Andy had the latest high tech paraphernalia technology installed in the office to enable him to work from home as much as possible. In memory of her Grandparents, Abbey had their portrait hung in the study where she would continue working from.

Opening her post after breakfast she almost dropped a letter from Sonya Day, she had thought it was another condolence letter. "Miss Forrest, please forgive me for being so rude to you. I'm deeply ashamed knowing you are in deep bereavement for your beloved father and now your Grandparents.

I hope you'll forget the words I spoke, and that you and Mr Byrne have a wonderful marriage. Sonya Day."

Abbey was amazed. Silently she passed it to Andy. His lips pursed as he read. 'She means this sincerely, Abbey. You're obviously setting a good example.' They continued going through the post.

Thirteen months after Abbey and Andy marrying, Abbey was delivered of a healthy boy 9 lbs 2 ozs. He was Andy's double, brown hair, but with Abbey's classical bone structure and curly hair. They couldn't stop crying for joy and thankfulness. Andrew Derbyshire's genes continued and he was going to be a seriously handsome boy and man. Named Grant Sebastian he was a happy, good natured baby and eagerly fed from Abbey until eleven months old when sharp growing teeth prevented this. Everyone loved him and Abbey and Andy knew they had been very God Blessed.

Twenty one months later Abbey was delivered of another healthy boy 9 lbs. 8 ozs. After the first weeks of morning sickness as she had known with Grant Sebastian she had a comfortable pregnancy keeping herself fit and eating healthily as always, running Sunrise Glow and enjoying being married to her Andy. This one, Quentin Andy, featured her dada and Granddada and was a contented baby. Andy and Abbey adored them both.

Just over two years later she was delivered of another healthy baby. All the babies had been born with a perfectly shaped head and features but Faye Didi being smaller was feminine with her small ears, rosebud mouth; long lashes already fanning her little chubby cheeks and the classic features following Andrew Derbyshire's lineage. She was a beauty as unknown to them Violet Markham generations back had been. She would be spoilt by her brothers but Abbey knew at nursery and school she would have lots of feminine company as she had.

'That's it now my darling,' Andy told Abbey.

'We don't want to later have any regrets, perhaps one more, Andy?'

'I'm sure this can be arranged,' he laughed.

'They are adorable.'

'They are, my precious, as their mummy.' Both deeply loving each other, they daily thanked God.

Didi and Russell visited often for a short time, staying in either Whitwell Wood or English Oak so Russell could take Didi dancing or to shows without disturbing the Holly House early to bed routine. Didi and Russell adored the children and Andy and Abbey was firm in not allowing them to buy expensive toys, bringing them up to enjoy simple pleasures and outdoor activities. Sharing love was enough. Andy's family who all loved Abbey and the children came often especially in the school holidays.

After another healthy boy was born Andy laughed, 'if they all want to go into hotel business, we'll be able to retire,' Andy laughed.

Agreeing this was enough despite she would have loved a sister for Faye Didi, was thankful she and her brothers loved each other and were good friends. They were all treated the same and deeply loved.

Lightning Source UK Ltd.
Milton Keynes UK
UKOW04f2352030714

234552UK00004B/40/P